THE HAPPENSTANCE PACKS

The WOLF, a BUTCHER, his DEMON, and their MASTER

By

Christopher S. White

DISCLAIMER

This book is a work of fiction. The characters, incidents, and dialogue are drawn from the author's imagination and are not to be construed as real. Any resemblance to actual events or persons, living or dead, is entirely coincidental.

Printed by CreateSpace, An Amazon.com Company
Available from Amazon.com and other retail outlets.
Available on Kindle and other devices.

DEDICATIONS

This book is dedicated to Kim, my brilliant, smokin'–hot, the-family-glue, bar-for-greatness, always-wears-flip-flops-even-on-cold-and-rainy-days, crazy beautiful, "brass taxes", dream giver, incredible mother, strong as hell, and amazingly tolerant wife.
I was not awake until I met you.
YAME.

There is no better part of me than my wife. I work to better myself so I can be better for HER. She is that incredible, and she is my Muse in everything I do.

Thank you, baby, for giving me my life - hell, for giving me LIFE.

This book is also dedicated to Amelia, my wonderful and vibrant daughter, who everyday reminds me that I have more energy, patience, creativity, wisdom, lack of wisdom, and humility than I ever believed I could possess. At six years old, she asked me if I knew when it was that I had grown up. At first, she was amazed when I told her the exact date and time of day; but then she thought about it and said, "Hey, that's when I was born!"
And I said, "Yep."

The reason I know there is a God, and that I am loved by that God, is because these two people have been put into my life, and have *become* my life.

I love you two so very much – to the moon and back!

Contents

"One person's crazy is another person's reality."
Tim Burton

"Know what? Fuck those guys."

Good advice; heard it somewhere.

CHAPTER **1**

NOW

Elbert Nachos and Walt Disney Cuthbert

*T*he *Old Dog's Wet Fart: A Fine Dining and Libations Experience* was a bar that, for all anyone around those scraggy parts remembered, had shown up decades ago on the side of that dirt road with none of the expected ceremony, creative advertising, or other relevant pomposities that are usually associated with an establishment seeking to earn its cash flow by servicing the local clientele.

Lore varied (as it will), depending on who you spoke with, as to the inception of *Old Fart* (as the locals would call it), because the full title required more thought and energy than most folks felt was necessary to adequately explain where they'd be for lunch.

THE WOLF, A BUTCHER, HIS DEMON, AND THEIR MASTER

There was young Liam Jones's grandpa, for one, who was sorely positive that before any kind of *Old Fart* sat on that land, there did sit an old plywood shack, attached to and built off of, the back of a broken down antique piece of rust, that resembled a Ford pickup. He remembered thinking that it looked like what he figured a "sick dinosaur'd look like". The truck's hood acted as the snout, and as the meager "found wood" buildings extended off the back of the old truck bed, the anomaly took on the shape of a fat belly and bulbous tail.

Another expert resident, Clyde Worthington, who hid his unusually large upper lip with a poor excuse for a full beard, said he read on-line somewhere that the local rivers in that area that had access to the inter coastal waterways of Nassau County were used to smuggle cocaine, whores, and immigrants for the local paper mills, crab boats, and farming needs; because of that, the area that surrounded *Old Fart* was used as a makeshift dry boat dock, because it was out of direct view of the river that ran almost alongside it. It was easy to get to, out of sight, and so was well used.

It was about twenty miles inland from the Atlantic coast on the Florida side of the Georgia border in an old (and almost forgotten) township of Barone. It had the anonymity of locations that were surrounded by flat land, hard soil, and trees. So many trees! Much of the acreage was used for growing lumber to supply the local paper mills with. A person could always recognize which plots were used for the tree farms, because all the young shrubs were lined up in neat rows stretching for miles back.

The general agreement was that Old Fart was originally used as some kind of fish camp and grew its functionality up from there. There were also stories about people using the hidden streams and small back roads to print and distribute counterfeit money, and - of course! - there was moonshine.

There is *always* moonshine, and there is always someone willing to get it to the people that want it. The Old Fart eventually was marked as the center of Barone and it had a large pole was driven down in the middle of it to show the exact center of the unincorporated town. And then, because there was no other place to put it, a jail cell was built underneath the structure. It also doubled as a bomb shelter, were that ever needed. Placing the jail underneath the local saloon may have seemed awkward at first, but it was quickly found that most of the people visiting the jail cell were the patrons of the saloon, and so it was very convenient to simply throw them downstairs until they'd sobered up the next day.

Regardless of how many stories there were about just how the Old Fart came to be, and how the township of Barone grew up around it, everyone knew that eventually, Elbert Nachos would go down as the man credited with the inception of it all. One day he came into that dense forested area and began to swing his hammer to the surrounding wood. Before long, there stood four walls and a roof. He cooked up some moonshine with a taste of honey so it didn't "smell like an old dog's wet fart" he'd say, and people actually showed up to drink it.

His reputation for being a man to cook decent swill spread and he built the place up. He added a kitchen wagon out back to make sure that the chili and potatoes were cooking at all hours of the day, and an upstairs lodge for people to crash and stay for the night.

The Wet Fart was built into a hill with lush trees and ferns lacquered with a particular sheen of green made for coloring books, but also with a hard, gray stone; stone that, along with some red clay from the Georgia side of the land, is considered a defining quality of the North Georgia Mountains and most other known locals for the state.

The building was old and solid. There was no rot in the wood and the stench of dirt, soil, sweat and whiskey was heavy once inside the large front doors.

A truck rolled into the gravel lot and up to the side of the building where it settled into a spot the way a bull might settle into a patch of grass. The driver's door creaked open and an older black man with heavy boots and fishing hooks in his ball cap stepped out to make his way up the front porch. He paused to pet the old dog who lay there most days, and then pushed open the front doors to make his way inside.

He danced sideways quick though, when two men came stumbling out dragging another guy with them because he was on the wrong side of consciousness. They were, all of them, seriously bleeding.

"Fellas" the black man greeted, and continued past them indoors.

His name was Walt. He was there every day for a drink and bowl of chili, except for Sunday. On Sunday, he waved the chili off " to give his insides a rest" he'd say. Instead he'd beg three drinks, or maybe four, or maybe just ask for the bottle so he could start the week off right on Monday.

He gave a nod to the bar tender, who in turn hollered back at him from behind her dark throne of heavy stained pine. "Hey Dis, I'll be right with ya – cleanin' up a small mess, kay?"

Walt smiled and settled into a table near a dim corner of the room to watch the buxom bar-keep tidy up the "small mess". She blithely pushed an unconscious man off of the bar in front of her and then quickly wiped up the blood, spit, and whatever else he had left behind while slipping from the long plank of stained wood with a wet towel. She might as well have been wiping up the sweat from a beer bottle, or the remnants of a bowl of chili that, although not completely finished by the previous customer, would surely be appreciated by the next one once it was added back inside the always hot barrel of chili in the back. Of course she'd never *broadcast* this spicy culinary secret; but then again, no one would ever ask her about it because she'd most likely give them an honest answer. It was all the same to her.

Walt's full name was Walt Disney Cuthbert, and this keeper of the bar was the only lady – nay, the only *person* -- who ever got away with calling him Dis, and on a daily basis.

Walt was, and always had been, a very cordial and pleasant person. People found it easy to like him. But as a child, Walt had problems with this.

He liked to fight, see.

And the problem for him was that people weren't hep to this; they didn't *want* to fight him.

They *liked* him, see.

Being rude wasn't something he did well. Never was. His mamma said that even when she "popped him outta her south mouth", and after an especially long birthing process, she swore that when he looked up at her that first time, he was apologizing for taking so long to arrive and that he really was *very* sorry if he had caused her any discomfort. And if it wasn't too much of a bother for her, could he please grab a hold of one of them large round fun sacks so he could suck down some breakfast? It'd been a long day.

Growing up, he tried using the color of his skin as an excuse to throw down, but that never turned out well; they were, all of them in those mountains, really fuckin' poor. Either they were dirty from the day's hard work and their skin color didn't show through very well, or they just didn't care. There were other, more important things for them to think about, like say, that scratch on their ass that wouldn't go away, or trying to remember if they had jumped in the river for a bath that week, or how they would be catching their next meal.

Racism only works when at least one party involved has money, means, or any kind of leg up on someone else and they can afford to entertain the more trivial and ridiculous matters of the world. As if the pigments of a person's skin has anything to do with - well, anything. And none of them in those mountains had anything more (or less) than the person over on the next muddy bank, and so that argument never worked out for Walt.

Then as Walt grew older, he began to take notice of all the visitors his mamma received at their house. He thought nothing of it, at first. She'd always entertained.

Mamma Cuthbert organized all the dances for the local cotillions and ran a prosperous catering company that was called on for most weddings and birthdays. She knew how to throw a party, it was what she was good at. But she also received visitors when she wasn't baking food to send out.

She'd smile at the door, give them all hugs, and let them cry on her shoulder if they needed to; some brought flowers, though always only the men. She'd make a real show of accepting that colorful and always overly odorous foliage by not just setting them aside on the counter, but while her guests were there, take the time to cut the stems under water, clean up the spare and dry leaves, and finally pick out a nice vase from below the counter to set them out in.

She said it made a man feel special when she'd croon over his offerings.

There'd always be her signature apple cornmeal biscuits fresh and hot on the stove, because she knew that'd be the first thing people asked for as they stepped inside.

Then his mamma would work the "1-2-3", a natural process she used to take control of the ceremony, as it were, in her home (she *was* the host, after all). She used the process to move her guests along from one intention to the next as a seamless, natural progression.

She explained the "1-2-3" to Walt like this: "After one great apple biscuit, two minutes of polite talk and three good laughs, people'll know good'n well that they had a proper visit in your home. And that counts for something these days. Folks want to feel proud about who they keep company with and where they spend their time. And when folks feel proud walkin' out your house, that puts you in good standin' with your town. That's a good thing Walt, to have reputation. *Good* reputation. That'll save ya more ways than one. Count on that, baby boy."

Also she explained about the three laughs. "Baby, there ain't a soul anywhere that don't feel better after they've laughed, and at least three times. One laugh, that's nothing, but it's a start. Two, ok, that's better, but it's forgettable. Three, that's the number. They can't ignore three. They be all better then."

And then Walt's mamma would take her guests, mostly men he'd realize, to the back room of the house where he was told he wasn't allowed. That was mamma's place, and it wasn't for him.

A little while later, she'd walk out with them again, her arm around theirs, and escort them to the front door. It really was all very proper and polite. It wasn't until later that Walt realized his mamma was *the* most respected escort in that woodland coastal region.

Someone looking in on this from the outside might assume that Disney would be distraught at learning of his mother's profession. On the contrary, this excited him! Finally, maybe he'd found something he could use to create a proper, fighting tension between other people and himself. He practiced in the mirror, yelling things like "Hey! What'd you say about my mamma!" and "Yeah, I know who my daddy is! He's the guy that's gotta kid that's gonna whoop yo ass right now!"

In fact, he did know his daddy. He died when Walt was much younger. That was when mamma started to "entertain" like she had.

Admittedly this was a dangerous, and potentially morally ambiguous, career choice. But she was a smart lady, and she was clever about how she ran her business. She made it well known that she would *never* sleep with a married man. Any trouble she'd have with a woman in town wouldn't stem from her amorous profession; more often, it'd begin from fighting over the fresh vegetables at market, or when she got into a political discussion about the bordering water rights with Georgia. They all knew she was adamant about keeping a marriage together.

There was this one time, Walt remembered, when he heard a ruckus in the back room, then saw his mamma pull a man out of the house by his ear – for real, by his ear! – to throw him out down by the road's sewer cap. The man limped away holding the side of his head, hurt and embarrassed. Once back inside she called the wife of that poorly behaved gent, and cemented his gloomy, immediate future. She hung up to let out a quiet "tsk", then laughed. The next day, a lady Walt had never met delivered a basket of fresh fruit to his mamma and the two ladies spent the afternoon laughing together on the front porch as old friends do.

The ladies in town knew that Mamma Cuthbert would shun every married man that approached her door. And they would also, in private, speak to her about personal matters that couldn't be discussed elsewhere.

The problem was that people liked and respected Mamma Cuthbert too much to take Walt seriously when he began to get snotty about her. He'd bring her up in conversation and say obvious things to make it easy for the other person to start a rub, like "Man, my mamma sho is cool. She's always having visitors over!" But instead of the smirk he expected, he'd get a look of understanding from the gentleman he was talking to and hear "Son, let me tell you about yo mamma. She is one hell of a good woman, and I am positive that the Lord has a fine house set aside for her after many glorious years on this great earth . Did I ever tell you I proposed to her once?"

The first time he heard about his mamma getting proposed to, he was appropriately shocked. The second time a man told him this, he smiled at the coincidence. And in line with that rule of three, the third time a man admitted to him a previous matrimonial proposal to his mother, it caused him to begin laughing in the poor man's face, and he had apologized as best he could between breaths to beg the man's forgiveness. Walt thought he might have to begin wearing a priest's white collar after that, because there were many other men that he would hear that confession from over the years.

"Mamma?" he asked one night, "You ever thought of getting married again?"

"Walter," she responded, "What made you say that?"

"Nothin' really. Just thought you might, is all. Some nice men out there and most seem to like ya. Only askin."

She laughed. "Well, I'll tell ya Walt, I've had a few suitors. Nice men all of 'em, and they'd have taken good care of me and you."

"Why didn't you say yes?

"Because," she answered, "There's only one man in my life now that means anything to me, and that's you, Walt baby. Ain't no other guy gonna get between us."

Walt smiled, and laughed. She'd embarrassed him.

"Plus, baby, I did the marriage thing. With the right man, at the right time, and got the right son out of it. There'd be no other man out there more perfect for me than your daddy. The way he was made up matched the way I'm made up, and perfect. We fit. There's some that would be close to measure, but none would make it. No sense in tryin' to make a life with someone else again. We do alright, me and you. This is good for me."

Walt's final step in working to rally rotten intentions toward himself was to act the town's sexual deviant. He hadn't had any real experience in the sex business himself, but at this point he was out of options! Racism hadn't worked. Having a prostitute mother hadn't worked, everyone still just *loved* her. The only thing he had left was to try and see if being queer would work. He knew he wasn't and didn't much care if someone else was, but this was a time when being queer wasn't yet cool, and he hoped maybe owning up to that would get him some fights.

The next night he was smoking weed with a pal of his, Buck, and in between inhales, he casually mentioned wondering if Billy Cud, that new kid down the road, had a cock that tasted as good as the joint he was working on. Maybe he'd go and find out.

He looked over at his friend, expecting a severe reaction. What he got instead was a shoulder shrug. "Don't know," Buck answered. "But hey, did'ya hear that Roy got his dick stuck in a raccoon's asshole? Yeah, that fucker's anus froze up so tight, they couldn't pull it off Roy until he lost his log!"

"You heard what I just said?" Walt asked.

"Yeah," his friend continued, "but here's where it gets fuckin hilarious. See, Roy's pecker wouldn't go down, he was too riled up with everything going on. So ya know what? His brother Cal had to hold the raccoon and jerk it back and forth, till Roy was able to finish off!"

"Ha! What happened to the raccoon?"

"Shit. That thing won't leave Roy alone, now. Sleeps by his window and waits for him to come out. Seriously, thing's in love with him."

Buck was quiet for a moment then said "Know what? If Roy can fuck a raccoon into loving him, he might could have somethin' special down there. Want me to hook you two up?"

Walt laughed and said thanks but no, he wasn't messin with a pecker that'd been up a raccoon's butt.

"So maybe that Billy Kid then?"

Walt realized that Buck was only trying to help him out and decided, rightly, that he was a good friend. He smiled and shrugged. "Nah. I just remembered he's from up around New York or some shit, so ya know he's a fuckin' sissy. I ain't got the time for that. Thanks, though." Buck nodded, and that was that.

Walt had tried every horrible thing he knew to try and start a fight, and none of them had worked. People round there were just too fuckin' tolerant, he thought.

Then one afternoon, after Walt had lost any hope of becoming known as a fighter, opportunity struck.

The local hardware and appliance store, Codges, got a TV. And the kids in town got their first glimpse of Mickey Mouse and all the other dirty rodents that came with him. They knew who he was, they'd all seen books and had the occasional doll, but the cartoons were something that were special. Almost no one had a VCR in town, or even a Beta Max - or a TV, for that matter. They'd seen them, but most of his crowd didn't have one in the house.

On Saturdays, Mr. Codge made sure that his supply of Walt Disney VHS tapes was plentiful and always playing for the kids' enjoyment. Because one, he was a nice guy; and two, because all the kids' parents were in town shopping, and this brought them to his store to spend their money.

It was inevitable that Walt's friends noticed that Walt's name, and the name of the company that made the cartoons, were very similar. Walt went home to ask his mom about this place called "Disney".

"I told you about that!" she said.

"No ma'am, you didn't."

"Could have sworn I did."

"Didn't."

"Well it ain't much, but your daddy and I took a trip one time to Disney Land, out in California, while he was stationed there for a time. We loved it so much! And I'll tell ya a secret…that's where you were conceived, child. 59', it was. So, we named ya for it."

It made sense, Walt was born in 1960. "For real?" he asked.

"I thought I told you that. I know I did."

"Didn't, mamma."

"Well…'bout time, I guess."

"Um-hm."

"Know what? I heard that they's buildin' one close to here, down in Florida. You wanna go when they do? It'd be so nice!"

"Um-hm."

"Good. Get me the rolling pin, please."

He passed her the rolling pin she needed for her biscuits, and walked out into the day thinking all that new information over he'd just had thrown at him.

And he smiled, because now he had an idea about some things.

The following Saturday, all the kids were in front of Mr. Codges TV, and Billy Cud (whose privates he never did get around to tasting) was the *first* to mention to Walt how funny it was that he shared the same name with that company who created the Mouse.

Walt took his time and looked at Billy real slow, like he'd just waken up. He'd been practicing for this. He knew how he wanted it to play out.

"What of it?" he asked Billy.

"Ha! Man, you got the Mouse name! Yo mamma named you that!"

"Are. You. Saying. That I'm kin to that mouse?"

Billy faltered, but kept at it, not realizing the brutal (excuse the pun) "mouse trap" he'd just stepped into and had no way of escaping.

"Well, maybe! That's some shit. You and that mouse got the same name."

"The mouse's name is Mickey. Not Walt."

"But he comes from Disney, right? So, that's funny! Hey, we got Mr. Disney over he-"

Walt slammed his fist into Billy's nose. Blood flew out and Billy stepped back. Walt prepared himself for blows, and folks around them backed up to make the well-known fighting circle that boys needed to work out any misgivings between them. This was an ancient ritual that some say began when young cave-boys would fight and begin throwing rocks at each other. The other cave-boys around them would also get hit with the errant flying rocks, and so quickly learned to move out of the way for the two combatants to work out their differences on their own, without innocent casualties.

Billy looked up surprised. "Shit man! 'the fuck!"

"Don't call me Disney. I ain't no mouse fucker. Never call me that."

Then Billy almost messed *everything* up.

He smiled, and to Walt's horror, began to try and *apologize* through blood lipped chuckles. He wasn't afraid - he thought it was hysterical! "Ha! Hey man, no problem."

Walt's inner consciousness took a split second to travel an infinitely long future path of life's actions and consequences, and realized that this could be what would *always* happen; he wouldn't get his fight, all his plans to become a warrior in the cave-boy battle circles of lore would dissipate, and he would die a very liked but completely unsatisfied old man. Only one option presented itself to him that allowed any chance of gratification. It was clear and solid in his mind, and he acted on it

13

immediately so that the infinity path of actions and consequences veered its course and presented an entirely new chain of possibilities in his life.

Walt saw this new Infinity Path before him and called it Good, and so he leaped at Billy as a dieter would at a pint of ice cream on their cheat day, before the opportunity of battle was lost.

Newly angry, he pushed Billy to the ground and kicked him in the leg. Billy, not a small kid for his age, rallied quickly and got back up. Still not understanding the "why" of it, he *did* realize the "now" of it, and shot back at Walt, toot sweet.

Neither boy was skilled in the art of boxing, so that scuffle quickly became a wrestling match on the rough sidewalk, which Mr. Codges broke up not long after it started. He didn't want business interrupted, and so he gave them both a smack upside the head (an adult could do that to ill-behaved boys in those days without being arrested!) to learn them a lesson before going back into the store.

Billy looked at Walt. Walt shrugged. Then Billy shrugged. And just like that, the beautiful condition that young boys possess in barrels, that amazing ability to lose interest in the *"then"* because it was no longer relevant in their immediate *"now"*, washed over their brains. The brief lapse in friendship was forgotten, and together they turned to watch more cartoons.

Walt's plan worked. Word circulated about his reluctance to be associated with the Mouse, and of all people, Billy was on the forefront of heralding that story to the public. Turns out, he enjoyed few things more than telling a yarn that'd make a man pee his pants from laughing; although he would admit, if asked, that his *favorite* person to make laugh was his Grandma Jo. Once he got her going, she'd pee completely through her clothes and the chair she was sitting on, and *still* she'd be laughing! His mom would run in and slap him with a towel because she'd be the one to have to clean it up, but it was totally worth it.

Billy performed the story of that day as if on stage at a night club. He'd berate Walt for being too sensitive, act out a slap stick routine of trying to talk through the mess of his bloody nose, and then finally make fun of Mr. Codges as a smelly ogre storming around the store and yelling at the innocent children outside watching TV.

Word spread as it does, and other boys thought it'd be fun to see if they, too, could get Walt's goat. And Walt made sure they knew that yes, they *could* try for his goat, each and every time. They'd walk away with bloody noses and hurt ribs, and Walt would laugh for the fun of it.

Older boys began to jeer at him, so he went after them as well. Walt found out, excitedly, that he wasn't as good at fighting as he thought he was, and on many occasions he thoroughly got his ass handed to him. But he was immune to common sense, it seemed, because he kept walking into altercations that were easily avoided and quickly lost. He got beat up a lot.

But for each loss, he would surely pick up a new trick to try during his next battle. This was fun for Walt, and regardless of how badly he got beaten, he would walk away smiling. Eventually, reputation happened, and folks'd say that Walt was a boy that liked to throw fists. Good ole' Walt D. Cuthbert, nicest guy around and had a mamma that everyone loved. Man, he'd throw down in a *second* if anyone likened his namesake to that of a cartoon mouse.

And that made Walt Disney Cuthbert very happy.

Walt continued to grow into a stout boy, and eventually his mamma, albeit she'd spoken otherwise, did end up getting married again. He was a good man, and was to become a solid male figure in Walt's life for years to come.

It was her late husband's brother that came to visit once his deployment ended. His name was Gill, and he hadn't ever met Walt and wanted to see the nephew he'd read so much about in letters. He was a few years older than his late brother, but Walt could see the resemblance in his uncle immediately.

He had a good sense of humor and, like Walt, was an easy man to like. Gill took to Walt's mamma instantly, which was not surprising; but Mamma Cuthbert also took fast to Gill, and this was a pleasant turn of tide. It wasn't long before Mamma Cuthbert quit her escort business and accepted the proposal of this new man in her life.

The town appreciated it as well. Mamma Cuthbert and her new man were respected. As far as Walt knew, no one ever used his mamma's past against her to damage her marriage with Gill.

Gill was a thoughtful man. Before he proposed, he came to Walt one day. His mamma was out at a function, and the two men went out on the front porch together to rock and drink the sweet tea she had for them the fridge.

Gill turned to Walt. "Dam. This tea, it's the best."

"Yeah."

"You think by the smell it'd be too sweet, but it's not. It's perfect. The taste coats your tongue, but don't ache your head with sugar. Out West, it's hard to get sweet tea. And when ya did, it wasn't worth drinkin'. This is perfect, Walt. Just like your mamma."

Walt, ignoring the compliment to his mother, asked "How else would a person make tea besides this?"

"Boy, you been spoiled! You've had it good from the start. See, it don't come sweet, not at first. You have to put that in there. And out West, like in San Francisco, you have to order "iced" tea, and then add the sugar yourself. I could never get it right as this. I finally just ordered Coke."

Walt laughed and waited for Gill to tell another story of how people did everything backwards Out West, or Up North, or Anywhere That Wasn't here. He liked Gill's stories. They weren't slapstick like Billy's, and not as crude. They spoke of other people in other lands, and ignited in him an interest in the world that would never be quenched.

Instead, Gill turned and looked directly at Walt, as a man does with another man. Walt met his gaze, comfortable and strong.

"Walt," he said "If you don't know by now - I love your mamma. And I love you, so very much. You're my nephew, but I've come to see you as my son."

Walt smiled, and nodded. He felt the same.

"I mean to ask your mamma to be my wife. And I'm asking you to give me your blessing."

Walt had an idea this was coming, but he was still surprised at the emotion that quickly built up behind face and in his chest.

"You need that?" he asked. "*My* blessing?"

The older man nodded. "Yes, Walt. I do. Because I'd have us be a family, a true family. To do that, I'm not just marrying her, I'm marrying you, as well. Ya ken?"

Walt nodded. "I ken."

Gill waited. He was a skilled story teller and purposeful speaker, and he knew there were times when words were no longer needed, only patience.

Walt wasn't a teenager yet, but he was almost there. He was old enough to know when someone was being sincere with him, and to recognize a moment of importance. He got up and walked over to Gill's rocker, which was more of a bench meant for two, and sat down beside him. They looked ahead at the street in front of the house, and he said to the wind, "Yes, sir. You have my blessing."

Gill said, "Thank you, son." and he wrapped his arm around Walt's shoulder, to draw him in close beside him. Walt let him and snuggled into his side under his arm. He leaned his head slightly onto the man's chest and smelled the detergent from Gill's clothes, along with the earlier sweat now dried from the day, and the slight tang of the oil that Gill liked to use in his hair. He also smelled the shaving cream from that morning, and he wondered if his dad had smelled the same way. He didn't really remember. He closed his eyes, breathed in deep, and decided that yes, this was the way his dad had smelled. And he had rarely ever been as happy as he was at that moment, on that day.

CHAPTER 2

THE MEN AT THE BAR

Their faces are hidden to Walt; he could only see their profiles. They were hunched over the bar, in effect creating their own cocoon of existence between only them, and on occasion the barkeep when she materialized to quicken their libation. Walt quickly assumed, and rightly, that these men were the cause of the former customers' misfortunes.

The man to Walt's left was strong and bulky; the man on the right was tall and lean. Walt saw his waitress offer them another round, and saw the man on the right wave her off, but the strong man on the left slapped his hand on the bar twice and pointed two fingers toward their glasses, which the waitress filled. The man on the left, the one who had brusquely ordered more drinks, turned his head toward the man on the right and shook his head, slightly. Pointedly. Scathingly.

The leaner man shrugged and tossed a drink into his grateful gullet. Walt had missed their earlier drinking appetites, and figured Mr. Right (What the hell was this? Reservoir Dogs?) would choke a bit. Not the case, it seemed. He handled it fine, and it satiated the ire of Mr. Left.

Walt continued his watch of the two men, and his curiosity must have pushed its way to the ambient senses around them, because the leaner man bent down to pick a black notebook up off the ground. And as he was bent over, Walt saw his head tilt a bit and look towards him. The shadows covered his face. Only his long nose was discernable.

No, not a *long* nose, Walt thought, but distinguished. Anyhow, Walt drew back his attentions once he realized they were being intercepted.

Then he gave his attentions to the man on the left.

He was intrigued by this man. The danger was palpable. He felt that this man could be trouble incarnate, but since up to now he'd been able to deal with any and all kinds of ill-behaved people in his life more or less successfully, he didn't know to be afraid, or worried. He had an ability to work with folks. He could tame wild dogs.

So, fuck it. He drained his glass and walked it over to the bar. He made sure his heavy boots made noise to help announce his presence. He didn't want there to be any surprises.

"Sadie!" he called out, obviously loud.

"Yes, Dis?" she answered, overtly sweet.

"The damndest thing here; my drink went and got empty!"

"What the ever-lovin' hell, Dis! Let me fix that for ya."

She did, and asked "You want some chili?"

"Well Sadie, I'll tell ya, and I mean this in the most respectful way possible - fuck no."

Walt settled in to the bar and Sadie gave him a hard glance. One that said he needed to watch his ass, cause these two guys just bounced around the brains in four other dudes.

Walt nodded and Sadie found the other end of the bar.

He took a drink and looked amiably down at the large man, the bully man, next to him. He saw the man's hands that were wrapped around the glass in front of him; saw that his knuckles were bandaged and bloody. Walt watched the man, not hiding it at this point, gingerly take the glass up to his mouth and truly – Walt was certain about this, this is how it was -- *enjoy* the drink. He inhaled the fumes before drinking the cheap whiskey (and it *was* cheap whiskey, but good as they come), and then exhaled through his nose, misting up the glass.

You'd think he had just discovered what it was to be hydrated. With anything, Walt thought.

The bully man pounded the glass onto the bar; sniffed mightily; cleared his throat.

"You didn't want the chili." said the man to Walter. Not a question, but still an inquiry.

"No." said Walt, "My stomach's not up for it today."

"You're drinking this bourbon, might as well peel paint, just fine."

Sadie hollered, "Shut it!" from the other end of the bar, and the bully man's taller partner leaned over a bit with a smile. Younger guy, Walt realized. A real slicked-back type. He continued his conversation with the big man.

"Well. This particular grade of paint thinner went and bonded with my DNA years back, so I'm good for this, ya see." He held up a hand and said "Sadie, this is good stuff, I promise. Please bring a bottle."

"We just keep making friends around here" said the younger man. "Must just be local type manners, right Coop? That, or this guy's hittin' on ya."

"Now why would you pop off to me like that, young man?" Walt asked. "You got no call for it."

"I'll tell ya why, sir. Because sir, I don't remember inviting you to drink with us. And I'm curious as to why you thought approaching us was good idea?"

"What's your name, guy?" Walt asked him.

The young man's eyes got wide and he yelled "Sadie! What's up with this guy? He lookin' for a three- way sausage train? That what we got here?"

Sadie, being a professional keeper of her bar and having known Walt for some years, was top notch at diffusing potential altercations that might occur at the work place. Not all of them, for sure, but a lot of them. Most of them, not including the ones that she had started herself.

She put on her best serious impersonation of a concerned citizen and spoke to Walt.

"Walt, sir, what's the trouble here? You trying to play with the butts of this here young man and his father?"

"Oh, he's not my father, Sadie. That's just crazy talk!" the younger man interjected. Walt recognized the heavy run of sarcasm in him, and realized he probably couldn't even help himself from doing it.

Sadie responded "Shit, sorry man. I meant your grandfather. He looks good for his age, ya know?" Then she leaned forward to the bigger man, who Walt had heard called "Coop".

"Sir," she continued in a purposefully loud and obnoxious voice, "you look good, sir. Is that why this man is hitting on you, ya think?"

"Ha! She called you my grandfather!" the younger man said, with an elbow.

"Ramos," the guy named Coop said low, almost in a growl, "please shut that fucking vagina you have on your face, that thing you call a mouth. This man wants to buy us a bottle, and we should let him. He either wants to drink – or do some paint work."

This earned him a middle finger from Sadie. He still had his head down toward the bar and hadn't looked up for a second.

"I'm Walt."

"Okay, Walt." said the young man. "I'm Ramos. This is Coop. Say, Walt, you with those guys that just left? You got anything you need to say to us?"

"No, I'm not with those fellas."

"That's good for you."

Walt looked over at the one guy still lying on the floor, and smirked. "Yeah, guess it must be." Then he leaned over and filled the younger man's glass with the newly arrived bottle. "Ramos, is it? Well Ramos, I'm not here to cause trouble. Or to pry."

"Tell me the reason for your visit, friend, and then I'll explain that you are, in fact, prying."

"Fair enough. Seems you guys are busy; having some kind of time today."

"Do you have pajamas at home that say, "My name is Captain Obvious" on them?" Ramos asked. He was rewarded with a giggle from Sadie, and that made him happy.

"And what I'm doing is buying a drink for some fellas that I think may have an even more of a tough time in front of them. And if they are so inclined to tell me their story, well…I like stories. I'm a sucker for 'em. Tend to get drawn to them, and this dude here, the one that don't talk…I bet he's got a fuckin story. Yeah?"

Ramos's eyes softened a bit and he lowered his voice.

"Thanks for the drinks, sir. Walt. We're ok. Been busy, is all. Gonna get busier. Got shit to take care of."

Walt nodded. "I know how that goes. I sure do." He finished his drink. "Well, I'll take my leave. I got some heavy thinkin' to do over yonder, ya ken? If you're ever this way, come on over to my table and we'll drink. We can talk if you want to. Or not."

The one who didn't talk, the one named Coop, looked up and smiled. "Thanks for the company. Sorry, not lookin' to hook up tonight, old man."

Walt walked away laughing, back to his table in the dark corner.

Coop looked back down at his drink. He felt things slow down and he pulled the gravity of the world toward him.

CHAPTER *3*

COOP

"**Y**ears ago, I killed men. And women. A lot of them, in one night. I exploded their blood into the cracked wooden floors of the rancid two-story building being used as a way station for young children, mostly Mexican, to come into this country illegally and then be used for prostitution.*

I pulled out hearts and kidneys, and I popped eyeballs from their sockets. I broke fingers and I wrapped my hands around the balls of the men who liked to abuse young boys and girls and then squeezed until those men were no longer men. Then they would beg me to kill them. I did.

Then I burned that fucking house to the ground, and those flames just about came close to matching my rage. I walked through the walls of fire, and I swear to you, I was not burned, not once. We were the same temperature, you understand? We matched. I stood in the flames and watched it all fall down around me, and I felt not a thing except what I had hoped would be satisfaction.

But in the days to come, I realized… I was not satisfied. And those flames; they matched my mood, but not my skin. I got burned. Not horribly, but I earned scars.

My name is Cooper Cornelius Happenstance. My brother would call me Cornhole early on, and my mamma liked to say I was her little Baby Corn. 'Course that made it easy for my peers to joke, and holler "Corny" and such, until I grew up a bit and claimed the pride, and the front teeth, of some bigger boys that hassled me one night by the lake.

After that, people just called me Coop. I preferred that."

The two men, Cooper and Ramos, stood and pulled themselves together at the bar. Coop threw cash down for the swill and Ramos slid his notebook, the one he picked up off the floor earlier, into his coat pocket, and followed Cooper outside.

Cooper's boots hit the porch outside the door. He stops to pull out a wooden match and lit it by striking it on said boot. The cigar fired up between his teeth. He's dressed in a sharp suit sporting a silver pocket watch. He puts his hands on his waist, stretched his back, and walked on.

Again, Ramos dutifully followed. He's wearing wing tipped shoes and a true hipster's wardrobe. He pulled a Berretta out of his pocket, ejected the clip and checked the bullets. He nodded and slid it back in, tucked the gun away, and straightened what he could of his suit that, after the melee they'd just been in the epicenter of, was showing off multiple tears and dubious stains.

As they walked to their car, their feet crunched on the gravel. They got in and the doors to their Dodge Challenger slammed home. The car rolled out throwing dust and rocks into the air.

They didn't need to talk. They had bloody, bandaged knuckles and sour, punched in faces. And yet, both were oddly introspective, and dare we say – optimistic (despite the circumstances)?

Ramos, in the passenger seat, wore a curious smile. He was beat up, but excited, and anxious about where they were going.

His eyes flashed red and he could taste the blood caked in his teeth. In the mirror, he looked no better than a ghoul with a sun tan.

Cooper had both hands on the wheel and stared straight ahead, jaw set. His eyes flashed yellow like a feral wolf on crack, and the scars on his face and neck seemed to light up with every muscle contraction.

The Charger burned down a dirt highway. Coop glanced over at a small sign sitting in the trees that marked what he was looking for. He slammed to a stop, backed up, and drove slow along the winding dirt path that was somehow labeled as a road.

They came to a stop in front of a cabin. Cooper turned the radio off and all went quiet. Every sound, every click, and every step echoed back from the empty trees around them.

In sync with each other's patterns, they were nearly silent as they ran into the cabin searched room by room, guns out and ready at all times.

"Anyone can kill, it's not a hard thing to do. Any person is capable of some kind of sadism, really. It's the living with it afterward, that's what's hard to do. Don't matter how good it feels at the time, and no matter how righteous the kill might be, a man has to become something Else *when he takes a life.*

Soldiers chalk it up to doing their duty, a job. Protecting a family from a home intruder is an easy one though; a man has to make sure his family is ok; the spray of the intruder's blood on the wall becomes an art piece to show off at dinner parties, depicting the once-threatened, but now prosperously continued life of their family. Although I'd imagine there'd be some undiscussed nightmares in that man's future."

They found a locked entrance and readied to break into the room behind it. Cooper stood back as Ramos kicked in the door and walked inside.

"Reconciling it afterward is the important thing. You either accept your actions because you did your duty, or you accept your actions because YOU ARE THE KIND OF PERSON THAT IS OK WITH THOSE ACTIONS."

Cooper heard Ramos speak from inside the now exploited room. "Oh, Fuck…"

He crashed in next to his partner and examined the scene. He looked at Ramos, and then back at what was waiting for them in the small, open space. Coop would never be described as a man of inaction; his very powerful and determined gait while moving toward any destination was well documented. But that was when he knew where he was going, or what he wanted to achieve.

This now, was not one of those times. He wanted to move, to create action, and his mind worked to figure *how* he could act and implement his mental energy into the world and get something *done*.

The action needed was less than a second away from clicking in his brain, he felt that, knew that, and tensed his muscles as he anticipated a quick forceful movement.

That final piece to the puzzle never had a chance to fit. One more second would have been *more* than enough time to get a clear situational picture, but for Coop one more second was more time than he had before an axe handle cracked him over the back of the head. Instantly, he found himself breathing in the clogs of dirt off the floor that his nose was now pushed against.

Coop was a very strong man. He instinctively began pull the gravity in from around him and to make himself the heaviest *thing* in that space/time area. He made himself the *reason* for his place in the universe. He used it to his advantage, and matter began flowing *to* him and *through* him, and he worked to get up off the ground. He began to get up, and ultimately, he would get up.

The hand tensely grasping the axe handle, though, knew full well what Coop was capable of and continued the barrage of heavy thuds. It came down again. And again. And yet again for good measure.

More hands grabbed the now limp body of Coop; any matter that had managed to pull towards him was now dispersed back into the local ether.

Coop heard a voice, like a whisper, *Oh shit was that too much? Is he dead?*

Then another whisper answer, *He's fine I'd be more concerned that it wasn't enough.*

His boots scraped as he was dragged across the floor, out the door, and into the open trunk of a car.

"A man takes account for what he does. And I did that; I took account of myself and I liked what I had become, and I became that person who claimed victory over a wrong done to him and his family, and who put away the bad men who had caused that suffering.

I gained my revenge, and so for a time, I became … victorious."

Coop's feet were gently arranged in the bed of the trunk and his head was propped up on a blanket. The lid slammed, and he was unwittingly carried to the next, or last, stage of his existence.

CHAPTER **4**

THEN

The Bonsai Tree

"**I**s that thing still alive?"

The question was irritating. So, she ignored it and kept working.

"Seriously… is it supposed to be falling over like that?"

Sam looked up from her desk and gave a look that she hoped conveyed a polite "Go Fuck Yourself." This was an office, her place of business, so of course she couldn't just come out and *tell* the young hipster-business hopeful guy that she had no interest in conversing with him, that she didn't want to flirt with him (although he did have nice hands and that was important in a man), and that this was her time of quiet reflection and focus. Sam needed this time because when her boss got back to the office, her time of reflection and relative peace would be over. Fucking Over.

So, this dipshit was sitting here trying to make conversation about something he obviously didn't understand. And Sam was in charge of this office, and she knew that it was unprofessional to curse and shout in an office, and because he was a potential customer probably waiting for Brenda (because really, who WASN'T fucking waiting for Brenda, yeah?) to get back, she had to be civil. And polite.

But not, she decided, conciliatory. Or overly nice. Or in any way curious about his well-being in the least little bit.

She decided to use the "Less is More" approach.

"It's a bonsai tree," she said, assuming that would explain all that needed to be understood.

"I know it's a bonsai tree," the young man replied, "I'm Japanese."

This caught Sam's attention, and she actually looked up at him. "You don't look Japanese. You look like a black guy."

"Well, I'm that, too. I'm like Tiger Woods. Mixed."

Sam kept looking at him. He thought he was being cute. "Tiger Woods isn't Japanese. He's Chinese. And Black. And Native American. And Caucasian."

"Ha! I know, right? He does this whole "'Cablinasian'" thing, or whatever. You think because he's a pretty good golfer, he should get to make up words like that?"

Then the guy put his phone on the couch and leaned over with his elbows on his knees, giving Sam his full attention and expecting a rise in the conversation.

Sam continued her look at him.

He sat there, smiling, elbows on knees.

They both kept looking at each other.

He's a salesman, Sam thought. *He's doing the "shut up and wait for them to answer" thing; he's daring me to answer, he's leaving it to me to become uncomfortable with the silence and feel obligated to continue the conversation. What an asshole. Brenda will love him. Plus, she's into black dudes now. Not the really black, night-time walking type black, but the lighter skinned, tight jeans wearing type of black. The Asian in the guy, if there was any, would probably really work for her while she goes and parties in that new sushi champagne bar that just opened up; I bet she asks him if he's been there yet. And I'll bet he has been there already.* Of course *he has. Fucking hipster. He probably waits until movies are in the dollar theatre before he sees them, cuz he's not that person who rushes to see the new popularity binges that everyone else rushes to see as soon it becomes available. But he will* for sure *be at the newest wine and art bar, like, opening night, because anybody who's anybody is going to be at the opening of Lush N' Brush, and drink the new local wine, and paint their shit designs on cheap art store canvas…*

She was picking him apart in her thoughts, and he was still looking at her. Smiling.

Sam looked back down at her plant, shrugged, decided she didn't give a crawling rat's fart about his little point that he was seemingly compelled to prove to himself, that point he had read in one of his men's magazines while he was taking a shit that said that thing about listening 80% and talking 20%, and also, once you said what you said, don't speak again until the other person does. He has to show that self-constraint, thereby showing his strength and control over the conversation. She just bet he was one of those assholes that as he shook hands, he brought his free hand up and grabbed the other person's shoulder, and squeezed, and felt like he was taking control, showing dominance, in that simple action.

What an *asshole*.

"So, you're not Japanese," she spoke out loud; a fact stated and put into life's swirling ether that could have been directed towards the plant, or to herself, or to no one in particular.

He sat back and relaxed his shoulder on the arm of the couch. "No. I'm not. I just said I was mixed, yeah?"

"You said you were Japanese."

"Ok. Look. (Sam smiled… she had irritated him) I don't have to be Japanese to see that maybe you're not cutting that tree right. It's leaning over the edge of the table, like it's about to puke, a little. And there's not a lot of green left on it. So, I'm thinking you're not trimming it right."

"Hmm. Did your NON-Japanese roots give you that thought?"

"My mom's Chinese. That's my Asian part. Ok? But still…"

"Well, then…" Sam replied slowly, like explaining the solar system to a three-year-old, "you should know that the art of trimming a bonsai is a predominantly Chinese tradition. It's a Japanese word, but a Chinese art form. So, you should know that this tree is being manicured precisely as it should be and being nurtured just as it needs to be. You should know these things, seeing that your mom is Chinese and all."

Cablasian guy had already picked up his phone and was scrolling through texts. That, or Googling bonsai trees. Whichever, he was astute enough to know that the conversation was over, and didn't feel that he needed to reply any further. Sam felt that way as well; this non-verbal agreement being met, they set there in the small lobby in relative silence, each making a real effort to focus on their own little projects at hand.

Then Brenda walked in and the silence broke, irrevocably.

The intern that had already been there for a few weeks knew enough at his point to get the hell out of the way and not make eye contact. Brenda would address you if she chose to. But the intern that had only started yesterday foolishly smiled and tried to get her attention. Brenda was on her blue tooth headset and maybe would have just walked right on by and not seen that new intern, but there was a brief lull in her conversation and Brenda wasn't speaking. The newer intern took this as a chance to get in front of her, try to shake her hand and say good morning.

Brenda stopped, looked at the stupid girl, and said "Move." The stupid girl blinked and had no response. So, Brenda continued to stare at her and watch as the girl's very soul was incinerated from within.

"No John, I don't agree with that, or those terms." Brenda said into her ear piece and continued to walk forward. The stupid girl just stood there, hoping no one saw that blasphemous interaction with the boss, and yet knowing that everyone did. *She'll cry to her mother about it tonight*, Sam thought, *and lament the fact that she was let go from her internship after just one day. Stupid bitch.*

Brenda walked by Sam's desk and wrapped on it twice with her knuckles. She then continued on into her office, where she performed a cliché, but effective, pithy door slam.

Sam got up and grabbed a stack of papers off the desk and steeled herself for action; the day had begun.

Brenda was still standing, waiting for Sam when she walked in. Sam took Brenda's purse, and helped get her jacket off, as she continued to speak into the air.

"No" Brenda said, "Andrew is handling this foreclosure." Sam stood back in the corner and out of Brenda's way, as she now strode to her seat behind her *very* contemporary desk. *The fucking thing is more glass than wood,* Sam thought.

Brenda continued her earpiece conversation. "Excuse me, we are not negotiating anything. I, and NOT that monkey turd Harold, am the executive on this account. I'm not approving any extensions. This should have been done last week, and the fact that Harold is talking about refinance options NOW is pissing me off. Fuck him. Fuck *them*. It's too late in the process to do anything about it, is my point. He keeps doing stuff like this, trying to hold things up, and be the good guy or something. And I can appreciate that, I really can, but in this case - it's just too late."

Brenda stopped talking and instead began to listen. Or rather, Sam thought, to think about what she was going to say next.

Brenda, Sam's bitch of a boss, sighed and looked up at the ceiling while shaking her head.

"Well, if he sent an email about it earlier, I *certainly* didn't see it. Of course not. No, nor did I receive any kind of certified mail regarding an extension. My apologies, but I just didn't get the word soon enough that we were going to try and rework the billing structure on this loan at all…had I known that that was a viable option, I would have *absolutely* done everything I could to follow through for… acceptable results. Harold says the tracking number shows it was received here, huh? Well, I don't know. Maybe an intern got it, I'll have to see. But really, would it make any difference? Really? There was no way we could have lowered payments to where that family could afford the place, and even if they *could* have afforded them, we've now put ourselves into a position where WE have to shoulder the burden of taking a longer time to pay our loan back. And if we do this for one customer, then we'll have to do it for all of them, eventually, and that'll be paperwork that I don't want to deal with."

She listened again, getting agitated.

"Well, Glory-Be! What the hell, John...then they shouldn't have gotten knocked up right after purchasing a house that they couldn't afford, right? That's not my problem. People make choices and people have to live with those choices. This is a business. A deal was made, and that's that. Now listen, I'll look for that paperwork here and see if it got mis-handled and we can talk again tomorrow, but John … I'm not granting any kind of extension on this."

Brenda viciously tapped her new Apple Watch and disconnected the call. Sam, because she considered herself an optimist, assumed John was done talking and had already hung up as well.

"Sam," Brenda turned to her, "my watch tells me that I burned a hundred calories walking up the stairs today."

"Fantastic."

"Your job today is to find me four reasons to leave here and come back. That's five hundred calories. I'm competing against Becky and Suze this week to see who can burn the most calories, and the winner gets treated to dinner at that new place, what's it called? Lush Brush or something?"

"Lush N' Brush."

"Yeppers. That one. And I'm not going to let those fat bitches beat me, Sam. I know they're going to cheat; Becky's husband - Jimbo? - is a trainer at PurposeFlex and I'll bet she has him wearing it all day for her."

"She'd cheat like that?"

"Seriously? Are you that dumb? Of course she would. She's not going to get off her own ass to do the work herself."

"Okay."

"I'll have to go to PurposeFlex to check and see if Jimbo's wearing that damn watch; and maybe I'll get a workout in with him if he's there..."

Brenda looked at Sam to see if she got her *not* so subtle innuendo. Sam did. Yes, she knew Brenda was screwing good ole' Jimbo, Becky's husband. In fact, everyone knew. Jimbo was the town slut. However, *not* everyone knew that good ole' Jimbo, big swingin' dick of Callahan, was *also* screwing Andrew, Brenda's counterpart in Foreclosures.

Brenda, not getting a rise out of Sam, straightened her back and pushed her hair behind the ears. Then she grabbed her boobs. She squeezed them, and pushed them up and watched them pertly fall back into place; she smiled. This was her new routine since she got them done a few months back.

"Sam, I'm tellin' ya… Dr. Lichtenstein is the *man*. I've still got major feelings in my nips! You should do this, really. He's amazing."

"Sure."

"Sam. Look at this. They look real, you can't tell the difference! You gotta feel these puppies, they are the bee's fuckin knees!"

Brenda began looking at her calendar, until Sam went over and decided to *actually* grab her breasts. Brenda looked up, more surprised at having her bluff called than of having Sam feel her up.

"Yeah, they're pretty good." critiqued Sam. "You'll have to give me his number. Will that be all for now?"

"Of *course* there is, Sam. I'm a busy bitch."

"For sure."

"What is the name of that dumb-bitch-intern that tried to corner me this morning?"

"Trinity, ma'am. She began a few days ago. She's from a small town near Valdosta."

"Whatever. When did that letter get here that John sent about the loan extension?"

"We received it yesterday."

"Ok, well… as I'm sure you probably suspected, Trinity messed that shit up, big time. She put the dam thing in the shredder bin by mistake. Unbelievable, right?"

"I can honestly say, I've never dealt with a worse mistake. Even with new interns, there's a line of errors that can't be crossed."

Brenda smiled. "Can her for that. She needs to go, today. I'll call John and let him know about our discovery this afternoon. And SHRED that letter. You've got it locked up, right? You'll handle it?"

"Yes. I'll destroy it immediately." Sam confirmed.

"Okay. Good. You know, if the Loan Department could do a better job of things, we wouldn't run into this mess. It's not *my* job to re-work *their* mistakes. I don't make loans, I close them. That's my job, and it's how I get paid. You feel me?"

Brenda looked at Sam, who nodded once back at her to show a full and clear understanding of the situation.

Sam asked "Anything else?"

"Yes. What is the name of that OTHER intern? That boy with the nice butt? The gay one."

"That's Claude, ma'am."

"Of course it is. Give him this watch and have him do five miles on the gym track. I need to get an edge on this contest."

"Got it. Here's your mail."

Most of it was orders from Amazon. *Some* of it *might* have been work related. Brenda screeched, "Oh good, my signed Mindy Kaling book! She is just so smart, ya know? *Really* unexpected from an Indian girl. You know she's from India? They are so repressed over there."

"And here," said Sam, ignoring any chance of more conversation, "is this box."

"From Amazon?"

"Don't know. Just has your name on it. In script."

Brenda gave Sam her Apple watch and pointed at her. "It's creepy, right? Look, there's no address on it. And this weird design in the middle. Whatever. That letter gets shredded today, right? And dopey girl gets let go. And Franz, or Fitz, or whatever, runs five miles with that watch on. We good?"

Sam didn't bother to correct Brenda on Claud's name as she walked out the door, but she did stop to say, "Oh, you have a guy out there. Says he has an appointment with you. Been sitting there for an hour? So…" No answer from Brenda, just a stare, "You want me to send him in? He's been here since before 11. He likes to talk."

Brenda looked through the window and asked "Is it the black guy out there? The one in the tight pants?"

"He's Chinese…some of him. Said he was Chinese."

"No shit? So, he's mixed." She looked down, then back up. "You think he's been to that new Sushi place?" Sam didn't answer, wasn't expected to. She wanted to see how long the inner monologue Brenda was having with herself would last.

Not long, it turned out.

"Let him sit thirty minutes, then have him come in."

"New intern?" Sam asked.

Brenda looked straight at her for the first time. And then smiled, which made Sam apprehensive. "No, actually. Potentially a new - office manager."

"I'm being promoted?" Sam asked.

Brenda's fingers stopped moving and her eyes settled on Sam.

"Ahhh… good" she responded. " You know what, this is good. We needed to have a good talk. It's been a while, huh? So let's talk, Sam. Have a seat."

Sam was immediately on guard. She knew, she felt, some shit was about to go down.

"I'll stand. I'm good."

Brenda smiled, and that smile said she could give a fuck *what* Sam did.

"Perfect. We're expanding, Sam, as you know." she began.

Sam raised her eyebrows, and shifted her head a bit, to show Yes, in fact she did know this.

Brenda continued, "We're getting bigger and we're getting noticed, and now we have to behave like the big boys, act the part. I need flash, I need bling, I want trend in this office. I'm looking to bring in people who know the town, who will make our division look good. I'm looking for someone who can handle that expansion, specifically in the direction of corporate recognition. These people would be working alongside you. *With* you. You'll handle what's here already, that's not changing. I'm just – I'm looking for someone who'll work on the other stuff, that – well, stuff that doesn't, ah, parallel, with your particular talents. I need someone who sells, someone who is, ya know, *out there*, and *in it.*"

Sam worked hard, real hard, to ignore her anger and keep her stare leveled, before she responded.

"Brenda, maybe you'll give me a kind of play by play here, 'cause I'm not feeling that I'm on the same page. We don't actually *sell* anything here, right? We foreclose on houses. How is this guy's, or anyone else's, sales ability relevant to us? The bank tells us which houses are in trouble, and then you go and shut them down. That's what we do. And we're thirty percent over quota YTD. What's the problem?"

Brenda said nothing. Sam continued.

"Brenda, listen to me. I keep your shit tight, and your business steady, you know that. I keep nonsense away from you. I keep your cherished private lists of foreclosed houses you haven't yet turned over to the sales people locked up, so you can use them as your personal vacation homes. And I make sure your letters, the ones that need to get shredded – *get* shredded."

Brenda replied, "If you mean you've done your J-O-B, then yes, you have. But when corporate comes down, we are *not* known for an office that shows them a hot night on the town! We are a lame duck division, and that has got to change. Shit, even fucking John gets that, and he always smells like a stank set of turd-dipped elephant balls. But, he takes the big boys and girls out, and he shows up looking the part. So, if I'm going to expand, we need a hipper, more in touch, staff. And also, those OTHER sales people you talk about? Those people that sell our houses after we foreclose them? Let me tell you, we want the best ones selling our houses. Not the entry level losers, or the long-living walking dead that only sell one house a month and then go around quoting Glen Gary Glen Ross to you. I want our foreclosures to be selling to the people that pay big bucks for them…the young hipsters, the older nostalgic's, groups like that. Plus, we need a stronger *in* with Hud 8. The low-end houses can be sold off to them, or better yet, we can get a military contract for officer housing! Let's get our midline houses out there for the government to buy and present it as turnover for them. This is the direction we need to push forward on, Sam."

"How does ANY of that concern us, Brenda? Your commission is not based on the sale of houses *after* we foreclose on them. There are no bonuses set up for the selling of these houses after we're done with them. That is not our job. Why are you concerned with *any* of this?"

"No, my commission doesn't increase with those sales. Nor do we get a bonus, or any say about how those houses are sold. But Sam, those sales people, they're big on kickbacks. Nice kickbacks. On so, so many levels. Do you know what Steve Rawls, over at Five Points Credit Union, gets from these sales guys?"

"No. I don't." Sam replied.

"That's right. You *don't* know. And that is why I'm looking to hire in new people, with different talents, for our division. I need people who have an idea about that sales world; people who know some things about … things."

"And. OK. And you think the Chinese guy knows these … *things*?" said Sam, whilst throwing up very large, and very "fuck you-ish" air quotes with her hands.

"To be honest," responded Brenda, ignoring the air quotes, "no, I don't. But he doesn't need to know them, because I believe he can look the part, create the image of production, and look all fancy while I get in and pull the right strings with all the right people. Pure decoration, Sam. He'll be outside, bull shitting with the bull shitters, while I'm inside, pulling on the right dicks to lure them to our list of primo houses that they can get quick and easy. Because we'll keep those houses off the market for them, keep them hidden in our little drawer until we're ready to pull them out. And then, when they sell them for large profits, we'll be handed these fat white envelopes with cash to show just how much they appreciate what we do here. That's the business, that's how we make money, and I know that you don't want to do that. Like you said, you…well, you keep the lists. And I appreciate that. You keep this place secure and steady. And most importantly, you know which lines not to cross. Because I know, Sam, that you are *not* a stupid girl."

Sam saw that if Brenda had had any mental guards, edits, or filters between her mind and her mouth when she walked into that office earlier, they were all gone now. Shut down. So Sam replied in kind.

"This is bull shit. You talk about bull shitting? *This* is some **bull shit**. I'm not sharing any kind of management position with him, and Brenda, I hope you know *just* how ludicrous this all is. You're playing with fire that's gonna burn ya, and hard."

Brenda came back:

"I felt I was being reasonable with you, Sam. What I'm trying to get across here is this that isn't something *against* you. Quite the opposite, in fact. It's something that's *for* the company and for the common good. But there you go with one of your "temperaments" that you always get. Sam, you have so many talents: discretion is one. Another is that you have a mind organized with compartments and drawers like I can't even imagine, and you never forget anything ever. And you file better than the Vietnamese chick at the salon can thread my eyebrows. You are a cornerstone of this office, Sam, a real key ingredient. But you aren't in the plan for this expansion, simply because that's not where your talents lie. You have a brain for numbers, but a look that says…mediocrity."

Sam faltered for an instant with her words. This infuriated her that a person like Brenda, a blonde fucking cockroach, could make her stumble on what to say next, just by using the grade school insult, "You're not attractive!" and "I'm prettier than you are!"

"Brenda, you're out of line. *You*, of all people, will not denigrate me. Not *ever*."

The beautiful lips on Brenda's face pursed forward to repel Sam's dead, hard stare.

Sam's pushing back, Brenda realized. *That's ok, smart dogs do that from time to time. But you have to keep them in place. Sam has been getting snippy lately; the idea of competition might put her in check.* Also, Sam had to remember who was boss here. Brenda couldn't go and *tell* her that, because if you have to remind someone that you're the boss, then…you're not the boss. You define that, and people recognize it, by your actions.

Brenda looked up at the words framed over her door, placed there so that she could see it over the heads of the people that were standing in front of her, waiting for her to determine the course of their lives. It was a quote from Eleanor Roosevelt, and it said, "Being powerful is like being a lady; if you have to tell people you are, then you aren't."

Brenda stood and walked around the desk, ending right in front of Sam. She pushed herself forward so her crotch pressed firm against Sam's hip, and then lightly put a hand around to the small of Sam's back before placing her face against Sam's cheek.

"You can push back, honey. That's ok, I understand. But don't *ever* forget your place. You've been getting snippy; if you want to rise up in the company and be part of the future path, then honestly, I think the idea of competition might put a fire under you. Also, you need to remember that I make those decisions, and not you…"

Brenda's hand brushed over Sam's butt cheek, held there for a beat, and then grabbed hold. Sam didn't move at the touch, but whispered "You've never seemed to question the value of my body before, Brenda. This is all bullshit. You know it is." She allowed a small pout to form at her lips.

Brenda had realized early on that Sam would need to be controlled, and quickly. She was a force of energy and emotion, and she was very smart. She couldn't keep her in the office without being completely under Brenda's control. She saw quickly that using force against her, or trying to push her around, wouldn't be effective. For most people, it would have. It was pathetic how easily folks bent under the fire of Brenda's temper. But Sam couldn't be affected by a pushy boss. In fact, Brenda felt that might work just the opposite; Sam would focus on being *against* her and Brenda would have let her go, and that would have been a waste of a huge asset.

And it was so obvious how Brenda would be able to attain her control. Okay, it wasn't right up there on the surface obvious, but if one was looking close enough (and Brenda was), it would have been spotted (and she had).

Sam had been eager to please her almost immediately after Brenda made it known, very subtly, that any physical affection between them wouldn't be rejected. Brenda certainly didn't mind having Sam drop to her knees now and again... really, it was pretty good.

Sam was a Giver.

Sam was a Giver, and Brenda was a Taker, and that's how it was. Yin and Yang, all that shit.

But their dalliances had been strained as of late. Sam was more addled, it seemed, than she usually was. And in addition, Brenda was trying, really giving a Girl Scout go of it, to get her husband in the sack more often. If she had to be married to the guy, she could at least get nookie out of it. That was one of the reasons, she privately told her shrink, why she even got married at all; to be able to get cock whenever she wanted it and without always having to go out and work for it.

But lately, her husband hadn't been around very much. So she'd gone off with women for long periods, to give a big "fuck you" to her ever-distant husband, and that was fun, but - she would soon remember that she missed the cock. Had to have it. Wanted it - always went back to it.

It helped, though, that she enjoyed women also. She was always amazed at how often these types of things happened in the workplace.

"The thing about bullshit, Sam," Brenda explained softly, "is that it's been known to roll downhill. Now you be sure to not step in it, ya hear? Or get your nose pushed in it, whatever." She squeezed Sam's butt hard, with a pinch that would leave a red mark. "My apologies; I misspoke earlier. Your body suits me fine, girl. I was trying to make a point about how I'm working to brand our division. Don't get grumpy on me."

And, that was the end of it. Brenda abruptly turned back toward her desk, leaving Sam far behind her.

Without even looking, she asked "Who's that box from again?"

Sam's teeth hurt because of the clamp she had them in. But, she did manage to squeak out "I don't know. Nothing's on the box. Just your name. As you can see."

"Right. Send over the black guy in about twenty minutes. And bring in coffee after you send him in. And Sam...that plant of yours is fucking dead. Throw it the hell away. What is that, like the tenth one? You have issues with plants."

Sam didn't answer. She returned to her desk and glared at the brown, tangled mess that was hanging over one side. With the thunder of hate boiling in her heart and her eyes a putrid tar-black coat of mud, she picked the plant up from the topmost stem and slammed it loud into the metal waste basket beside her desk. The can's metal rung with the recent tumult, and the sound of dead leaves settling to the bottom marked yet another death in the vicious cycle of Sam's bonsai's.

At the disheartening noise, Cablasian guy jumped up away from his Twitter feed and looked over to where the explosion came from. He saw Sam sitting at her desk, applying makeup, oblivious to any alleged clamor. And as a credit to his fellow man, and to show that the male human species of this planet *is* actually evolving and maturing a bit in this new age of technology (which many scholars debate over - many claim that the male human is the most rapidly *declining* species on the planet, actually thought to be "DE-volving"), he wisely chose to not say a word about it.

CHRISTOPHER S. WHITE

CHAPTER **5**

THE BLACK NOTEBOOK OF CLIFF RAMOS

There was this local BBQ place that Cooper and Ramos liked to eat at, and that's where they were now.

Coop took a break from gnashing his teeth and looked at Ramos, "Captain asked how you thought I was doing?"

Ramos had his face down deep in pulled pork and his answer was garbled, "Yep."

"Um hm. Did you answer him?"

"Yep," uttered Ramos, with his voice still in the meat.

Cooper sighed and set down his tea; then he pulled out a small pack of wet wipes from his inner jacket pocket and motioned for Ramos, who'd finally come up for air from his pork and was covered in sauce, to take them.

"Here. Wipe your damn face" he said.

Ramos started to giggle, he couldn't help it. "Why do you always carry those things around? Is that for me? Do you carry wet wipes around for your partner who is a grown ass man?"

"I carry these perfectly moistened towels with me because sometimes, boy, a paper towel just doesn't cut it. You need something extra at times to get the stink off. And also, after two years of working with someone, you get to know their habits. And you act accordingly. Proactively, say."

"Like how? What are *my* habits?"

"Like now, for instance, how you tend to use your *face* to eat your food, as opposed to just letting your fingers, or hands, or God forbid even some silverware, help to shovel it into your mouth. It's like your face goes to your food, as opposed to the other way around. See here? You are completely leaned over your plate. Nose, inches from the table. You're inhaling that honey mustard-flavored ripping's of pig flesh like dogs sniff farts. I mean, I *know* your hand has to be in there somewhere, but honestly? I can't see where your arm ends and your long horse face begins."

Ramos thought hard for a reply. He found one, "I should think that speaks for the quality of food at this fine establishment, sir."

Coop considered this, drank more sweet iced tea, and eyeballed Ramos. He'd decided he wasn't going to respond to him. Just look at him.

And Ramos, knowing full well that Coop had pulled back, smiled. And continued, "Seriously, though. Isn't it slightly embarrassing to always carry those around in your pocket? And you can't blame this on Baby Girl. I know three year old granddaughters get messy, but come on, right?"

"The wipes do help with Ally, Ram. The girl puts on a princess dress, and then goes out to jump in the mud. It's good to be prepared. And to tell you the truth, I ain't never had a man come up to me and say how embarrassing it is to be carrying around wet wipes. So, I ain't never had a reason to think so."

Ramos responded dryly, "That's 'cause I don't know any men stupid enough to say that to you. Most have an appreciation for their prized external tender parts."

Coop nodded and continued, "She's a special girl, Ally. Smart. Way smart, and fun. And beautiful, like her mamma. I tell you, there ain't never been a more beguiling child than Ally. She expects your love, demands it. And she gets it."

"I do know. She's special. All those astrologists got it wrong...the world don't spin around the sun, it goes around Baby Girl. And she'll tell you that, for nothin'. Can't believe she's almost four."

"You makin' the party?" Coop asked.

At that, Ramos lost any geniality in his voice. "Coop. You honestly think I'd miss a party for Ally? Or anything? Ever?"

"No. I truly don't."

"I'll be there. Only Death himself could keep me away, and I'm not so sure even *that'd* be enough. And I'll come packin' wet wipes, cause a wise man once told me that was a smart thing to do."

Cooper leaned in to Ramos and got his elbows set on the table. "What'd you say to El Capitan?"

Ramos was young but tall, very smart, and quick. He had a sense of humor that some folks did not appreciate. Cooper could handle him though and could see when Ramos was trying to think up a real smart-ass remark. Which on a typical day, was always.

"I told him you were being an asshole. *Still* being an asshole."

"Well, hey. No one expected *that* to change."

"That's what I said, too!"

"Um hm. Anything else?"

"Yep. I told him I thought that you had gotten even *more* grumpy. And he didn't believe me. He said he's known you since I started to jerk off, and that it was *not* possible you could get any grumpier than you had been up till now. So then, because he's the Captain and all, I said ok, you're probably right, Coop's still the same grumpy asshole. Just older, I guess. That must suck. Coop, ya gotta tell me, does it suck getting old? Cause I bet it does."

"You're never gonna find out, Ram, you keep on talkin'."

"Sure, I got that. Don't get your Depends all wet." Ramos wiped his hands and dropped the wet wipes onto the now empty plate of the pig's flesh that had been ripped from the bones of the butchered swine. The aura of the pig still radiated from the dish, Cooper thought. "He's worried about ya, is all. I told him you were doing great." He shrugged his shoulders, yawned, and sort of... let his eyes wander down to the plate below him.

Coop had witnessed this before. "What are you seeing this time?"

"Why do you say that?" Ramos asked.

"Because I can tell when you go into one of your trances. Like some epiphany explodes inside your head, and it gums you all up."

"So?"

"So that means I have to listen about it later in the car, where I can't get away from you. Tell me now. What'd you see this time?"

Ramos smiled and indulged himself to talk of his inner thoughts. "Just an idea, really. An observation. We just inhaled this pig's flesh, that had been ripped off its bones while being, literally, butchered. We just ate the outer covering of a once living being. And then we seasoned it, and savored it, and made it a treat. You wouldn't even know it was flesh we were eating if you didn't already know any better."

"This that animal rights thing? About going into a grocery store and not seeing the face on the meat we buy? Saw it on Netflix."

"Interesting. But no, I didn't go there. I don't buy into that rationale. Rather, I saw us as divine beings. We didn't just inhale this creature, we butchered it, and seasoned it, and savored its juices on *our* terms, not on his. We sucked in this creature's cosmic energy, but we did it by drowning it in Carolina Sweet Sauce. No other creature can even *think* of doing that. They eat it as they get it. But not us. We not only take its life as we please, but we also butter it to our tastes. That's kind of amazing."

The waitress, Dana, walked over. "Hey Wolfman, you carrying out cheesecake today?"

"No hon, let's save it for tomorrow." Coop answered. "Sam's coming home early tomorrow, and we're gonna have a movie night with Baby Girl."

Dana smiled. "Sounds good. I'll have one that's fresh and cold ready for you all." Coop came back with a "Thanks, babe" while putting down his standard twenty-dollar bill for the meal.

"One of these days, she's gonna smack you for calling her "hon", and "babe," Ramos said.

"Maybe," Coop answered, "I would definitely deserve it."

Ramos, against all his best efforts, had ended up idolizing Coop, in his own way. And it was small things like this that Ramos could not get enough of. Shit like calling waitresses "babe," and them not getting offended.

It wasn't a Southern thing either. Ramos had seen plenty of that in New York. And it wasn't an age thing, he'd seen young guys do it, and old. But Ramos had tried it, and it had never worked out well. He'd always earn a stare that marked him as a creep.

And the twenty-dollar bill thing? Coop always had the money cordoned out for the week, for the lunches he paid for. And it was never a ten, a five, and some ones. Nor was there ever any hard change involved. He kept it to the least amount of bills as possible. Ramos asked him about that once, and Coop replied that paying for something shouldn't be a show; that it wasn't a time to brag. Just pay for it, tip well, and keep it cool. That gets respect.

And Ramos bought into that. He loved seeing it. Coop wasn't an old guy, somewhere in the top half of his forties, but the term "Old Soul" never applied to someone more appropriately. He was solid and built harder than most stones that ran through the North Georgia-mountains. Coop was about the age Ramos assumed his own dad would have been, had he not died when Ramos was very young. But regardless of his respect for the man, Ramos made sure to not make Coop a father figure. That was important to him from the beginning of their partnership. This was his career, this was his path, and becoming emotionally intertwined with Coop would not help him to complete what he was meant to do.

Still, Coop had gained his respect. Not his trust, not completely, because he trusted no one and never had, but he'd admit to anyone that if any man had gained the largest amount of trust in his life, then it would be Cooper.

THE WOLF, A BUTCHER, HIS DEMON, AND THEIR MASTER

Cooper Cornelius Fucking Happenstance. The man was funny. He played the "I'm just a simple man; a redneck with a cause," card, but that was bullshit. Ramos saw through that almost instantly upon meeting him. Rednecks don't wear tailored, contemporary Brooks Brothers suits; nor do they carry a pocket watch, one in particular that Ramos had always been fascinated by; nor do they keep their boots polished to a high shine, even though they always refer to them as their "shit kickers."

No, Ramos - known as Ram to Cooper when they were getting along, or as "Bam Bam" when Coop thought Ramos was acting particularly annoying, which was often – saw quickly that his partner and mentor, Coop, was a very intricate and multi-layered man. But like most works of art, Ramos would think, they are simple and perfect from the outside when you first look at them. However, it's when you begin to stare into that tangled mess of brush strokes do you begin to understand just how gnarled and mangled, or rather intricate and dimensional, that this piece of art really is.

And Ramos, he knew art. Like Christian scholars who could quote the Bible line by line, Ramos could name practically any piece of art hanging in any museum anywhere in the world. He put these pieces of canvas to memory as a courtesy to those that came before him; he would give them that dignity. But beyond that, the majority of the work that had ever been created meant nothing to him. Most artists tried and failed to live up to anything that really stood the test of being unique through time. He felt the same with books...there are many, many, great books out there, but only a few of them are truly fantastic, truly a mirror of the human soul that created it.

Ramos considered himself an artist. So, he kept his black notebook with him.

The leather was real, and he had bound it himself. He had made over a hundred leather notebooks in his life, each meaningful and poignant to him. The paper was special as well, very high-end stuff. His view was that if he was to pour his brain onto physical matter, that matter should be worth having his brain poured on to it.

Ramos didn't bother to thank Coop for the lunch; it was Coop's day to pay. It was expected that Coop pay that day and getting thanked by Ramos would have just annoyed him. Plus, when Ramos payed for it the next day, he knew he'd get no gratitude from Coop. It was what they did.

Ramos asked, "You think if I ordered as many pies from Dana as you did, she'd tell me why some folks around here call you Wolfman?"

Coop pulled out his watch and checked the time. Ramos liked how it snapped shut. "*You* can't get the pies from her that *I* get from her, boy. So, no, I don't believe she'd talk to you."

"You sayin' there's *no* chance I could buy her pies?"

"It's not up to me who she sells her pies to, Shit Stain, but I'd imagine that she prefers a more established, reliable clientele. One that's more deserving, and can always be counted on to *pay*. Now, I could be wrong about that, but probably…I'm not." Coop winked at him, and walked off to hit the head before they left.

Ramos smiled. He had heard a handful of townies call him Wolfman from time to time, and that was always met with a gruesome visual smack down from Coop. He never berated them, but it was made clear they should keep their mouth on a leash. But with Dana, she got away with it. Coop let it slide with her. And *only* her.

Dana walked over to the table and smiled down at Ramos. And he smiled back up at her, as well.

She said, "I'll tell you why he don't get into trouble with what he says. He's easy on the eyes."

"Those eyes are a lot of things, Dana. Easy ain't one of them."

Dana appraised him. "You've got nice eyes, honey. You should let me bake you pies, sometime. You'd like 'em."

"Oh, I know I would, ma'am."

"I ain't talkin' like that, don't get pert."

"My apologies. How'd you mean?"

Dana looked over to Coop as he was returning to the table. She ignored Ramos's question and asked him one of her own, "If his eyes are so hard for ya…why do you like him?"

"You don't know that I do."

"Of course I do. I listen to everybody talk. This is my place."

Ramos nodded. "Okay, but what makes you think I like him? I know I've never said that."

"Cause I ain't fuckin' blind, sweetie."

Fair point, that. Ramos answered, "I don't trust people, Dana. And I mean nobody. But I trust him more than most. And that stands for something in my book. So, to speak."

"You mean that old leather thing you carry around?"

"The very one."

Ramos looked away then, and Dana knew that part of the conversation was over. She switched tracks.

"I'm serious, baby. You let me know if you get an itch for my pies. You'd be surprised."

"Thank you, ma'am. But I'm partial to other…crusts."

"And which would those be? I'd make some inquiries for ya."

"I appreciate that, but no. The ones I want are the hardest to get, Dana. Only I can procure them. And I haven't been properly satiated in a long, long time."

"You must be starving, then."

"Ha! In the worst way." he agreed.

Coop walked up. "We got appointments."

Ramos decided to razz him. "I bet her pies are delicious, Coop."

That earned a slight tick, but then rather disappointingly Coop said, "They are. Let's get rollin', Bam Bam.

Ramos gave Coop a blank look and thought to himself: *Cooper. What do I even know about him? Much more than he'd want, probably; quite less than I prefer, certainly. He called me Ram from the start, which was nothing original. But then he came up with "Bam Bam" for when I got into his skin something fierce.*

That little insult allows him to fight back without losing his cool and yelling at me. Two little words, and they speak volumes. Less is more. It's his way.

Yet, it's insulting in my *way. I've killed for lesser insults. He even claimed space in my book, by my hand, in my words. I wonder if he knew how close he was to death in this world, and immortality in mine. I wonder if he would have cared. I wonder if, despite my best efforts, I would have been able to immortalize him at all. Is he powerful enough to defeat me? Is he that strong?*

Possibly he is. He's intricate and multi-layered. And like many of the best movies made, they speak simply but shout in puzzles.

I found I wanted to create a chapter for him, about him, and so he would exist indefinitely. But I've held back completing the chapter, because I felt his story wasn't complete.

So like a blanket, I keep my leather book with me at all times; to record the lives around me.

They walked out, in line as always. Coop blazed a path and Ramos plowed it down.

At the car, Coop said "You were making too much noise while you eat. Do you listen to yourself when you eat? It's loud."

Ramos saw that he *had* bugged Coop this morning, and he called it a win.

"Probably, I haven't," he answered blithely. "Do you ever listen to yourself when you talk? Most people don't. We tune it out. We hardly ever pay attention to our body's little peccadillos. We take our actions for granted, but do you realize just how telling a person's voice is? Their language and how they communicate? It's fascinating."

"Um."

"And what's especially perverse," Ramos pressed the point, because he had read something about this topic the other day and had been working to find a way to put it into conversation, but mostly because he knew that this would annoy Coop, "is that a person's outside language doesn't always match their inside language. The outside voice and the inside voice aren't the same."

Once in the car, Cooper looked over and eyeballed Ramos. Ramos nodded back at him and began to flip through his notebook. "You have one voice; comes from your throat," Coop stated.

Ramos froze, his finger stopped dead center on some – random? – notebook page. Did his ears deceive him? Was he hearing voices? It seemed to him that Cooper had just *acknowledged* Ramos's flippant remarks, and was now *pursuing* a line of inquiry for discussion. Amazing!

"See?" Ramos looked up and smiled, "People say you aren't a fan of conversation, but you and me, we know different! You truly *are* a natural for good repartee!" Ramos continued, excited to be explaining philosophical theories in the car right then, "So, there are two "you's" Coop. There's the Inner You, the child, the thing that cannot resist temptation. It cries, it whines, it wants to be satiated; it is a slave to its wants. And it has no idea that any other part of you exists.

"Then there is the Outer You, the guy you see in the mirror. This is the Main Man, the Real You. He is not only aware of himself, but he can, when he chooses, also be aware of the Inner You.

"You ever think about what your Inner You sounds like, though? Ever paid attention to what your voice sounds like when you read quietly to yourself? What voice is that? I don't know about your voice, but I was paying attention to mine last night, and I was surprised to learn that I use my *child's* voice to read to myself. Once I realized this, I immediately switched to my regular voice, of course, but the point is, until I was aware of my Inner's voice, it was that of a child. A fucking child, Coop!"

Cooper stared ahead; Ramos knew now to stop talking and let the information percolate in his brain for a hard second. Finally, Coop answered, "Is this useful information to have? 'Cause Ram, I know things, like, which ones of my toes are longer, or that the hairs on my knuckles lay pretty flat...but that information about myself, it's useless. Does me no good. If I could delete it out of my head, I would. It takes up empty space. And you have to ask yourself Ram, what good is that information you just gave to me? I'm not going to use it for anything."

Ramos leaned forward, and the leather of the black notebook creaked like an old man as his weight pushed down on it. "Because Coop, once you are *aware* of your Inner guy, you can begin to shape him; mold him; change him; make him more like you, more like the Outer You that is aware of everything. Like when I realized I was reading books to myself in a child's voice and then manually changed that voice in my head – I updated my Inner Me, so to speak, made it more like the Aware me. I took control of my Inner self. The closer I come to connecting with my Inside Self, the closer I am to truly understanding how I tick.

My random thoughts now carry more weight, my dreams at night now have real meaning; I get to be a part of my organic computer as it comprehends and manages my day to day everything! There are emotions, memories, secrets, desires, that have all been buried. In a very real sense, I get to uncover buried treasure, and it's truly exciting. To me, that is useful." Ramos leaned back and snapped his notebook shut.

Cooper responded, "Interesting."

Ramos nodded. "I thought so, too."

"But I wouldn't go too far into matching up with your Inner You. Just yet."

Ramos's face fell a bit. "Why?"

"This is how I see it. If something is buried, as you say, then someone buried it. There was a reason for it. You uncover something special like that, you might just also uncover *why* it was buried, and it may not be a pretty thing."

"I don't need pretty, Coop. Nature's not pretty; Life is not pretty. Things decay and rot, and people commit horrible acts against each other that even animals won't do or even consider. Our entire existence is not pretty, and I don't need it to be. I'd rather have truth."

"That truth you speak of, Ram, it's relative. Your truth is my punchline. But I understand your point. Also, though…a man lives on hope and ideals. You take away that inner voice that believes it can have all the happiness it wants, and you take away hope. You take away the desire to be a superman, and you kill the need for living up to ideals. A man needs to be able to sink into his desires for a time."

"Tell that to addicts."

"I do. Everyday. You know I don't drink anymore; and I know that that is something I cannot ever do again. But deep down, there's a hope that I'll feel cold whiskey on my lips again. And that when I do, there will be no shame, no judgement, no circumstance. The smart me knows that this can never happen. But the child in me doesn't accept or understand that. And I'm glad for it, because that allows for bend. And bend gives strength. Skyscrapers aren't steady, they rock back and forth. They were designed to do that. If they tried stand rigid against the wind, they'd break. But, let them bend a bit, and they hold up. Same thing for a man. He needs to have some small hope that he can surrender to his desires, sometimes. Even when he knows that it would be detrimental to him and his if he did."

"Self-Introspection is a good thing, Coop. That's how we grow as people."

"It's only a good thing if a person can accept what they find. For better or worse, you are who you are. If you can't come to terms with what you find, then it will do you no good to find it."

And then, as it was with them, silence. The topic was discussed and then dropped.

Coop put the car in gear and drove, while Ramos opened his notebook and drew circles.

CHAPTER **6**

TREE SPIKES AND COPPER WIRE

Ramos looked up and saw they were heading into one of the many off-path rural fields one finds in that area. "Somethin' Bout a Truck" was playing from the radio (yes, the radio, as opposed to satellite radio – Coop refused to listen to anything but local AM/FM channels), and Ramos might have thought this was some great meaningful coincidence, seeing as they were *actually* in a farmer's field right now; but he didn't, because if he thought THAT as a coincidence, then every fucking song playing on this fucking channel would have been considered a meaningful fucking coincidence, because it seemed they were *always* in some fucking farmers field.

He turned the radio off and asked, "What's goin, on here?"

Coop smiled. "It's a surprise. You'll like it."

"Please-Please!" whined Ramos, "tell me we're putting the hammer down on J-Walkers again. Fucking assholes. And then we're pulling the " bad cop/worse cop" routine on people that violate parking down-town. Please! Tell me the Captain's pissed at us for something and has us looking for whoever's breaking into parking meters again. That was such a great day!"

"That *was* a fun day. We'll definitely do that again." said Coop.

"But that's not it?"

"Nope. It's better. Something we'll both appreciate."

They drove further and further into the surrounding acres of trees until they became utterly secluded. Coop turned right onto a dirt trail that appeared out of nowhere, like one of Harry Potter's rooms of requirement. A clearing appeared, and there were some patrol cars pulled over at a site down the way. Ramos immediately got happy when he saw who was at the center of the commotion.

"Fuckme. It's Boogles." he grinned.

Coop got out, took off his coat, and straightened his sunglasses. Ramos followed suit, but tucked his notebook into his back pocket.

The young man apprehended between two cop cars was trying like hell get out of his handcuffs, was incessantly yelling at the officers about personal rights and the struggle for human longevity.

"Come on! These are fucking tight! Listen to me, ok? What other fucking species on this planet loves ourselves as much as we do, and yet work so hard to kill itself off? I'm not here to harm human interests, man, I'm here to help save our race! YOU and YOU need to think OUTSIDE of that puny fucking existence you've allowed yourself to be trapped in, man! Each of you, you're elephants at the circus."

"What'd you call me, boy?" asked Cop #1. "An elephant?"

"YES! I DID!" the young man hollered out with even *more* conviction, now that he saw he was being listened to. "You are both elephants at the zoo! You've got so much power, so much strength, and yet all it takes to hold you back is a small, weak string that's staked into the ground. You've had that string tied to your leg since you were a baby and you couldn't break it. But now, you're an adult and you can TOTALLY break it. You just don't know you can. Break the string, man! Hear what I'm trying to tell you!"

Cop #1, who is a really big black guy, looked at Cop #2. "My daughter turned Dumbo on TV the other night. And dude, I couldn't watch it. That shit is sad, man."

Cop #2, who was a medium sized but wiry MMA type replied to Cop #1: "Seriously? You didn't watch it at all?"

Cop #1: "I watched some, but walked away."

Cop #2: "What about Bambi? Can you watch that?"

Cop #1: "Oh yeah, I can handle Bambi. That wasn't too bad."

Cop #2: "But the mom still dies, right?"

Cop #1: "Yeah, but...it's not bad. Just a gun shot, and Bambi calling out. Then the rabbit shows up, and it's ok. Plus, he meets his dad later."

Cop #2: "But the mom still dies. That doesn't make you sad? Always did me."

Cop #1: "But it's not over done. It happens, and then moves on. "

The young man, at this point, realizes that he has lost their attention. "I am not talking about fucking Dumbo!"

Cop #1 Continues: "Plus, did you know... the kid who voiced Bambi ended up being some bad ass in the marines?"

Cop #2: "For Real?"

Cop #1: "For Really Real. He kept it a secret, and then just before he retired, his boss called him up for some pain in the ass job. He said no way, and his boss tossed him a file that said "Confidential" on it and said 'Major Bambi, unless there is information you don't want leaked to your men, I suggest you have that job done by the end of the week,' or some shit. See, he never got billing for it on the movie itself, and he figured that info was gone. He didn't want folks knowing about it in the military. But, you know…they found out."

Cop #2: "Crazy. What's he doing now?"

Cop #1: "Like, Ted talks and stuff. On tour. Totally embraced his Bambi. Loving it. Heard the guy talk on the radio, he's pretty stout. So, Bambi's ok."

Cop #2: "But not Dumbo?"

Cop #1: "Fuck to the N-O, man. That scene where his mom's rocking him in her trunk while she's locked up in that box? No way. Can't handle it. I don't watch that movie."

Cop #2: "Yeah. That was sad. I get you."

The young man took advantage of the lull. "Ah, can we take these cuffs off now? Seeing as I *didn't do* anything wrong?"

Cop #1 looked down at him. "Hold up, man. These guys here want to speak with you."

The young man looked over at the two smiling detectives walking toward him, and said "Fuck."

"Boogles!" Ramos shouted out. "What the hell is going on here? Are you ok?"

"My name's Woody, asshole. Same as it was when we were in high school. Or to you, it's Mr. Dent."

"Oh. Well, Mr. Dent... what's this you're up to today?"

"Nothing. 'Cept trying to save all your asses, *again*."

"We were told you know this guy?" Cop 2 asked.

"Yes. We do." Coop answered. Unlike Ramos, Coop was not smiling as he approached Woody. "What you have here, gentlemen, is yet another example of a man who is lackluster, but trying to live up to a dull shine. But see, he ain't got no shine. Tries to think he does, but he don't. Just causes trouble."

Woody had heard this before and was no less mad at having to hear it again. His mouth spoke before his brain thought. "I had enough shine for Sam, a few years back. I was good enough for her then, and to be your grandkid's daddy, man. Just never enough shine for *you*?"

Ramos pursed his lips. He loved Baby Girl and was even more unhappy about Woody being her biological daddy than Coop was. Sam was special to him.

He looked to see Coop's reaction, and Woody's head dropped as Coop got up into his face. "Shine? You fuckwit. Shine don't make a daddy. Being *around* is what makes a daddy." Coop looked up at the two cops and addressed them, as Woody sulked.

"Yeah, we know this guy, fellas. Not only is he under major surveillance by authorities because he's fond of spiking trees and digging sink holes in land that's due to be developed, he *also* likes to blow up machines. Large machines, that cost a lot of money. Oh, and, he is now being considered for the theft of about a ton of copper wire from local neighborhood construction sites. You been stealing wire, Woody?"

"No."

"That sounded weak." Ramos said. "Not sincere."

"It's the truth. I didn't steal no wire." Woody said.

"Come on, Boogles. Just tell us you did."

"I didn't fucking steal no wire, asshole."

Ramos went for another dig. "Admit it Boog, and we'll go easy on ya."

"The only thing I stole from you is your woman, man."

This was not the movies. Ramos could not haul off and hit the guy and not expect charges against him. Instead, he stood there, and looked at him. And saw in his mind dark lines being drawn down Woody's face, and around his abdomen; then back up and around his neck; then around his ears, and eyes. This would be the track Ramos would use to carve the skin off of him, while he was still alive.

The lines were clear on Woody in Ramos's mind, and he moved on to pull out his blade and begin to slice – not cut – where the lines began, and make sure that he collected neat piles of skin.

His thoughts were not seen, but they were felt. What were thoughts but a form of energy, anyway?

Coop felt the energy and said to the cops "Thanks guys. I want to talk to him. Then we can take him in, if it warrants. You get him for anything?"

"No," said Cop 1. "Just trespassing. And a dirty fucking mouth. Resisting arrest could work, but the land owner says he'll let him off with a warning if no harm was done."

After the cops took off Woody's hand cuffs and began to walk back to their car, Woody called out toward them, "Whatever! I didn't do nothing! You guys ain't shit!" Then he began to laugh. "You cry because of Dumbo! Fucking Pussy!"

Cop #1 turned around and Woody shut up.

When they had gone, Coop asked, "What are you doing out here, Woody?"

"Hunting."

"For what?"

"For a mission, man."

"If I search around those trees, will I find a bag of spikes anywhere?"

"No, you won't."

"No, we won't. But if I were a betting man, I'd wager that by tonight, there'll be spikes in those trees. Probably those trees over there, the ones with green plastic bands around them; Those were the trees you marked for spikes later on."

Ramos knew Coop didn't care for Woody, but he also felt that Coop was too soft on him. Did Coop think Woody was too weak, or that he couldn't take care of himself? Ramos could see where Coop might get a "Wile E. Coyote" vibe from Woody, impressed as a sort of a frenzied, helpless animal running in circles that might evoke empathy. But Ramos had known Woody a long time, and he knew that Woody was *anything* but helpless. He was not a big guy, but he was always a fighter. He was a scrapper, and he mostly fought against people that he had *no* business messing with. The larger the opponent, the more willing Woody was to go after him. If he had fear, Ramos never saw it. Usually he got beat down, and in a bad way. But he always got back up, and he never stopped fighting against those he felt deserved his vengeance. Most of the football team, all of the bullies, and the lion's share of the punks in school had, at one point, went up against Woody for one injustice or another.

On one hand that was noble, but on the other, it was a false kind of glory. If you keep throwing yourself against a brick wall, you know you're going to lose, which carries a kind of comfort. There aren't any unknown possible outcomes. You'll never have to live up to the responsibility of what happens if you actually *win*. When a person wins a fight they gain a title, and with that title the victor has the responsibility of honor, of reputation, and of possible repeat performances to prove the validity of the first victory. When a person loses a fight, they still gain the respect of having fought, but that's where it ends. No other responsibility is demanded and the loser gets to move on, content that they fought the good fight and could look in the mirror with pride.

Ramos hated Woody because he had decided to throw himself at Sam years back, when Sam and Ramos were dating. Woody knew he could never sustain a girl like that, but he went after her anyway, to say that he did. Also, he and Ramos had been fighting for years, and asking out his girl was a tactical gambit that ended up working much better than he could ever have truly wanted.

It surprised both the men when Sam showed herself open to Woody's outlandish courtship. And when Baby Girl came along, it didn't surprise Ramos in the least that Woody was never around to be a father.

Ramos thought of pushing back in to Sam's life at that point, but by then Coop was his partner, and Ramos felt that barging into his daughter's life would not be appropriate. But lately, conversation with Sam had been increased and the intensity between them reappeared. Sam was his future, he was sure of it. He'd be a loving husband to Sam and a great father to Baby Girl. She would be his own, the daughter that was rightfully his.

So, he didn't like it when Coop would give Woody little bits of parental advice, in hopes that maybe he'd follow it. Ramos didn't want Coop giving him any chances.

"Come on. Get in the car." said Coop.

Woody's ire immediately flared. "We going to jail now, for nothing?"

"No, we're taking you back to town. Ramos, call that land owner and tell him the news about the trees, and they'll know to set up a guard around them."

They drove out. Ramos got on the phone, and Coop spoke to Woody.

"Should I even feel the need to ask why?"

"Ask why. *Please*, ask why. Mr. Happenstance, I'm trying to stop the corporate machine from killing our Earth's crust and making it impossible for humans to survive."

Ramos, now off the phone, smirked. "You worship Mother Earth or some shit? Part of that cult?"

Woody rolled his eyes back and took a lecturing tone with Ramos. "Mother Earth needs no protecting, Cliff. There's nothing we can do to her that she can't bounce back from in a billion years or so. We are insignificant to her. But we *can* hurt her enough so that she kills us off. We can break down the only environment in the universe that sustains us, and she'll let us do it. I'm trying to stop people from taking a shit in my living room, and then expecting my kid to clean it up."

Cooper jumped in. "The only thing your kid needs from you, dipshit, is to show up. Which you've not ever been able to do. That's all she needs. Ramos is more of a dad to her than you've ever have been."

"Oh, Ok. Right. You want me around? So you can berate me some more? You just can't stand that your daughter ever got with a guy like me. That she didn't end up with Ramos here, or some other asshole."

"Regardless of my feelings for you Woody, you have to remember that the best thing you have ever done with your life is to help create Baby Girl. That has been your honor in life, to be a part of that. Good for you. But that's not being a dad. A dad shows up. A dad is around. A dad teaches, and supports, and is just...*there*. Don't ever call yourself that in my presence again, unless you begin to *be* what you say that you are."

At this point in his mind, Ramos had not only stripped Woody of his skin, but sliced him into chunks of raw meat, set them in freezer bags, labeled them, and stacked them in the garage freezer so he could eat them over the winter.

He said, "Even explaining that to him is pointless, Coop. He's got other priorities."

Cooper looked at Ramos and acknowledged that as truth, then turned to Woody.

"Have you been taking copper wire, Woody?"

"Why do you keep asking me that!"

"Because it's my job to. There have been thefts recently, and on a fairly high scale. This is something that does not fall in the misdemeanor category. Have you been involved in that at all? If you have, you need to tell me."

"No, sir. I haven't. Isn't me. Even if those new sub divisions do deserve it because they mowed down miles of forest land to be built, but no. I didn't do nunna that. I don't mess with it."

Cooper inquired further, "You know who would? You heard anything?"

"I would imagine that the scrap metal recycling plants could tell you who sold them what, right?"

His tone was not smart, but helpful. Coop answered with patience.

"Not always. We've met with the metal plants multiple times and asked them those same questions. Generally, they are extremely willing to cooperate and don't want any part in receiving stolen product. The problem though, is that this stolen metal gets broken up into smaller amounts before it's ever taken to a recycler for resale; then it's taken out of state, where chosen "locals" can dispose of it for cash. At this point it gets hard to trace. Not impossible, but hard. It's easier if someone hears something about it, or can lead us in the right direction."

Woody shrugged. "Sorry. I really don't know anything."

Coop was satisfied with his answer. "Fair enough. I believe you. But I know you'll say something if you find anything out, right?"

"Yes. I will."

"Because if I find out you knew, it'd be bad. Understand?"

"Yes."

"And," Coop continued, "I don't have to remind you that coming back here to spike trees and sabotage the land against the developers is a bad idea?"

"Yes." Woody agreed again.

"So why do I feel you're going to keep on causing problems out here, Woody?" Coop pushed.

Woody responded, with obvious passion. "Because, if I can make it too expensive for these land rapists to continue their work, they'll eventually leave. It's all about the money for them. If the cost of developing the land grows beyond their profit margin, they'll drop the project and get out of town. And that would be a win."

"I hear you. I do. But it's against the law, and if someone gets hurt from the other side…then you got to jail, son. And you don't want that."

Ramos cracked his neck at the mention of Woody being called "son" by Coop. He knew that was unintentional, but to him, it was uncalled for.

The trio drove into town and Woody was dropped at the nearest bus stop. Ramos and Coop leaned against the Charger and watched him scamper off, much like a weasel would through a forest.

"What's up with you?" asked Coop.

"Remind me what tree spiking has to do with anything."

"Woody's peculiarities aside, it's a potentially dangerous thing for everyone involved. Tree spiking is an age old guerilla tactic used to stop companies from clearing land. First, a guy will go in and scout specific trees. Second, he'll return maybe a week later, usually at night, to drive metal spikes into various parts of the previously selected trees. He'll spike the bottom, the top, and the middle of the trunks. If done right, no one will ever know exactly where the spikes are. So when the company comes and clears the land, and the trees go to the lumber factory, the metal spikes will destroy an enormous amount of equipment when they are cut into."

"But at that point, the trees are already cut down and the land is cleared. How does that help the guy who did the spiking?"

"For that particular parcel of land, it doesn't help at all. But it will cost the lumber company a lot of time and money when their machines are destroyed, and that's when the spikers start to get a foot in the game. Later, that same lumber company will come around again for more land, and again, the so called Eco Terrorists pop out and spike the trees. But *this* time, they *tell* the company after they do it. They don't say *which* trees of course, but they *will* disclose which acres of land have been compromised. In addition, they might mention that there are tiger teeth hidden in the roads to pop tires on vehicles and sugar poured into gas tanks of the construction equipment at night. The hope is that the real estate company will decide that the risk, and the cost, of continuing that development project is too great and just walk away."

"The spikes just stay in the trees?"

"Yeah, but spikes don't really hurt 'em, as long as that's all they are. Trees just grow over them after a time."

"So by stopping Woody, we're protecting these companies' pocket books?"

"Maybe. But really, we're protecting the Eco Terrorists. Because the development companies, they're wise to these tactics. They know what's up. And I've seen what happens when these security companies get a hold of a nature crusader. It ain't pretty."

"I can imagine" said Ramos. Coop pressed in on him some more.

"For real, Bam-Bam. You're being a bitch. Talk to me."

Ramos broke. "That fucking guy, Coop! I mean, I *know* you don't like him, but it irritates me to think that you may, deep down in that cutesy little heart of yours, still have a soft spot for him."

Coop laughed, and Ramos continued.

"You don't need to be giving him advice about how to be a dad, Coop. The guy ain't never gonna show up for that. I still won't accept that a guy like him could, in any way, have helped to bring a girl as incredible as Ally into this world."

"Calm down. I'm just talkin' to him for information. You know better than anybody, when he starts yelling about the environment and thinking he's been unjustly accused, there is no dealing with him. If I'm gonna get anything at all valuable from him, it's easier just to keep him calm. It's funny how a little guy like that causes so much trouble."

"I'll never underestimate the trouble that guy can cause." said Ramos. "In high school, even though he wasn't very big, he was always a fighter."

"And you respect that."

"The tenacity, maybe. Or the lack of fear. But not the reasoning behind his actions. He would fight just to fight. To show that he could. And that's what got in me and Sam's way, years back. Man, Woody *knew* he could never get a girl like Sam, not long term, but he went after her anyway when she and I had split for a little while. He did it only to say that he did. And to spite me."

"You believe he did all that to spite you? Why?"

Ramos shrugged. "You know the story. And...I was never that nice to him. We had our issues."

Coop already knew the answer but he asked, "Remind me, why'd you and Sam break it off?"

"I don't know...she talked about getting her life together; I was looking at colleges. Perfect storm, but it should have been temporary. And then *everybody* got surprised when there seemed to be any reason at all for her to go out with Woody, and not a week after we split. And then boom...Baby Girl came along. And *nobody* was surprised when Woody wasn't around for that."

"You could have come around then. Why didn't you?"

"Different reasons. I spoke to Captain about it. We both agreed that chasing after my partner and mentor's daughter would not help to create a perfect union between you and I.

Coop nodded. He had suspected as much, but had never asked about it. "While I respect your decision, and Captain's judgement - you could have gone back to her, Ram. I wouldn't have stood in the way."

"I know that now. That's why I hate him, Coop. He stole a piece of my life. I love Ally, and I feel that she's mine anyway. And I'll always care for Sam. That's no secret."

CHAPTER 7

THE BOX

Brenda Leighton watched Sam close her door and thought about how best to proceed.

The girl was smart, but plain. And belligerent. And surprisingly good at "Tongue Lingus." And that was fine, because Brenda had recently discovered she didn't mind getting her legs spread for a lady that knew how to move a good tongue. Not long ago, she had been out to lunch with Rosa, this hot Latina realtor that was selling all her shit houses to HUD. As long as the houses were standing upright and had running water, they could be moved. These were the houses that weren't worth the money to rebuild and were usually located in lower income areas.

The initial deal between the ladies was this: After Brenda foreclosed on a property, she would (with Sam's help) hold it off to the side on a "classified list" that realtors did not have access to. Rosa then reviewed the list and identified the specific properties she could sell quick and easy to HUD. After each sale was complete, Rosa gave Brenda one percent of the sale price in cash, under the table. There were at least ten of these houses being sold every month, and they became very happy with the results.

They met one afternoon for lunch and began toasting their new-found prosperity; red wine turned into whiskey, and that working lunch became a happy hour. Brenda found that Rosa handled bourbon better than most men she knew; Rosa laughed and said it was because she had graduated from the University of Georgia – folks there drank that shit for breakfast!

As the sun morphed from a bright lemonade to a dark, early morning pee color, Rosa asked if any other kind of houses were available for sale. Brenda laughed, pulled keys out of her purse and dangled them in the air. "Let's go!" she said.

They caught an Uber and Brenda took Rosa to a house in Fernandina Beach. It was a posh area of town on Amelia Island along Fletcher Ave, which ran along the shore. They could hear the surf beating the sand as they giggled up to the deserted beach mansion. "Ok, bee-otch…welcome to mi casa!" Brenda said, and pulled out the keys to open the front door.

The house was great; granite everything, good hardwood - it smelled of money and art. Rosa looked over at the hallway table and saw yellow sheets of paper wrapped in plastic laying on it. She walked over and picked it up.

"Is this a foreclosure?" Rosa asked. When Brenda lifted up her shoulders, innocently showing the face of an angel, she laughed.

"I take full advantage of the perks I have access to!" But what Brenda didn't tell Rosa, was that she had been using these locations as her personal vacation spots for over two years. Once she realized that it wasn't terribly difficult to "hide" these foreclosed houses for small amounts of time (six months at most), she obtained for herself a P.O. Box mailing address, put most of her clothes in a climate-controlled storage room, and left her husband at the house whenever she felt suffocated by her living situation (which was often). She kept some personal belongings in a light, easily movable bamboo rolling case and was able to move from house to house as she saw fit. She liked the novelty of the different locals, but was usually bored with them by the time she left.

She also liked moving from house to house because it allowed her to not think about her rapidly failing marriage. He was older, and very suave. His wife had died five years back, and Brenda met him not long after at a new restaurant's grand opening. She was there for the scene, he was there because he had financed the project.

What landed Brenda on him, besides his paycheck, was his attentive performance in bed. He would go down on her for days, and would constantly give her massages and make mad love to her whenever there was a free second. The sex was good, but what she really liked was the attention. If a man was this attentive in the bedroom, then that must transfer into other parts of their lives, correct? Brenda could not get enough attention, or focus, from anyone. She would do anything for a person in a relationship, whatever they needed, as long as they reciprocated by immersing themselves into her daily dreams and considerations. Anal sex, group sex, bondage, role playing – she'd do it all, and she enjoyed it. But for her partner to receive all that from her, *she* had to be their focus in life. There was nothing that could mean more to them than her.

But he was not attentive to her like she would have him be; he was always traveling to meet his kids somewhere, and to see his newly arrived grandchildren. His family was nice enough, and they included her in their lives almost immediately. It was obvious, though, that Brenda was not going to be number one in his life. She was the comforter, the play-thing that he needed to mitigate the sadness of his deceased wife. She would live well and be surrounded by nice people, but she'd never be the priority for him. As time went on, they grew apart. Divorce was a hassle so that never happened, and when he was home they had a good time.

Brenda began to step out at night, and he didn't stop her. So, she kept on with it. And one night, with a guy's dick in her hand in the back of an Uber, she realized she didn't want to go home. She looked at the dude sitting next to her, felt his legs begin to spasm, and watched him put on quite possibly the most unattractive "O Face" she'd ever engineered. Well – maybe not the *most* unattractive, but it surely landed in a respective Top Five list. The dude finished up on her hand and collapsed back into the seat, just letting his dong flop atop his designer jeans. The Uber driver turned off the video he had just made from his phone and texted it to his boyfriend; Brenda reached into her purse for a pack of wet wipes (the flushable kind, so she wouldn't have to use the sandpaper offered at most public restrooms) to clean the ocean-scented baby batter off her hands, and she realized that she still had the key to the latest house she had foreclosed on that week.

So she kicked the overly appreciative dude out of her ride and diverted the driver to a cute little house in a neighborhood on a lake. It wasn't the fanciest house, but it was exciting walking into someone else's past life. She took off her clothes and slept on the floor naked in a back room facing the lake. The windows were open to let in the smell of the man-made expanse of fresh water and the overhead fan kept a breeze on her skin that made her nipples erect. The carpet was new and she wiggled her bum into a comfortable divot; then she flipped over on her belly with her hand between her legs and *thrice* brought herself to a dull-eyed, fully sating, growl inducing climax.

Brenda had slept deep that night. In the morning she sat nude on the back porch and let the breeze creep up between her legs, and she decided to stay at the house for a while.

Thus, her habit of staying away for long periods at her foreclosed locations was born. And she found other people, and other ways to bring attention to herself.

THE WOLF, A BUTCHER, HIS DEMON, AND THEIR MASTER

This particular house that she and Rosa went to that night was one of her favorites. Even though the Atlantic Ocean was just over a single sand dune and held an unquestionably strong allure, she liked that this one had a pool in the back. With a pool, a lady didn't have to worry about hungry fish nibbling at her private parts while she took a midnight swim.

Rosa had no idea that Brenda spent so much time in these side houses, and she didn't need to. Brenda could tell Rosa thought they were spontaneously breaking the rules, and that it was fun for her. So Brenda played that part up to increase the excitement.

An iced bottle of bourbon was pulled from the freezer and the two went out the back door and onto the currently deserted beach. Soon after, their high heels and panties lie forgotten on the sand while they tumbled naked into the ocean together. They played and kissed and laughed and felt each other up while the salt water hit their lips and the sand ran between their toes with the tide.

But as with many, if not most, ocean-side romantic romps it was soon realized that the sand, and shells, and driftwood on the beach made it very uncomfortable to continue horizontally, so they ran back up to the house and fell into the clean water of the available swimming pool.

They had swum in the unlit pool and made slow circles around each other.

Brenda had kissed girls before certainly, but it had never amounted to anything significant. She suspected it would that night, though. Rosa floated over to place light kisses all over her face, and it was exhilarating when Brenda's ass was firmly grabbed so their wet bodies were pulled together. Their hands and tongues explored the inches of each other in the pool. Soon Brenda found herself sitting out on the edge of the pool, palms behind her on that scratchy cement and her soft butt getting rubbed raw, while Rosa's head thrashed between her very wide open, very spread legs.

They made their way back into the house, but not any further than the lush living room carpet, where they basically spent the next few hours doing to each other what every male beyond the age of fifteen searches for on the internet.

In the morning, Brenda looked up when Rosa walked out of the bathroom, all showered and dressed. Rosa had no makeup on, had her hair pulled back in a tight pony tail, and was still, if not more, as beautiful as she was the night before.

"Fuck," said Rosa, "I completely forgot I have to meet my fiancé's parents for brunch today. I gotta go, bitch."

Brenda laughed. "You need a ride?" Brenda had no intention of driving her any damn place, but she figured she'd at least act the part. But Rosa, the professional that she was, already had things taken care of.

"No, I've got a cab coming. But here, we have time for a quick breakfast." Rosa had made two mimosa's and handed one to Brenda. They discussed a new batch of houses that Brenda had just written up, and Rosa again began to ask her about selling higher-end homes, similar to the one they were in now.

Brenda explained she had top sellers already in the McMansion Market that took care of those things, but she dangled the carrot to let Rosa know that. So if she kept on making money for them both, they could look at getting her into the more expensive housing market.

Rosa left when the cab arrived and Brenda went upstairs to soak in the garden tub. Business had continued to be good since then, and she had recently given that house to Rosa to sell.

The thing with Sam happened purely by accident. Brenda had walked in on her crying in the bathroom one day, something to do with her tyrannical, environmentalist boyfriend. Sam had just finished up hiding a batch of houses for Brenda in the paperwork, and Brenda was concerned that could unravel.

So, she put an arm around Sam and took her back to her office. She told Sam that she would take care of her; that it was ok. Brenda felt some kind of power move could be used here, so, emboldened by her tryst with Rosa, she took Sam's face in her hands and kissed her.

Sam let her, because Brenda was the Alpha. Sam was not a lesbian, Brenda knew, but hell, Brenda didn't even consider herself one. She just had fun. But she wanted Sam emotionally, possibly shamefully, attached to this job. So, over the course of the week Brenda threw passes that Sam intercepted, until one day – touchdown. Brenda had been sitting in the chair behind her desk watching Sam pick up papers that had fallen on the floor, and while Sam was on her knees in front of her, Brenda reached out to firmly pull Sam's head into her crotch.

Of course she expected some pushback, or maybe a little fuss, about the impropriety of an office romance. But it was a nice surprise when Sam not only went straight to work getting Brenda's panties out of the way with no obtrusive discussion, but then was also *quite* adept at the downtown work as her pouty cheeks pressed against the inside of Brenda's thighs and her tongue did gymnastics inside the opposing labia.

It was done; Brenda was shown to be in charge and Sam would continue to make sure that the foreclosures that came through their office were categorized properly so as to maximize Brenda's profit margin.

Brenda looked at her pile of mail and spotted the mysterious brown box lying atop the printed-paper atrocities promising nothing but boredom and tedious work. She picked it up, saw there was nothing on it except her name, her full name, Brenda Thomas Leighton, and a small something branded in the top right-hand corner. It looked like a "T" but she couldn't make it out. And she got irked by the spelling of her name…she previously went by Brenda T. Leighton, but then dropped the T while she tried out being known only as "Brenda L" or just "BL." Those didn't work, but the "T" stayed gone after she went back to simply being known as Brenda.

The cardboard was thick and had a thin, brown hemp rope strapped around it with a buckle on top the long part of the box. It was a long box, no more than six inches long. She pulled the strap back to unlock it from the buckle, and then loosened it again as she pulled the rope off of the box. The top pulled off easily and she paused.

There was another box inside. On top of the box was a circular handle, and there was a word written on the handle: KEY. She picked up the KEY and saw three prongs sticking out the bottom of it, and supposed those prongs fit into the three neat holes she saw at the top of the box.

The fuck? She thought. This *had* to be a VITO package, she knew it. This was one of those idiotic sales letters that were used to get through to the **V**ery **I**mportant **T**op **O**fficer of whatever company a sales person was trying to get a meeting with. Shit like this was entry-level sales; it was tacky and embarrassingly outdated. But Brenda would grudgingly admit: she'd sent out quite a lot of these in her first days of sales. They didn't always work, no marketing gimmick always does; but when a VITO package *did* land a sale, it was generally a large one.

The idea is to get noticed. So if the package is interesting enough and important-looking enough to get the VITO in question to actually open it, that is considered a **win**. A VITO receives a large amount of mail every day, and looks at little to none of it. But if that VITO notices, and then physically looks at the special package, odds increase dramatically for the sales person who sent the letter to get a meeting with the VITO, a.k.a. the Decision Maker, who can instantly deliver a sizeable increase in business to the soliciting company.

Brenda got annoyed. This was some measly sales person's gimmick wasting her valuable time. Did they think she was the type of executive that appreciated this bullshit? But then, she thought she might be flattered a bit. Someone out there obviously knew she was a VITO, and was worth the time to put together a VITO package for her. Damn right, she was important and people knew it. She deserved a package like this, even if it was pathetic.

CHAPTER **8**

COOP AND THE VIKING

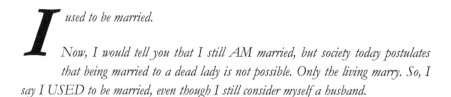

I used to be married.

Now, I would tell you that I still AM married, but society today postulates that being married to a dead lady is not possible. Only the living marry. So, I say I USED to be married, even though I still consider myself a husband.

My wife is - or was - a Social Worker. There was this one kid, a girl named Maria, that she took a special interest in. She knew Maria came from a shit background, and for whatever reason, she made it her mission to rise her up above the sludge she was born into.

I kept telling her to not get so invested in these kids - they just kept breaking her heart. No amount of time spent with them seemed to matter enough. Plus, she had a kid at home that needed her.

But she persisted. And one day, she took Maria back home to the squalor that she lived in, to try to talk to her folks. She didn't find Maria's folks. But she did find that Maria was living in a brothel and had been smuggled over from Mexico to work there.

See, my wife was the kind of government worker that city planners salivate for. She accepted her insult of a salary and worked more than three times the hours of folks making three times what she did. It was her fuckin' badge. It made her proud…She did her amazing work despite her bad pay.

My wife did not make it out of there alive. Her body was found a few days later. She'd been beaten, raped, killed, and then branded so as to make an example to anyone doubting the strength of that organization.

The Captain was the one who notified me and brought me to see her. He asked me, as I fell to my knees and held my love's head in my hands…He asked me "Do you want justice, or do you want victory?"

I kept my eyes on my wife's lips, which were now cracked and sore, and tilted my ear towards The Captain. His words were simple and should have added together easily, but the implications unbalanced them. He bent down and his bushy eyebrows bore into my temple's soft spot. Cigars, coffee, and the usual morning shot of bourbon (double shot, it smelled like today, to deal with recent circumstances) drenched the small air between us and stabbed onto my cheek. It wasn't unpleasant. I'd come to appreciate that smell over the years. It was the smell of collusion; of importance; of secrets told and kept; of delicate fucking issues being dealt with indelicately. Again, he pressed his point.

"I'll ask only that one time."

"What's the question?" I asked.

"You heard me fine."

"She's gone. What's the difference?" I asked. Oh My God, her nails still looked good. But there was blood under them.

"You're stalling. But your wife is lying dead here before us, so I get it. Regardless, you must hear me on this: I am giving you the option to control the outcome of the

retribution on these heathens. Either we allow law enforcement to pull them into its system and whatever justice it deems fit for them, or… we keep the system out of this, and I tell you the location of where your vengeance will be found."

My daughter Sam was pregnant. The dad was an idiot conservationist, but that was still her baby coming, and it was a grandchild my wife would never be able to meet. These people put me in the position of telling my daughter that her mother is dead. These people took away my wife.

"We work for pennies, risking our balls every day for this job and getting nothing back for it except pain and heartache. This is when we get one back. This is something I have in my power to do for you. I will go with either decision you make, but that decision has to be made now."

I made the decision. Really, that's a lie. There was no decision to make. I just acknowledged the truth of things. I was given an address, some pictures, and a few names.

One name, in particular: Alejandro Morales. The Captain explained this was the man that made all relevant decisions. I would know him by his "trinity;" three identical tattoos, always visible - one on each forearm and one on the top of his chest. They were all the shape of an Odin Hammer "x'd" with a battle axe. Coincidentally, this was the same image branded on my beloved wife laying broken in front of me.

"See, he fashions himself a Viking, Coop. He's Mexican, though. Dude's from Quintana Roo, on the very South end of Mexico - next to the Yucatan Peninsula. And that ain't got nothing to do with Scandanavia. He did grow up on boats, though, and fell easily into pirating. So now he thinks he's Rathgar Lothbrock, right? A Viking King Incarnate, or some fucking thing. The man's delusional but still very dangerous. He's a big dude, a skilled fighter, and never shows mercy. But he's vain, and he's convinced that mortality is something only other people deal with. He is your adversary. He's the one that killed your beautiful wife. He is the one that must die."

It was Friday, and the system didn't start up again until Monday, so I had some time.

THE WOLF, A BUTCHER, HIS DEMON, AND THEIR MASTER

Soon I sat in my car, out of sight from the building Captain told me about. It was in the middle of this small town named Callahan, but it was the kind of small town that always felt bigger than it was. It had stories, and history, and lore. I watched people enter and leave. I sat for two nights and I kept my body and mind nourished by the handles of bourbon at my side.

On Sunday night, I opened my car door and looked in the trunk. There was a toolbox and I grabbed the large hammer I knew was there. I walked across the street towards the building; as I approached the front door, I grabbed ahold of a trashcan from the sidewalk and threw it crashing into the front window. I heard yells in Spanish and of people scrambling. I stepped through the shards of glass hanging from the window frame and stood still a moment on the wooden floor.

Folks came running into the room. I'd been noticed, so…I smiled at them, and made a show of taking off my jacket, and placing it on a nearby chair. I felt the surrounding air begin to pull toward me as I became the heaviest object in that building. I controlled the gravity we were all in. The people hesitated and tried to guess my move. Which was: pulling the .45 out of my holster, and putting two bullets into the first two fucking heads my sight landed on.

From there, I became a God. I had vengeance and power and righteousness with me, and I buried into my enemies as a bull does to a group of naïve tourists in Spain. The clip emptied quickly and I holstered my weapon. The women around me were trying to get the kids to safety, and the men worked to organize themselves against me; but how do you organize against a hurricane? Their folly amused me. I continued my vengeance.

I squeezed enough blood out of that place to sate a hundred Aztec gods that night.

Going from room to room, I sunk my soulless metal pounder into countless more skulls; the long wooden handle of my hammer was worn by years of use and fit easily in my hand, without once slipping out of my grip.

I found the man I was hunting. Of course, he was waiting for me. His figure was impressive, as it was meant to be. He wore black skin-head Doc Martin boots, slim jeans, and no shirt. The sides of his head were shaved, but his hair was long over the middle and hung down to his shoulders in one strand.

I entered from the corridor. All the others in the room stood back and kept their guns holstered. I assumed they had been ordered as such, but it wouldn't have mattered. I owned their lives already, and I feel they knew that.

Alejandro stood and smiled. "Not that it matters," he announced, "but I'd like to know why the Gods showed you the way to my warrior's manse. Is it money? Reputation? Competition?"

I looked at him and knew this was my man. The tats matched, and I noticed he had bright gold and silver Rolex and Tag watches banded around his wrists and forearms. I realized that was his equivalent of taking a prize from his battles, a trophy from the people he has dominated. A Viking tradition, if what the books say is true. They would take a gold or silver armband, and the more armbands one had, the more revered he was.

"You are Alejandro Morales." I spoke.

"I am." he answered.

"My wife is lying on a slab because of you. My daughter is without a mother, my unborn grandbaby without a grandma, and I'm without a wife."

Alejandro nodded and remained silent, so I continued. "You branded my wife and that led me to you. Your stench of shit showed me the way. I am insulted that a peon like you was ever able to affect my family's life."

He smiled. Not a mocking grin, but a full broad show of happiness. "Ah. Vengeance. Yes, Ok." He walked around his desk and stood before me across the room. "I remember your wife. She was the Social Worker? The one that tried to take Maria away and show her the good life? Ha! There is Maria now, look there..."

I looked to where he pointed. There was a girl standing in the corner, trying to be invisible. I knew it was her.

"She brought your wife to me. And I would have you know ... I had your wife. I fucked her asshole, you understand? I made her taste me and swallow what I had to give her. And when I was done, I gave her to my men. Every man in this room ate a

piece of her soul, and fucked a chunk of her body. She died screaming. So…I understand your vengeance. I accept your challenge."

He was baiting me and doing a good job of it. But I stood back and felt the mountains I grew up in as a child in North Georgia boil my blood. The hard stone concreted my soul; the wood nymphs that I used to play with as a child whispered in my ear and promised me retribution.

I began rolling up my sleeves and made a show out dusting myself off. "Okay, Slick. I'm going to…I'm going to let you watch your heart stop beating, while it's in my hand. Got that? That's how this is gonna end."

Alejandro pulled a battle axe off the wall and swung it around to show his dexterity with it. I wiped the blood off my hammer, and after a thought, I pulled the .45 out of my holster. There was no more ammunition, but I turned it around and held it by the barrel, so I could use the butt of the handle as a sort of blunt instrument. I'm right handed, so I moved the gun there before securing the hammer in my left hand.

I'd like to say it was a battle to make the gods proud, but really, it ended … expeditiously. The fates had already written and published the ending, the credits had already rolled on the consequential movie.

"Inevitable" is the word.

I walked toward him as he leaped up with a battle cry to rally his spirits. If you could have put that leap in slow motion, really, it would have been impressive … every muscle was taught, the eyes were vicious but smart, the axe flew prominently over his head, and his hair sailed out behind him. Every inch of him was the epitome of what a warrior is expected to look like.

He landed beautifully. I stepped aside as the blade came down, and then jumped back as he reversed his swing around in a powerful twist. I knew he was fast; I saw it when I walked in. So, I let him go through what I figured was a dance routine he had practiced before. It was used to put an enemy off balance and make them unsure of their footing.

CHRISTOPHER S. WHITE

The dude was big, and I lacked the motivation to box him twelve rounds, so … when he got to what I thought was a stopping point in his routine, I moved in at the end of a swing and brought the gun butt down on his face, and I mean right between the fucking eyes, man. In a slighter dude, that might have been considered a kind of lobotomy, but for this guy, it just stunned him. Then I brought my hammer up and with both hands brought it down onto his right kneecap. It shattered like a virgin on prom night, just fucking exploded. As he fell to the floor I stepped on his arm holding the axe so he couldn't flip it up. He looked at me and I saw that his eyes were still that of a warrior, and so as a sign of respect, I proceeded to give him the pain I had promised I would.

My hammer swung and came down between his legs, and I'm certain his testicles split like grapes. He realized his new reality then, and began to experience a fear and pain that he never believed could exist. Then - I did what I told him I'd do. I turned my hammer around and used the claw to rake the heart out of his chest. I did it turned backwards, with my boot pushing down on his chin and the angle of the cut going up under the rib cage, so I got the least amount of resistance. I couldn't be too slow, I didn't want him bleeding out.

I dug my hand into his chest for his heart. It was still filled with blood when I pulled it out, and I showed it to him. And I was so happy to see that, one, he was still conscious and knew what I was showing him, and two, that the heart was able to beat a couple times so that the blood poured over his face and he got to see his most vital bodily organ working without him, and he was able to feel his death with full comprehension.

Honestly, I hadn't known if his heart would still beat after I pulled it out of him. It sounded good as a threat, but was that even possible? Turned out it was! I smiled as I showed it to him like …. well, like a dad that had told his kid that something could be done, and I did it, and I say, "There son, see?, I told ya. There it is, right there!" And he'd say, "Gee dad, that's swell!" And I'd try to play it cool and say something like, "Yeah, it's pretty good, isn't it?"

I squeezed the organ, and blood spewed like water out of a sponge. I jammed Alejandro's heart into his mouth as I got up to take account of my victim. I was amazed to see that his eyes were still following me, even though his body was bleeding out and his brain wasn't receiving any oxygen. I knew the gods were smiling down on me, and I reached down to pick up the mighty battle axe he'd attacked with. I raised

91

the weapon up over my head and brought it down hard on his neck, then did it once more, and that mother fucker's head limped away from his useless body. Then I tossed the axe far away from the body, so there'd be no chance in hell that his soul could be accepted to Valhalla. They had to die with a weapon in their hands, right? Stupid fucking rule, but then that's what makes something a religion…stupid fucking rules. I'd abide by them.

I picked his head up off the floor so I could look into his now (unfortunately) lifeless eyes.

There were a handful of others in the room; I think maybe a couple of them had tried to walk towards me in some gesture of reconciliation. Perhaps they wanted to show me that since I had defeated their King, I was now their new Master. But I had no interest in being a king, or any kind of leader for them. I didn't even want their respect or their apologies, if they had any. So I threw the head towards the crowd of them, and as their eyes followed its path to the floor, I picked up my hammer and broke the skull of the first one of them I could reach. The rest came at me then which was good, because I didn't want to chase them, and I ripped each and every one of their throats out. Every. Fucking. One of them.

I stood in the building and the blood of my victims vibrated with applause at my decisive victory. I stood and felt what it was like to be a hero. I stood because I knew if I tried to move just then, I'd fall and not be able to get up for a long time.

And then I saw her, still in the corner, terrified and staring at me with her makeup smeared on her face. It was Maria. It was the girl that had brought my wife here and gotten her killed.

I walked to her, and at that point, I don't know what part of me wasn't covered in blood. She began to pee her pants. "You brought her here, to this?" I said. She had no answer for me. "Did you see what they did to her? Were you here?" She still didn't answer, but I felt that she had been there.

Hanging on her throat I saw the necklace my wife had given her. I pulled it roughly off her neck, and in the process ripped most of the front of her shirt off.

I think at that point, I believe she thought I might rape her, and that she was relieved by that thought, because she knew she might live through this if that was the case. But no. She was going to die. And she did, as I grabbed her neck and squeezed and didn't stop until her body was limp. When I was satisfied she had no more breath to give, I let go and her body hit the floor.

I had done what most victims never got to do; I had found my attackers and avenged my wrong, in the most basic and satisfying way.

The headless Viking Mexican from Quintana Roo lay prostrate on the floor. This guy had watches up and down his arms that were nicer that any I had ever owned. There was one, a Tag Heuer, that I noticed. I pulled it off of him and admired the large blue facing lined with bright silver numbers. One rule Vikings had, I heard, was to keep battle treasures from those they had conquered. I liked that. See, it made sense.

I never had worn a watch because I didn't like how they would cinch onto my wrist all day, but…I did have it made into a very nice pocket watch. The silver band was melted down and made into a part of the chain for it, and I earned more than enough money to have a sturdy silver case and latch made for it by pawning his other watches and having the various silvers and golds melted down for their worth.

I carry that watch to this day. And to remind me of my victory, I had Alejandro's symbol engraved onto the back of it; an Odin hammer, crossed with a battle axe. I usurped his symbol, downgraded his importance, and sent him to the underworld with no significance. If he chose to show his symbol to others down there, they would ask him "Why are you showing me Cooper Cornelius Happenstance's symbol?" And he would scream because he no longer had an identifying "nom de guerre."

Of course the Captain made sure none of my vengeful slaughter would have ever been connected to me, and afterwards he actually ended up getting major props for the decrease of the city's prostitution! Since I burned down that operation, which was the centerpiece of the enterprise, there were few people who still dared to deal in young women. I mean there were always a few that tried to push the line, but it was easy enough to track down those stragglers that were still trying to rake in a buck. From a criminal standpoint, illegal prostitution had become very taboo.

THE WOLF, A BUTCHER, HIS DEMON, AND THEIR MASTER

After my victory, I assumed that I'd earned some sense of peace. I couldn't imagine that the fire in my soul wouldn't have been sated by the fury of that night. I waited, and spoke very little and worked to remain calm.

But the pulse of the souls I conquered never stopped beating. In fact, it got louder and I felt an elation that I'd believed was extinct from years back. I tried to take care of Sam, but emotionally, what she needed to get, I couldn't handle that. Not because I didn't want to, but because I didn't have it. Paying the bad guys back for the wrong they did is one thing…assuaging the anguish of a daughter that had lost her mother was another.

I felt guilty, a little.

See, I was gifted with the retribution she would never have. The lack of that, I think, affected her more than I could ever realize; but the gain of it, I'm sure, affected me more than I was ever ready to admit.

CHAPTER 9

SAM

Thank God I was able to NOT fucking laugh when I opened the door to Brenda's office. It probably wouldn't have looked good if the first thing I did after finding her body, slumped over on her desk like she was passed out drunk, was to giggle like a silly bitch.

I was sitting at my desk, looking at websites of local nurseries to see what other kinds of bonsai's they had in stock. The Cablasian guy was still working furiously to ignore me, when we heard, "Ah...Fuck!" come out of the office Brenda was in. That in itself was not unusual. Actually, it was quite normal.

What made it suspicious was the frog shaped tape dispenser that crashed through her window and landed in the lobby, and the subsequent "thump" sound that followed; and then the silence. Really, it was the silence that was odd, because that is *never* what a person expects to hear from behind that door.

So, I walked over to open said door. Cablasian guy followed after me; I guess he realized he should at least *act* concerned, since his potentially new boss could be in there, and if he wanted the job then he should portray himself to be a "part of the solution."

According to Dr. Phil, the first thing a person must do to fix a personal problem is to be able to realize and then admit that there IS a problem. Once that is agreed upon, a person can then get on with fixing what it is they want to fix about themselves. This is a difficult process for some, because it involves serious introspection and the ability to handle uncomfortable changes.

As for me, I *like* to make things better about myself – and anything else I deem imperfect, which are most things. I like to tweak something until it is perfect, and then tweak it some more until it's even better. Those bonsai trees were my latest project. Those horrible little plants had been refusing the next level treatments I'd been administering. I watched all the YouTube videos about manicuring them, and how to maximize their vibrancy (allow for plenty of sun while still keeping the roots protected, etc.). I kept clipping, kept cutting, beyond the point the videos I watched said I should go.

But those bonsais, they kept dying. There was no reason they should have done anything but thrived and continued to grow more beautiful than they were organically ever meant to be. My treatments were that perfect. It confirms to me that there are things in this world that just do not want to better themselves, or to become more perfect by harnessing the inner power of themselves.

If a plant has to die while trying to achieve perfection, then so be it. Perfection is a noble cause and at times only attained with the ultimate sacrifice. I wanted to make these bonsais perfect; but I hadn't got there yet. I wouldn't stop until they *were* perfect. I would know I had achieved perfection by, when I look at a bonsai, I'd instantly know that it was shaped as it was meant to be shaped. It would be balanced as it was meant to balance. It would be exquisitely positioned from every angle. And most importantly, I would know it was perfect because I would immediately be happy.

My house is like this. The inside is perfect, but it doesn't take much to mess it up. It is a constant exercise in attaining a perfect "fung-shui" of solitude.

In high school, people wouldn't do projects with me because I never quit critiquing the assignment and making minor changes up to the last minute. They didn't have the patience or the far-sight to see that what we were working on should be perfect.

My dad has always laughed at this peccadillo of mine. He thinks it's cute. But his head lives up his ass, so I could give a shit.

Woody, I think, was a project of mine. He was the ultimate fixer upper, and I'll always believe that's what pulled me to him. That, and the fact that he was very well hung. He never lasted long, but he was able to jump back up to full attention in minutes and continue to do that for as long as he needed to see the night through.

But he became distant, especially when I began to turn the screws on him. When I really began to sculpt him, and try to cut out the bad parts so only the good ones would thrive, he ran off. Got scared I guess. Not everyone can handle change. Ally misses him, but he knows he has to go through me to get to her.

If I'm being honest with myself, I should have stayed with Cliff years back. But he was already perfect. He was the house that didn't need any maintenance. I mean, everything needs fixing at some point, I could have found something; but Woody was easier. Cliff and I did have our time, though. We were together, and it was good. But I chose Woody, even when common sense yelled that I shouldn't. I made Woody my choice, maybe because I was scared of losing the control I had on him, and of having someone who was my equal to contend with.

But recently, Cliff and I have been reconnecting and I'm thinking that he's more of a project than I had first imagined. That's attractive to me. He'd be more aggressive and so harder to handle, but that'd be fun. And Ally loves him, of course. They are so damn good together.

Brenda was a project of mine, as well. I wanted that promotion she was hiring for, and I didn't want some moron to stop me from getting it. This was *my* office, *my* project, *my* little world I had helped create; it would be sustained according to how I felt it should be.

Brenda was a bitch and difficult to deal with. I couldn't change how she acted, but I realized I could change how I dealt with her. You can't control most things in life, but you can control, sometimes, how *you* decide to be. So, I looked at myself, and I decided that I wasn't being helpful enough to the organization. I knew I could be more helpful, more willing to be on "Team Bren," and that is what I focused on.

I looked at what she really wanted in life. She wanted to be seen as a bad ass and to be beautiful. She wanted pleasure and money. She wanted to be a Rock Star.

So, I cooked her books for her. I knew what she was doing, and I made it so that she could sell and use the foreclosed houses at her discretion.

Eventually, she made her personal intentions known to me. One evening, some files dropped off her desk and she motioned for me to pick them up. I got down on the floor and found I was directly in front of her. She was sitting in her chair with her legs wide open in front of me. It was obvious she was making a show of dominance over me (eye roll). But I went with it. I figured if I was going to jump into it, I'd hit it like a bullet to force my own upper hand.

I stared directly into her eyes and began to push her tight-fitting dress up from her knees. She was surprised, I could tell. That was good, she didn't think I'd step up to this. But I knew she played around with ladies on the side, and that was my angle. I'm a fucking Baller, and this would give ME control with whatever our relationship was.

She lifted her hips and I pushed the dress up around her waist. I wasn't surprised she wasn't wearing any panties. Of course not, this was Brenda! But as she lifted her soft thighs to the side, I'll admit I was impressed when I looked down on *the* most well-manicured pussy in town. It was truly spectacular. And I could appreciate that! It wasn't sloppy, or out of place. This was the epitome of the perfectly proportioned porn pussy, and that agreed with my fung-shui balance sensibilities. If there was any woman I was going to go down on, it should definitely be one that took pride in making sure her V-Town looked good.

And, I was excited. Being a novice at this, I was curious to see how I would do.

My guess is that I did pretty well. It didn't take but a few minutes until I felt her stomach tighten up, and I tasted her release on my face. Then she became limp and purred while I kept my tongue on her just a bit longer, as a kind of post-coital back scratch. Afterwards, I seemed to be well inside her good graces during work hours, which made my life easier. So hey - mission accomplished!

But then, she became difficult again. I got displaced somehow. She was slowly pushing me off to the side and keeping me away from the game. So today I was online shopping for new plants to trim (can ferns be trimmed?) and meditating on ways to handle Brenda's new personality of the week, when the tape dispenser came crashing out of her office window. Now I had Tiger Woods guy behind me, looking all "Oh, my God, what's that!" at the sight of Brenda incapacitated on her desk. I looked at him with obvious disgust. This idiot was who she wanted working here? Fucking Bullshit.

He ran around the desk to pull her head up but she just fell to the floor when he moved her. Her perfect tits, the ones she was so proud, were facing pertly up in the air. They had no idea anything was wrong, why should they? They were perfect! Tiger checked for breathing then tried chest compressions. But he gave up on that because her fabulous tits kept getting in the way and he couldn't work with her chest without totally molesting her. So he just began to shake her, like she might wake up. This guy was pathetic.

"She's dead, dude." I said. He looked at me and either didn't understand what I said, or was just not computing what he saw. This did not fit into the reality he had planned for himself today.

His chest compressions were useless... one look at her, and I could tell she was done. The frozen expression on her face was like a person who had sucked a huge lemon and failed. She also had this plastic looking shit all over her face. And it was all up in her nose and mouth, so I knew she wasn't going to be breathing without Roto Rooter coming and cleaning out those airways first.

And kudos to me... I absolutely held back from making a crack about her looking like she just got a facial from the new local gang bang club that just opened up...

I walked back to my desk and got the phone. I thought about calling 911, just to piss my dad off. He'd have to hear about this from the circuit board, and he might not even get assigned to come over here. But no, the benefit of being a detective's daughter is that I could control which officer showed up at this scene, and that it wouldn't be some newbie beat cop.

Or I thought, should I call Captain, my Godfather, directly, and have him call Ramos first? Because he would, he and dad had been pissy with each other lately. Captain would call Ramos, that creepy fuck, and Ramos would be the one to tell dad about what happened here, and that would for sure irritate him. He'd want to hear about this first hand. Having his partner tell him something about his daughter to give him information he didn't already have would rile him up. And that is *hilarious* to me.

Ramos would like it. It was obvious he was into me, and I had politely (what I consider polite, anyway) refused some of his not-so-subtle advances. I know dad gave him shit about that. This would give Ramos something to throw back at him.

And dad would HATE that!

So, that's what I did.

As always, the Captain's voice was slightly more smooth than paved gravel, and harsh as brine.

"This is Captain." he answered. No pretense. No lead up. Not even a "the" in front of Captain. Just…Captain. What a fucking pig. I loved him.

"Sweety! Good to hear from ya. How's Ally?"

"She's good, Cap." I didn't embellish and kept my words short. I knew he'd pick up on that quickly.

"What's wrong, kid?"

I told him about Brenda. "Jesus fucking Christ! What kind of place you working at over there? This is the boss with the great tits you work for?"

"Yes." (eye roll).

"That's a shame."

"She was a bitch."

"They all are, honey. Except you, of course.

"Of course." (smile).

"I bet her tits still look good, though." This was how he thought humor worked.

"Her tits'll look good in a hundred years. They'll be the only things left."

"That's good, right?" I could hear his chair squeak and I knew he was leaning forward to put his cigar down on the table.

"Who you gonna call?" I asked.

"Who do you *want* me to call?" he asked back.

"Whoever. It'd piss dad off to have to hear this from Ram, yeah?"

"Yeah, it would. I'll do that."

"Good. What should I do until they get here?"

"Just close that office door and don't let anyone in there."
"Okay."
"You still working on those bonsai's you talked about? They're fucking great, aren't they?"

"They all keep dying."

"Because you keep abusing them, kid. Cut 'em and leave 'em alone!"

"Whatever."

"Yeah, ok. Give Ally a kiss for me."

"Come over tonight, we're doing movies."

"Isn't this your dad's movie night? I'm not interfering with that, girl. Your dad would have his period right there on the spot. I'll come over this weekend instead."

"Whatever." He was right, though.

"Stop with this "'whatever'" shit. I'll knot your tongue up."

I sighed dramatically.

"I'm calling Ramos now. Sit tight, kid."

CHAPTER *10*

THE CALL

Ramos got the call from the Captain.

"Who is it?" came from Cooper.

And because he knew it would piss him off, Ramos held up his hand to signal he'd be with him in a minute.

"Shit. We gotta go see Sam, Coop. She's at her office, and her boss is dead."

"Is Sam ok?"

"Yeah, she seems fine."

"Her boss – the one with the great boobs, right?"

"She's the one that's been giving Sam a hard time lately, really up in her shit. You know she had her working most weekends?"

"I know. And she's dead?"

"Yep."

"But she *is* the one with the nice ta-ta's, yeah?"

"Yes. She has excellent ta-ta's."

"Ok then."

CHAPTER **11**

THE BOB SIMMONS T-SHIRT

"**Y**ou killed another tree? Boogles might get upset."

Sam turned and looked at Ramos, who had walked up behind her. His notebook creaked in his hands. "Stop looking at my trash, creep." This wasn't said unkindly.

"I'll look at anything of yours that you want me to." Ramos replied. This wasn't said UN-creepily. And Sam wasn't unpleased at the remark.

"You need to stop calling him Boogles. Really pisses him off."

"And yet...that information only throws more faggots on the fire, Sam. I will not stop, not ever."

"That's mean. And just now, very rude sounding."

"Sam, it is one of the few pleasures of my life that I get to address him by, what I consider, is his true, God-Intended name; I take it as my personal responsibility. And, I feel I'm owed it, so … there ya have it."

He could be SUCH an asshole, Sam thought. But really, he probably does have a small right to it. She could understand Ramos's animosity toward Woody.

Ramos looked up to see Coop over by Brenda's office door, talking to the medical examiner. He had come in like a bull, made sure Sam was ok, and then went straight to work; and he was out of earshot now. Ramos had tried to get in first, to be the one to reach Sam, but he wasn't going to try and beat out her dad for that.

"Ally doing ok?" he asked.

"Sure. Running the house, as usual."

"I got the thank you card she made, I appreciate that."

"She wanted to do it. Made sure I put it in the mail. She loves those Play-Doh sets you always get her."

"I got the card on my fridge. Looks good. You know, Sam, how I feel about her. And about you."

Silence, so Ramos changed the subject.

"You doing ok?" he continued. "Other than this whole "'boss dying in her office'" thing?"

"I'm good, thanks. Don't you have a job to do?"

"Yes ma'am, I do. And I'm doing it … taking care of the witnesses, probing for information and making sure all angles are covered. Coop's bulldogging the M.E. right now, getting facts – it's how the process works. I'll go over in a few minutes when he's ready."

"What information are you probing for?"

Ramos affected a look of serious discussion. "Okay, well first of all - who's that Chinese guy over there?"

"He's Cablasian."

"Like Tiger Woods?"

"Obviously. He was here for an interview."

"Another Intern?"

"She goes through them like Kleenex."

Ramos glanced at Sam's neck, and at the V of her blouse. She had terrific skin. Sam noticed his visual inquiry but didn't call him on it. She kept her eyes toward his.

"And, where are you planning on being this weekend?" Ramos continued.

"Excuse me, how is that relevant?"

"You're a witness to an unusual death, Sam, we may need to follow up with more questions; we can't have you leaving town right now."

Sam was disappointed at his straight answer; it seemed logical.

"And," Ramos continued "that old hipster movie theatre in Fernandina is playing Bond movies all weekend."

"TNT is doing the same thing on TV. And my couch is less smelly than that movie theatre."

"Right, but they're doing a salute to Bond. Playing the good stuff, the old stuff. We can drink some whiskey and watch some Bond. And talk in English accents, drink some wine …"

Dammit. He was irritating, Sam thought, how he always picked up on the simple things. He knew she crushed on Bond.

"What kind of wine?" If he answered this wrong, she could blow him off. The "whatever kind you like" wouldn't work for her; nor would the "I don't know, like a Chardonnay or something?" sell out.

"A stout red one. A Zen. I picked up a new box yesterday, thought I'd try it," Ramos answered.

"What brand?"

"Dirty Panties." Dammit. That was a good one. A local North Georgia winery had recently put that out and had been successful at picking up on the new wave of good box wine.

Again she tried to blow him off.

"I'm not in the mood to go see Roger Moore. He's not as good looking as he thinks he is." Actually he was, but she would never admit it. Guys like that have enough going for them.

Ramos was not deterred. "Ok. That works out, 'cause I got tickets for opening day. Starts early, like 10am. And they are running *every* Bond performance chronologically. I mean, they're going way back, showing all the Bonds that weren't Connery or Moore. I thought you'd like that."

"If they're showing the George Lazenby Bond, that doesn't qualify as unique. The poor guy's manager was an idiot, told George to *not* sign a multi picture deal. We may not have had to sit through Roger Moore if Lazenby had stayed in. But everyone knows about George."

"Ah, I'm not talking about George, sorry. I'm talking about Barry Nelson, baby. The first, *first* Bond, from that old Casino Royale TV special they did in '57. They're running it first, as a promo."

Dammit, Sam thought.

"And then," Ramos continued, "they're even having the local theatre group do a reading of that South African radio show they did? Remember? That's the one there's no recording of, just the script? You can't tell me that ain't cool."

That *was* cool, Sam thought. But that date would be trouble. Nothing easy would come of it.

"AND... they're giving out Bob Simmons t-shirts."

DAMMIT! Sam could no longer deny him. Bob Simmons, for those in the know, was, technically, *the first* Bond to show up on the big screen. Under the EON production team, Bob Simmons was the stunt guy for the film Dr. No, and *he* was the original one who walked out in that famed beginning sequence, turns to see there's a gun on him, and shoots at the camera. Sean Connery did that scene in subsequent movies, but Simmons did it first in Dr. No. He had a hat on, so it worked as kind of a generic-spy-looking thing, but still - Bob Simmons was the first Bond on screen.

And that would be a cool fucking t-shirt.

Ramos smiled. He knew Bob Simmons would nail it, saved that one for the closer. "I'll pick you and Ally up at 8. We'll do breakfast at The Sloppy Pancake. I know Coop and Ally are going to the zoo that day, so we'll drop her off after that. And then we'll go watch Bond."

This would be perfect for Ramos. Coop would see them together and it would be his way of getting back in the picture. But, to be safe, he'd talk to Coop first to make it respectable.

"Ramos!" Coop called across the office, and Ramos turned to do his duty. It was easy for him, not like it was for other cops, to change mentalities for the job and for at home. As he spun around from Sam to Coop, his face contorted from nice and happy to serious and focused.

He pulled out his notebook as he walked in then nodded to Coop who began to list details.

"Suffocation, basically. See all that white stuff on her face? It's not just there, it looks to be sealed in her nose and throat, making it impossible to breath."

Ramos walked over to the body and began to look it over. He scribbled notes in his book.

He asked Coop, "They say what this stuff is?"

"Not yet. Lab's gotta process it. But from what it looks like, she was opening that box there - this stuff shot out of it and congealed into her breathing passages."

Ramos instantly began poking through the box. "Oh, man. This is cool."

"What is?" asked Coop.

"See this? There's a CO2 cartridge inside, and that's what powered the explosion of material. It was set to go in this little pipe. Once the box was open, it triggered the CO2."

"And what actually triggered the CO2 cartridge after the lid was opened? Can you see that?"

"I'm guessing ... this. It opened with the key and lock there. Once that lock was opened, it activated the cartridge. One shot. By making the intended receiver of the package unlock the shooter, it mitigated the chance of the material going off during transit. That's smart."

Coop felt he had enough data to begin the investigation. "First thing we look for is, where'd the box come from? Check and find tracking numbers, the whole bit. Probably won't find any, but let's rule it out anyway."

"Ok."

"We'll start interviewing the folks here, but from what I heard so far, no one knows how the box showed up. I expect we'll need to focus on the *why* someone would send her this package; that may show us the *how*, as well."

Ramos moved close to Coop and spoke quietly. "Sam. She could get more involved than we want in this situation. You know that she was having a hard time with her boss."

"Yeah. I'm with you. Here's how we do this: still do the rounds of interviews, it's expected. And that includes Sam. We make sure all information goes through us before it's sent anywhere else. Got me?"

"I got you. Expecting any trouble?"

"No. I'm sure everything's fine. I do, though, want to make sure there's no chance of any shit thrown where we don't want it to go."

"Understood," confirmed Ramos. "And if something were to come up that might be a problem for us?"

"Then we deal with it, we move on, tidy things up, and we put a pretty pink bow on the end of this case, like we always do. But I am sure, Ram, that everything will be fine. Because we will make sure that it's fine. You got me?"

Ramos looked over at Sam. "Oh yeah. I got you."

CHAPTER **12**

CIRCLES TURN, BOXES BURN

Ally, aka Baby Girl, aka the oldest five-year-old that Ramos had ever met, was out the front door and on the front porch yelling, "Rammy!" before Ramos was able to finish parking his car.

"You stay there, Ally! Car's still moving, wait till I get to you!"

"Why are you taking so long? C'mon!"

"I'm coming!"

"No, you're still talking! You need to get out the car and walk!"

With the car finally parked, Ramos ran up, lifted her high, and began gnawing on her leg as a good monster should.

"Here's what we can do! I've got these books to read, then we can play scientists, and then you can be monster and chase me. Ready?"

Ramos put his forehead against hers. "Baby Girl, I would love to play today, but me and your mommy are going out for a while. I promise, I got you next time. Done deal, kid."

"Fine. Mom!" she yelled.

Sam called out that she'd be ready in five. Ally led Ramos to the kitchen table and showed off the ingredients she'd be mixing up while she played scientist.

She looked at Ramos and asked "If we live on a circle, why don't we fall into the sky? Are we upside down? We live on Earth. That's our planet."

"Kid, your brain is amazing. What made you ask?"

"I saw about space on TV. And you always answer questions, you give me answers." She shrugged.

"I'll always answer your questions, baby. Count on it. And this," he said while pulling over paper and a crayon, "is why we don't fall into the sky…"

They leaned toward each other on the table, heads close. She kept hollering out questions, and he kept answering them.

Sam walked out and thought about how those two were always in some deep conversation. Ally always asked Ramos things, because she knew he'd answer them directly. Not without tact, it'd be age appropriate, but between them, they'd covered death, math, good and bad people, souls, space, and Lord knew what else. She kept teasing him that she'd need to schedule the "now you're a woman" talk with her in a few years; he'd answered that "no, that was gonna be Sam's party."

They were so alike, those two. Not for the first time did she notice how Ally used many of the same motions and gestures that Ramos did, like her ways of talking, moving her hands – small things. That in and of itself was not surprising, Ramos had always been a part of her life. He'd always been there.

And also, not for the first time, she'd questioned her choices over the years. And that was something that she did *not* do very often, if at all.

Sam had no personal inner struggle, no ego turmoil. Some had called her a narcissist, and they weren't wrong; others had gone so far as to use the term sociopath. Maybe they weren't wrong, either. But that didn't bother her, because whatever she was, she was.

She didn't hold grudges; rather, she removed - or avoided - whatever it was causing tension in her life. And once she chose the direction, that was it, it was over, done and done. The past didn't exist anymore and she was only concerned about what was in front of her face at the time.

She came up behind Ally and kissed her head. Ramos stood, picked her up, and gave her hugs. "Ready to go?" he asks Sam.

"What were you all talking about?" she asked Ally.

"Mom, we're not gonna fly into the sky, don't worry about that."

Sam made sure to look relieved. "Whew! I'm glad you said that, because I was getting worried. But how do you know?"

"Because Earth is a circle, and it turns fast, and it sticks us to the ground."

"Earth is a circle? I thought it was flat, like a box or something."

"No! It's a circle, mom, for real. If it was a box, it wouldn't spin, and then it would probably fall into the sun, and we'd get burned and have to wear sunglasses and band aids all the time!"

Ally looked at Ramos to confirm her knowledge, and he nodded his affirmation seriously.

"I can go to the movie with you guys," Ally continued, "if you want me to. I can make sure people are quiet around you so you can hear ok. Want me to?"

"How would you quiet them down?" Ramos asked.

"I'd throw popcorn at them. And if they kept talking, I'd put it in their mouth, and if they got mad then you can go and arrest them."

"That's a good plan."

"Yeah, it'll work," Ally agreed.

Ramos laughed. Sam said, "Baby Girl, your granddad is waiting for you. He said he's got all new things you two can mix up as potions!"

"All right! Let's go!"

Sam told Ally to use the bathroom first, and when she was gone, Ramos whispered to Sam, "Coop said that? Does he know she's gonna use every drop of shampoo, dish soap, shaving cream, and ketchup that she can get her hands on?"

"Ha! Hell no, dad didn't say that. He has no idea. I told him she'd just sit there and watch Teen Titans."

"You are a bad daughter. Just horrible."

"I know. I've made peace with it," she smiled.

"I'll pray for you, dear heart." Ramos squeaked in his best holy roller impression.

"He'll be fine. He's been teaching her to fight, so now she's all about how she can "'karate'" people.""

"Good for Coop," said Ramos. "I expect nothing less. A girl's got to be able to take care of herself. Boys are awful. I know. As the mother of a little girl, you should be very worried. About everything."

"About what?"

"I'll tell you what. About all those swingin' dicks out there when she gets older! A parent of a boy only has to worry about that one swingin' dick, but the parent of a girl has to worry about *all* of 'em!"

"Dammit. You're right."

"Don't worry. I'll be around to deter unwanted callers."

As they were all walking out the door, Sam saw Woody pull up in his old truck. Ramos stopped on the porch, holding Ally's hand. Ramos thought it was interesting, and was glad to see, that Ally didn't leave his side to go see Woody. She stayed right with him and made no attempt to move.

Ramos also noticed that Woody didn't seem to realize that. His attention wasn't on his daughter, it was on approaching Sam.

"Sorry," he said. "Got some tools around in the back shed, was just gonna pick them up. Wasn't planning on disturbin' ya."

Sam said "Not a problem, Woody. We were just heading out, so take your time."

He nodded then seemed to finally notice Ally. "Hey Al, how's it goin'?"

She kept hold of Ramos's hand while she smiled at Woody. But she didn't say anything, which for Ally, was very circumspect.

Sam interjected to break tension. "Ok, let's get buckled up! See ya Woody."

"See ya Sam." he answered and looked at Ramos. "Actually Ramos, I was gonna call ya. I may have heard something about that stuff we discussed, I wanted to mention that."

"Fine, sounds good Boo...Woody. Is it crazy urgent?"

"I wouldn't think so."

"Ok. Do me a favor if you can ... either call or come by the office on Monday, and we'll make sure to go through everything you have. That work for ya?"

"Yeah, that'll work."

"Good, I appreciate it. I'm sure it'll help a lot." Then Ramos jerked his head towards the girls waiting for him in the car and said he had to get going. He walked off with his back toward Woody and never once looked back at him.

At Coop's house, Ally yelled, "Hey granddad!" and ran past him into the house. He heard her in the bathroom, bumping things around, and called out "You ok in there stinker butt? What're you doing?"

"I gotta get shampoo and soap! And shaving cream!"

"Why?" he asked as Sam and Ramos walked up.

"Potions! How else are we going to make potions! Duh-uh!"

Coop looked at Sam and asked, "What are we supposed to be making?"

"She'll tell you, don't worry. Just make her stay in the bathroom – it'll be easier to clean up."

Coop looked at Ramos. They had spoken earlier about he and Sam going out, and what could potentially come of it. The answers Ramos gave Coop were the right ones, and he gave consent to their evening out. Not without reservations, but he kept those to himself.

Sam and Ramos drove off, and Coop went in to mitigate the mess he knew was being made in the other room.

That night, when Ramos dropped Sam back home, it wasn't nearly as late as she would have liked. It wasn't even nine o clock.

Ramos had treated her with all the respect and dignity that one would imagine a princess was entitled to. He laughed, he joked, and he flirted, but he was always on guard against any other person, or threat, that could have harmed her. She was completely protected inside the invisible cocoon he spun for her. He was the dominant male wherever they went, there was no one that could have caused trouble for them that he wouldn't handle quickly.

She liked this security; she likened it to what those pathetic little girls in the vampire romance books felt when they had a mighty one-hundred-year-old blood sucker, trapped in an eighteen-year-old's hard body, looking out for them.

They held hands, they hugged, and they watched James Bond at his best. Then they got FROYO, sat on a bench, and talked. She asked once about the Brenda case, and he waved it off. He explained that it wasn't worth mentioning because she had nothing to worry about from it, and then promptly changed the subject.

In the car later, it was her that got out of line, not him. While still in the parking lot, she straddled him in his driver seat and immediately felt him harden. But to his credit, he somehow managed to get her back in the passenger seat, explain it wasn't time for that yet, and not concurrently insult her feminine wiles.

She knew he wanted her, she could see him undressing her with his eyes all night. And yet, he was the one that pulled back.

Which probably, now that she thought about it, was best. If they had fucked in the car, it would have been fun. It would have been great. And the next day, she would have found a reason for it to be weird. That might have ambushed anything that could be realized from this second chance romance!

He walked her to the front porch and Sam thought *fuck it, Ally's at dad's for the night, I'm inviting him in, this is happening,* and when she turned to him, what she saw there for a half second made her think he was going to take her there on the wood planks. She would have bet on it. His eyes almost glowed and she saw no mercy in them, and she accepted it immediately.

Instead, he pushed her up against the banister and, beginning at the base of her neck, inhaled every scent her could find from her. He was plucking at her soul the way he explored her natural perfume.

She tilted her head forward and inhaled his aroma as well, and they stood head to head appreciating each other, silent.

He smiled, took her hand, and lavishly kissed it. Then he winked, said he'd see her tomorrow, and drove off with a few honks into the night.

CHAPTER *13*

THE BROTHEL MASSACRE

"Happenstance. Ramos. In here, please." Captain opened the door while they trudged into his office. They waited for their boss to close the door, and the three stood in a loose triangle in front of the desk.

"You two feeling frisky?" he asked. "Energetic, rested and all that?"

Ramos, ever the boy scout, answered, "Yes Sir." Coop chose to answer the Captain with not a word, just a slow nod, and an understanding that they were being set up for some shit.

The Captain wanted his attention, hated when guys acted like a cool slacker, so he pressed his question to Coop again, "Happenstance, you ok? Feeling well?"

"Yessir, Captain." he responded this time. "I appreciate you checking after our health and such. That's nice. And how're you, sir?"

"I'm well, Happenstance. Good of you to ask."

"My pleasure, sir." Coop replied.

The Captain gave the two men his measure, then decided to begin. "We have a mess to dive into, fellas. A real mess. A big pile of rhinoceros shit, truth be told."

"Smells bad?" asked Ramos.

"How shitty?" Coop asked.

The Captain leveled his dark eyes at them, and they could feel their chests being pushed on with some invisible finger. "Smelly enough to offend my delicate fucking sensibilities, boy, and shitty enough for me to consider sending in two men with your particular talents to see to it."

There was only one thing that Coop knew of, after all these years of working with the Captain, that would set him off on a path of destruction. Only one thing pierced his psyche above all else, and he would ever attack it with all the fire and lightning available from his soul. Coop asked a question, already knowing the answer.

"We got kids again?"

The Captain nodded. "Not sure. Heard something about it. We got an address on a house that may have some activity on it."

Ramos asked, "Where'd this information come from?"

"Where ever it *had* to come from, you nosey shit. Point is, I got wind of ill news. I don't like it. I want it checked out, discreetly and with full applicable prejudice."

Both men were familiar with this not-oft spoken set of instructions.

Coop asked, "Similar to what we saw before?"

"Possibly. Ramos, you weren't around then, but Coop will get you up to speed later. This is some shit we wiped out of this town for good, years back. Now we are just recently getting information about it again. Young kids, illegals, being traded around like cattle."

"You suspect pros? Some kind of organized way of moving human traffic?"

"I do." the Captain confirmed.

"This information is reliable?" Coop asked. "We've had eyes on the activity?"

"Would I mention it otherwise, Happenstance?" the Captain asked strikingly.

Coop responded smoothly, "I only ask, sir, because it's like you said ... you're not sending standard infantry to check it out, you're sending *us* - with prejudice. I'm not questioning your target, but rather the source that gave you the information."

"My apologies, Happenstance. My ire, maybe my age, got the better of me. You are right to ask about my source, and I'll tell you that this is a top source, by a top man, and I can completely validate what I'm telling you now."

Coop nodded his agreement, and Ramos, being Ramos, began to speak.

"Captain, by top men, you mean..."

Coop caught him up before he was allowed to continue, "Bam-Bam, DON'T you fucking MENTION Raiders of the Lost Ark. Do. Not. Do it."

Ramos looked hurt. Coop asked, "Was that what you were going to do?"

"I'm impressed you got the reference."

"You are a fucking child. Sorry, Captain. Please continue."

The Captain ignored Ramos's attempt at humor and continued.

"In sum, I believe children are being smuggled across the border and delivered to various brothels for prostitution. In my book, and really that is the *only* book that matters: This is the most serious offense in an already offensive society."

Coop replied "Ok. Give us the info you have, we'll give it a look tonight. And if there is anything to take care of, we'll do that."

"Dam right you will!" the Captain expelled, his ire returned. "Hear me now … if this turns out to be what I suspect it is, and I'm not saying it will be, but if it *does* turn out to be, I want you to have a boy's night out, you understand? I want righteous fury to reign down on these miscreants. I can accept many things about human nature, Happenstance, I can understand most things men do. But pimping out our children, abusing them in sick ways even animals couldn't think of? People who do that are not people. They are demons. And they need to be exposed, and after that, they need to be eliminated. Completely eliminated so that no trace of them will ever be found. Are we clear? Ramos?"

"Of course, sir."

"We're clear, sir." Coop also said, but hadn't needed to.

Then the Captain, cleared of his anger for the moment, lightened his mood and became more of an administrator, and organizer.

"Good. I'll discuss progress with you when there is progress to discuss." He turned and sat behind his desk, leaving Ramos and Coop standing.

"Now, tell me about this thing with Sam's boss. We get specs from the egg heads at the lab?"

Coop let Ramos respond to this, it was in his wheelhouse.

"Yes sir. And really, it's interesting stuff. There was a white powder packed tight into a small cylinder, hidden inside a box that Sam's boss, Brenda, opened. But to open the box, she had to use a key, turn some knobs … What happened, is that when the final latch was turned, it activated the CO_2 cartridge inside, which shot out the white powder. This powder was mostly flour-based, believe it or not, and was created so that while it's in a dry, sterile container, it remains in powder form. But when it comes into contact with any other moisture, it instantly gels up into a quick-drying goo. Once the powder hit Brenda's skin, it found enough moisture to activate the gel forming particles in the powder. Brenda starts inhaling, the powder goes inside her nostrils, and her throat, and then hardens in there almost instantly. And as a backup measure, it also covered her face externally, so that it locked in the powder that had already made it into her air passages. Even if there had been EMT's standing beside her at the very second she opened the box, she'd still never have had a chance."

"Son of a turn-pike whore…who thinks of this shit? Any word on how the package got there?"

"None so far," Ramos continued. "We do know that it wasn't sent through the mail, UPS, FedEx, or any other major delivery company. Also, we checked with courier services in town, and still nothing so far. For now, we're looking to find any existing motives from employees, past and present. Brenda was not a well-liked woman, and we've found plenty of folks that were more than happy to let us know what a bitch she was. But nothing's rang a bell with us yet."

"What did Sam say about all this?" the Captain asked softly.

"Same as the rest of them," Coop answered. "That she has no idea how the box got there, only that she and Brenda noticed it in the mail pile that morning."

The Captain leaned back and thought for a moment before addressing the men again. "If these interviews lead anywhere that could be harmful to certain people ... let me know. Bring that to me. Understood? That is clear?"

They each nodded just once, already having had that conversation themselves. They were not surprised to hear this from the Captain, however they were still relieved to have it told them.

And the Captain, having said what he had wanted to tell them, no longer had use for them at that moment. He dismissed them as his brain was already digesting information from a nearby to-do file, with "That is all gentlemen, thank you. Now get the fuck out."

That night was as dark, and as black, as the business was at hand for the two men that appeared out of the shadows; this suited them perfectly, it's preferable when the weather is on level with one's own mood.

They had considered trying to find a side entrance less visible from the street, but ultimately decided on the front door; less of a chance of tripping over shit.

The door's lock stood guard against them. Cooper asked, "Want me to get this one, junior?"

Ramos looked it over and replied, "Yeah, it looks to be standard. Shouldn't be too hard. All yours, old man."

Coop made quick work of it with his boot heel and they walked inside.

Ramos looked around and said "Place is nice. Look at these magazines: Architectural Digest, Pottery Barn. Trashy stuff, man. Wasn't this place supposed to be a brothel?"

"You disappointed it's not?" Coop asked.

"I mean...kind of. You have this vision, you know, of like a Dusk Till Dawn bar, but less vampires, right? But chicks still swinging from the ceiling and stuff?" Ramos explained.

Cooper had his weapon at the ready and focused on searching the house.

Ramos did the same, but kept talking. "Captain was worked up about this place. I hadn't seen him that way before."

"This is his Achilles; the one thing he can't stand. You'll learn that about him. What men do to each other, as grown men, is one thing. He sees that as a kind of nature. But when kids are involved? Forget it. He loses his shit."

"You feel the same way?"

"I'm ok following his lead on that."

"You dealt with this before, he was saying?" asked Ramos.

"We had a – poison -- in town once, and it got worse before it got better. But it did get better. After a huge amount of bloodshed, it got better. And all that poison, it started out very similar to this."

They continued to search the house. Quick and quiet, aware of each other's movements. Ramos spoke to Coop in a low voice, "This feels good that we're out again, Coop. Doing stuff that needs doing. It's been too long. I was getting edgy and shit. You understand?"

Coop nodded to himself and said bluntly that yes, he understood very well.

"There's something here tonight," Ramos continued. I can feel it. I can smell it."

Hearing this, Cooper looked directly at him. "You gone out recently?" he asked, showing concern.

"No. Not recently," Ramos admitted. "But I've got plans on the books; things I've been looking at, so…"

"Don't neglect it, Ram. Don't get hungry. I won't lecture you about it, but I can tell you plainly…You have to feed it some, or else it takes too much from you."

"I know. I *know* that. I've got it covered. What about you?"

"In truth - I could use a night out."

Coop paused silent for a beat. "You hearin' that?"

"Yeah. Through that door, past this hallway. People in there. And music. And not for nothing, but I was wondering when you'd pick up on that. For real? You just now heard it?"

Coop turned away and could hear Ramos smiling behind him. "Bam" he said, "remind me when this is over to ram my foot up your ass. Sideways. 'Kay?"

"I will, sir, but you keep making these promises…"

Coop didn't mind these little tangents of his, these jokes. That showed he was psyched up, getting ready. He knew that if they went any further, they'd for sure be seen if anyone was looking, so he chose to not look like he was sneaking around. He holstered his gun, straightened his coat, and walked ahead purposefully. Ramos followed his lead, only he was sporting a large grin, and a hard on, at the thought of imminent action around the corner.

They entered a hallway that had a door at the end of it. Along the hallway were dark little niches that couldn't be seen into. The light was low.

Neither of the men said it, but they both had a snap memory about the Wizard of Oz, and that long tunnel Dorothy and her friends had to walk down for the high man's audience.

Side by side, with Ramos instinctively hanging back less than a foot to create a staggered shield wall of sorts, the men walked calmly down the hall.

As expected, two men stepped out of the shadows, one from either side of the hallway. Coop assumed there were more guys hiding farther down the hall.

"Hello gentlemen." Coop greeted.

The lead guard, the one who had stepped out first, raised his hand to advertise that Coop shouldn't waste his words on him.

"You're in the wrong place, fuckers. Leave the way you came." was how he introduced himself.

Ramos heard this, and knew it was time to light these two assholes UP! But before his fists could put action to these thoughts, his mouth fired the first shot.

"Oh!" he said, "well okay, this just became awkward."

Coop heard Ramos begin to heckle and didn't stop him. The kid was amped up, cocky, and that's when he was at his best. It told Coop that Ramos was confident about what they were up against that night. And it allowed Coop to look around to figure the terrain. Incredibly, Coop couldn't make out any other guards in the hallway. Surely there had to be more! But he didn't find any. Didn't mean they weren't there, but if he couldn't spot them by now…they probably weren't. Liking the chances even better now, he stayed put in front of the lead man and just eyeballed him.

Meanwhile, Ramos worked the guards.

"You don't think you made it awkward, just then? When instead of introducing yourself, you decided to just insult us for potentially being lost? Excuse me for saying so sir, but you need to work on that. Think of it as a life opportunity. A solid introductory statement is *so* important when meeting new people - you know, in Toast Masters, the first speech you give is called the Ice Breaker, and it's used to tell about yourself and experience what it's like when speaking to an audience. Normally the Ice Breaker isn't scored in any way, and this is the one speech given that usually gets no critique at the end. But if you had used that as your Ice Breaker in a meeting, it's doubtful there would have been anyone there that didn't give a helpful critique of "'That sucked",' or "'Try again",' or better yet, "'Don't do that again, ever.'" See what I'm saying? You need to be more fucking polite, Dilbert."

He got no response from either of the two guards. So he smiled and winked at them.

But still, no movement. What did he have to do to provoke these guys?

Coop asked "What's going on in there? Sounds fun."

Then the backup man, in his own attempt at verbal warfare, finally chimed in. "It's your funeral, asshole."

Coop continued to laser through the lead man's eyes, and slowly he pulled the energy and the weight of the room around them to himself.

Ramos, after hearing the backup man's quip, snorted, "That was pathetic."

This apparently was too much for the backup man to take. He had considered himself a sharp-tongued wit, and Ramos was showing him up as an imbecile.

"Asp!" he yelled to his lead counterpart and flicked out his arm to unleash an extending baton. It was obvious he watched too many movies, because it was almost like he struck a pose after brandishing his weapon.

The lead man, aware it was time for action, didn't pull an Asp baton, but rather a stun gun with an obnoxiously high voltage. In a close quarters confrontation, Coop thought, a baton is almost useless if it can't be swung around; the stun gun is a better choice of weapon over a baton, so he gave the man silent props for good preparation.

A note to the reader: These two guards get beat down, and very badly.

What's more, they are beat down **so** *quickly (it was clocked at under seven seconds) that it borders on, nay crosses into, the pathetic. Honestly, this part of the story almost didn't make it to print, except to say something like "they came up against two black-hearted foes and struck them down quicker than it took them to think about doing it." That would have been fine; it works and sounds snappy. But in the end, this lackluster confrontation stayed on page because, in the interest of literature, it serves the reader to know more about how our two anti-heroes think and operate. It may also serve to create more of a connection between the reader and the characters in the story. Because as we all know, it's not how* **well** *a book is written (And thank the heavens for that! Wouldn't you say that this novel was a "good try" at best?), but whether the reader comes to know and associate with the characters and how well that happens.*

On with the story, then. Apologies for the interruption.

And, it began. The lead man decided on Coop as his target, and his plan was to use his forehead to break Coop's nose, then finish him off with the stun gun. Thing is, Coop figured it'd be something like that, because he saw the man's neck twitching, ready to smack his head forward. So, when the man came at him, Coop simply stooped down, moved to the side, and used his tremendous hammer of a fist to break the ribs of the backup dude, who meanwhile was focused on Ramos and also the fact that, surprise! his baton was forced flat against the close hallway wall and he wasn't able to bring it up for a swing.

Next to them, the lead man fell forward a step, missing Coop completely, and instead encountered Ramos, who by then had pulled two very sharp knives out of a specially made sheath attached to his back. These knives were also special made; each had two sharp edges and a deadly point. There was no "safe" spot on the blade, no flat edge. Nor were the knives serrated. These knives were made for killing, and for doing a lot of it at one time. And while a serrated blade is wonderful for gouging into an opponent and opening up his belly and watching the insides spill out, the problem is that the knife's serrations can get mired in the belly and refuse to come out very quickly. While this might make a great one-off kill, it's not a good situation to be in while facing more than one person at a time.

Therefore, these knives that Ramos carried were more like stilettos in the sense that they were essentially nothing but killing blades. They would slide into an enemy like butter, and then retreat back out again, just as smoothly, to move onto the next target.

Ramos sprang at the unfortunate man as he stumbled forward. He threw his left hand around so that blade cut neatly through the neck's jugular, and then spun so his right shoulder pushed the man's back up against the wall behind him, and that allowed Ramos to plunge his right-hand blade into the offending hand that held the stun gun, essentially stapling the palm to the wall.

Cooper had finished up by then. After having no less than four of the ribs on his left side completely shattered by Coop's fist, the backup man was forced to obey gravity and began to just - crumble. But Coop caught him as he fell. He locked the dude's head in between both his hands, and simultaneously pulled up and twisted left with tremendous force. The backup man was immediately dead as he was basically decapitated, but still had his skin to hold the bowl of meat he called a head, albeit much looser, to the body. The spinal vertebrae attaching the skull to the body not only was snapped, but completely broken in two halves.

That body, now more like a liquid puss balloon, squished as it hit the floor. Coop looked down and thought it funny that the hand was still trying to find a way to move the baton into a useable, offensive position. He bent and wrenched the baton out of the man's hand, inspecting it. He grunted with a sort of appreciation of the thing, then twisted slightly and pushed the three extended pieces back in to one smaller piece. Then for lack of a better place to set it, he slipped it into the back pocket of his pants, where it fit nicely and enabled him to reach it quickly.

Ramos's attacker was still hanging to the wall because of the knife embedded in his hand. The man might have used his other hand to pull the knife out, but instead was using it to wrap around the front of his torn neck, to try and contain the endless flow of blood from pouring out of himself. It did no good.

Coop watched as Ramos stood in front of the man, peering into his soul as it prepared to leave the body. But Ramos got bored and decided it was taking too long. This was a big guy, it might take a while. And so to speed up the process, he drove his free knife directly through the top of the rib cage and into the slowly beating heart of his victim. The man died, Ramos pulled both knives free, and Coop straightened his tie before moving on.

Cooper motioned towards the rear door where the party was obviously being held. "Hey, look here, Ram. There's a back section of the house we haven't seen yet. Shall we?"

"Oh. Yes please." Ramos replied.

With their guns still holstered and their alternate weapons sheathed, the two warriors pushed open the double doors leading into a larger room. The party room.

They took in the scene, as they themselves became a part of the scene. They were in a club room, with girls dancing and men drinking. There were also strobe lights, loud thumping music, and small bars set up sporadically around the room so that no one waited for a drink.

THE WOLF, A BUTCHER, HIS DEMON, AND THEIR MASTER

A well-dressed young man in expensive jeans and a t-shirt walked up smoking a cigar. He saw them, these two impressive looking men, assumed they were here for the celebration, and went over to introduce himself. He was the host, and it was up to him to make sure his guests had a good time.

As he approached them, a natural apprehension began to loom, although there didn't seem a reason for it. The two men standing there had no weapons, and no looks on their faces showing that they meant any kind of harm. They presented well, in sharp suits and stocky builds. But still, something was off…

The host looked around them, through the still open doors they had arrived from. He saw the two guards lying on the ground and smiled. Smiling was his automatic reaction when a stressful situation came about. He found that worked better than gasping, or screaming, or standing there looking worried as the people around him might be trying to decide to kill him or not. Smiling usually allowed him a few extra seconds of observing the activity and deciding on a course of action, and that had allowed him to remain alive thus far.

He was no longer confused, it made sense now. Still smiling, he understood the situation now. These two men, although having no weapons in their hands, were still a deadly threat: *they were* the weapons.

The young man was still a handful of paces away from the two new deadly arrivals, so he felt a modicum of safety and a confidence that he was able to retreat without harm. He rolled his eyes and shook his head, scolding the two men in his way, and then laughed. Coop and Ramos laughed with him. It was all very funny now that they everyone understood each other.

The party had another guest that was also very interested in the men who had just arrived. It was Rosa, friend of the late Brenda, and as she was settling in to do her own business with some of the girls there, she saw the two men and guessed correctly that death came with them.

Using her infallible womanly instincts, which had always served her so well and would continue to do so that night, she disappeared behind a tall pillar in the back of the club room, pulled out her phone and made an urgent call. Then, without waiting to see if the threat of these two men was real or not, she opened a well-concealed back door and got the fuck out of Dodge, as did a small group of other ladies that hadn't got completely fried that night and so still maintained the ability to recognize a serious problem when one came around.

Our young host, meanwhile, had also realized that these men should not have been there (and then thought or, if these men *were* meant to be there, that would surely mean that he and his men *shouldn't* be there, because they were opposites from these men. Nature demands balance, and if both factions were existing here, that would create an imbalance and would require an immediate correction. The only way to do that would be to remove one of the factions that resisted each other; for some, this speaks to the ideas of fate and karma, but the young man - who really was very wise for his age - knew this was none of that, only nature asserting itself. And yet, was it really *asserting* itself? Really it was just "being" itself), and so he raised his arms in a commanding order and gestured toward Ramos and Cooper. Men appeared from every corner and shadow in the large room, and all were targeted toward the new arrivals.

The wise young host ran off then, but saw something, before he'd fully turned away, that he'd never forget as long as he lived.

What the young man saw were the eyes of his new opponents.

A wolf flashed within the profile of Cooper; a butcher, maybe a demon, in Ramos's.

The host retreated, certain now that his life was no longer measured by years, or decades, but rather by seconds and, if he was lucky, minutes.

Ramos and Coop pulled away and separated to opposite sides as they made their stand against the men approaching them. This was not discussed between them, it was just done intuitively. Both moved to their own corners and took stock of the battle ground they had chosen. Later, they would come together again and fight in tandem, but now, the idea was to separate the mass of oncoming enemies and thus weaken the brunt of the attack. Also, it allowed them to take charge and dictate how the battle started. Once that was done, and the numbers defying them had cordoned off a bit, they would draw back to a stronger position of attack. This position would be one that they, and not the enemy, would choose, and would allow them to plow into the head of the beast, the bulk of the horde, and rip it to shreds from the inside.

What followed was nothing less than one Epic Fucking Battle.

Cooper roared mightily and smashed into the first tangle of men as would a human wrecking ball. His force was devastating; every punch he threw carried the weight of a bowling ball hurtling towards the ground after being tossed from a hundred-foot watch tower, and every piece of flesh that his hands were able to grasp either broke or tore apart as easily as an old mother breaks the morning eggs to feed her family.

Ultimately, Cooper found himself not just surrounded by his enemies, but also by the newly dead. Live men were trying to get a hold of Coop, but the wall of dead men made it difficult to get to him. And truth be told, when men saw what Coop's fist did to a person, they were hesitant to go near it. They thought they might have better luck fighting a twenty-foot-tall grizzly bear instead of this man, who to them seemed like a wild animal, like a cunning boar that could dance around its enemies and inflict mortal wounds when it decided to attack.

Coop, while not ungrateful for the mounds of dead and wounded men making it difficult for his attackers to reach him, also realized that he was not able to reach them either. He couldn't wait around, he had to thin the heard quickly or else risk them being able to mount a successful counter attack, probably with them being able to find and use firearms.

He was about to make a charge through the insane rabble, then stopped as he remembered the new toy he had picked up just a few minutes earlier.

He retrieved the Asp baton from his back pocket and heard it click true as he flung it down and it realized its full potential as a hard, merciless weapon.

Coop walked out of his "man-made" cocoon slowly, methodically, using the baton to reach over any obstacles and lay out men that hadn't been able to reach him previously. Faces broke and wrists snapped as Coop forced his way to a more suitable clearing of death mongering.

A group of about five men all were able to jump on him at once, and this might have proved a good strategy at the beginning of the battle; but at this point, none of the five jumpers were able to get a good hold on him, and their idea of being able to muscle him to the ground was just ridiculous. Coop supported their weight as they tore and punched and kicked at him. Some were even trying to get their pocket knives out at him, but he just kept walking forward slowly, minding his step and finding the most advantageous play afforded him.

Finally, he was able to swing the baton up and at the closest assailant, and it connected on his ear and crushed some of the temple. That man went flailing off, and then the rest was easy. He threw men away from him, one by one, then searched for other potential attackers.

Eventually he found himself torn and bloody, but alive as hell, on the opposite side of the room from which he had begun, faced toward the remaining force of men that wanted him dead.

Ramos, while also strong and able, instead used stealth as his primary weapon. Like Coop, he had also ran towards his attackers at first, but veered at the last minute to jump up onto a nearby table and use his forward momentum to leap over the heads of opposing men. This aerial maneuver allowed him to land behind the first ranks of his attackers, but it still put him directly in front of the rest of the men coming at him.

Fortunately for Ramos, these new men were not expecting to see him so quickly. The element of surprise was his, and he used it to dictate how he wanted this gruesome melee to play out. He unsheathed his blades and began to madly accost his enemies. They hadn't known he was coming, so even though he was in front of them, he was able to strike with deadly efficiency at their masses.

Knees broke as Ramos smashed them with his boots, and the floor became sticky with blood flowing from the targeted wounds he sliced into his adversaries. He knew that many of his opponents had guns and the idea was to not give them a chance to use or aim the hot steel before Ramos could get to them. Keeping the horde grouped together like a crazed den of hogs was an effective way to do this.

Eventually (meaning, in real time, like ten seconds), the front line that Ramos had jumped over did turn around and began to come back in his direction. And that was fine, because now, Ramos had the rear line in panic and disorder, and the ones who weren't already dead were quickly dying from blood loss or were next to someone who was, and the idea in their heads was to find safety as soon as they could. The men began to run away from the source of death (Ramos) and tried to merge back in to the main herd of their peers so as to achieve safety in numbers.

The panicked rear flank crashed into the oncoming front line, and the disorder increased as men decided whether to help those that were wounded, try to regroup and keep fighting, or just get the hell out death's sight, if that was still even an option.

It wasn't.

Coop and Ramos joined back together and stood against the men they had not been able to kill, or to wound sufficiently enough so that they were incapable of further defiance. They figured there were just under twenty men left opposing them. Twenty mortal men against two unnatural warriors, and the odds seemed so woefully stacked against that group of men, but still they worked to band together and achieve victory from the mouth of defeat!

This was not a popular opinion among the ranks however, and a few of the remaining mortals got the idea that they might plead for mercy and live another day.

And then, as an inspiration, their mighty leader ran in to show them how a battle was won. Our young man from earlier, the wise host with a mind for philosophy let out a ferocious battle cry and lifted a baseball bat high in the air to show that the real battle was not over; nay, it was just beginning!

"Get *up*!" He yelled, "Feel the strength in your arms, harness the power in your legs! These men are wild animals, but what are we? We are warriors!" His men felt vigor rise in their souls, and they looked to him for the divine gifts of power, and strength, and fortitude.

The young leader continued his dramatic speech. "We are the men who control the night! We are the dominant force in this room, not because nature decrees it, but because *we* demand it! Rise up men, Rise up! We will defeat these demons! We will be victorious, and we will piss down their skulls and fuck them up their dead asses as we dine on the meat of their loins that we have cooked in our fires!

Follow me, my warriors! Follow me to victory!"

He truly was an inspiring leader. Men who's muscles Coop had pounded into hamburger meat and who's veins had been sliced by Ramos's blades now began to rise up off the ground with renewed hope and begin to join their comrades for the next wave of battle.

Even Coop and Ramos were impressed by this bawdy upstart; this young man in the expensive bedazzled designer jeans that came forth as a prophet, as a demi-god that chose this time in the world to reveal himself and lead his men toward their glorious and hard-won victory.

The Twenty Men now became The Thirty (or so) Men, and they came together in a semblance of organized ranks, with the young host, now the Great Warrior King, at their front and center.

No one drew guns or found their rifles, even though they had had time to get them. They didn't intentionally refuse them, the idea simply didn't occur to them. This was a special fight, one that history would never sing about, but should.

This was man against man, flesh on flesh, and this battle would be won by fists, and sticks, and stones; the tools that men have been using since men were men. It was hard, it was cold, and it was right.

Ramos and Coop squared their shoulders and steeled themselves against the oncoming tide of inspired anger. They watched as the horde opposite them gnashed their teeth and rolled their eyes and pounded their fists and yelled to the gods for a battle that would define them as heroes, as warriors.

The Young Host again raised his battle bat high towards the gods, although it could have been the Reaper's very own Scythe, on loan to the young man for the purpose of harvesting two particularly rough stalks of corn. And he lowered the bat/scythe toward the two men opposite, and the two men in turn bent their knees and readied themselves for a killing charge.

The angels cried, and the demons hollered, and every sprite moaned in ecstasy when he uncontrollably ejaculated all over the willing bodies of their lovely fairy counter parts, as the power and purpose and tenacity filled the very ether around the potential battle.

The Young Host's Scythe swung down and split the air that it traveled through, leaving rips in the realm of time and space, and the horde that he commanded moved forward to claim their victory.

Battle cries roared, the fire and determination of their human souls were turned up to ELEVEN, and the brave men waiting to do battle believed they heard righteous lightning crack upon them and it lit their eager faces. Fate was theirs to mold.

Only - it wasn't lightning that cracked above them, but rather, it was the bullets flying out of the pistols that Coop and Ramos had kept hidden until now. Each man had two guns, and each man was putting bullets into the heads of the army approaching them, one at a time.

It was a slaughter. A fish in a barrel had a better chance of surviving than the unlucky assholes that were facing off against Coop and Ramos that night.

The two men spent all their rounds, reloaded with fresh clips, and continued their butchery. No one remained alive, not even the Young Host. Their pistols fell empty once more, and again they reloaded with their final clips of ammunition and they continued to shoot every single-body in that place; even though they were already dead, it was going to be doubly so.

The angels were too stunned to cry anymore, and the demons were so mad at not being able to witness the perfect battle they couldn't even speak; instead they just kept flicking the two remaining live men the bird and silently mouthing the words they physically could not get out of their mouths. The sprites found their libidos instantly limp, and the fairies flew away to clean themselves up, disgusted with themselves for being covered by sprite-spouge for no damn good reason such as this disappointment of a battle ending.

"I'm gonna call Cap." Coop said. "You need anything?"

"I could use a drink." Ramos replied, "And I should probably change into some new pants. I'm a mess."

Coop motioned, "Bar's over there. Pour me a Co-Cola if they got it. Nothing I can do about the pants, though. Lot of blood tonight. Soda water ain't gonna help with that, I think."

Ramos smiled and turned to Coop. "Wasn't the blood that soaked my pants, Coop. I blew loads tonight! I came all the way down to my socks, sure as shit!"

Coop said, not unkindly, "You are a sick fuck." and walked away to make the call.

CHAPTER **14**

THE CAPTAIN'S DEBRIEF

The Captain was in a good mood.

CAPTAIN: So, you two ok? All good?

COOP: We're good, sir.

CAPTAIN: Get a good run last night? Exercise some demons, et al.?

RAMOS, answering directly: Yes.

CAPTAIN: Good! Glad to hear it. You know, my nose is a kind of divining rod, of sorts. I can sniff things out, that's my talent. I can smell what people need, what they want, and how to connect them with that. Last night, as horrible as it is that it existed - that was an opportunity for you two boys. Your needs cancelled out that atrocity. It waxes fucking poetic, me thinks.

RAMOS: Cleaning crew find anything?

CAPTAIN: Did we find anything, you ask? You mean other than a bunch of dead bodies and blood all over the walls? Not really. We did find some cash, though, which here … have a taste.

The Captain handed both of them an envelope that was nice and heavy, fluffy, and felt exactly like what an envelope filled with a lot of under the table cash made from busting up a criminal enterprise should feel like.

CAPTAIN: Also, there was some paperwork found in a safe. It didn't look like there was much of a permanent office set up there, so it was made to be mobile and able to move out quick if needed.

COOP: We know who owns the house? Who put all this together?

CAPTAIN: Some of the men we found used to work for The Viking, if you remember that dude. Leads me to think that some of that old crew are trying to get back into business. But the house itself, that was interesting. It was still owned by a bank. It had been foreclosed on just a few months ago.

COOPER: Which bank?

Captain handed him the paperwork and he read it over.

COOPER: That's the bank Sam works for.

CAPTAIN: Yes. And that boss of hers that just died? That house was being managed by her department.

COOPER: Ok. So, her death may have a link to this. Could be how these people got into the house to begin with, maybe.

RAMOS: You're thinking Sam's boss pissed off some of these people from last night? And they sent her that package?

CAPTAIN: It's a theory. You got another one?

RAMOS: No. But I inspected that package thoroughly and saw how it was put together. I have a hard time believing that the assholes we found in that place had the ability, or imagination, or the fucking lack of ape hands, to put together something as pretty as that box was. It was a nice package.

COOPER, leaning in: You don't think there's a tie-in, here?

RAMOS: Let me rephrase. I don't think that *those* guys are a tie-in. They were thugs - muscle. If there is any kind of connection, then it's from someone that managed those guys. Someone with intelligence. Someone with a creative mind. There may be a link, but it's going to be higher up the chain.

CAPTAIN: I hear you. Good thinking. Let's start climbing that chain. And men, do I *need* to remind you that last night is *off* the books? It never happened. It will never make it to a police report, ok? That was for the common good, and sometimes that means that our wonderful system of bureaucracy needs to not be burdened by the shit stained underwear of society.

COOPER: Understood. You got anything else for us to look at?

CAPTAIN: Possibly, yes. But listen to me now ... do *not* go doing this on your own, without my say so. Got me? 'Cause last night, I had you walking into a focused operation, with good intel. I had a cleaning crew standing by. I knew specifics, all the when's and where's involved. I made sure it'd be a clean hit. It was organized. Do not, I repeat, *do not* go into a situation like that without my direction or knowledge. You understand that? I don't want you two getting hurt, only because you are unprepared.

RAMOS: That's sweet, Captain. Thank you.

CAPTAIN: But really, Ramos, I just don't want to deal with the headache of a legal fallout if you two fuck something up. I hate red tape. And I don't want attention that I didn't condone. The easiest way to keep your house clean, Ramos, is to never make a mess in the first place. That means being organized. Are we clear about this? Tell me, so I know, that we are clear about this.

COOPER: Yes. We are.

RAMOS: Yes. Crystal, sir.

CAPTAIN: Good. Get the fuck out of here.

CHAPTER **15**

WOODY'S INFORMATION

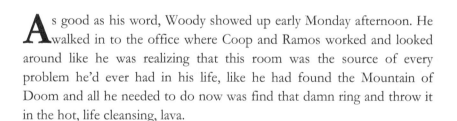

As good as his word, Woody showed up early Monday afternoon. He walked in to the office where Coop and Ramos worked and looked around like he was realizing that this room was the source of every problem he'd ever had in his life, like he had found the Mountain of Doom and all he needed to do now was find that damn ring and throw it in the hot, life cleansing, lava.

RAMOS: I thought you said you were going to call.

WOODY: You also said I could come by, so…I came by.

RAMOS: Fair enough. Let's talk.

WOODY: Actually, Ramos – if it's ok – Cooper, do you have a few minutes? I may have some info for ya.

COOPER: Sure. What about?

RAMOS: I thought you said you wanted to talk to me?

WOODY: Yeah, but Cooper's here so … Coop, you mind if we go someplace private?

RAMOS: This about Sam, Woody? 'Cause if it is, you can say what you came to say right here.

WOODY: No, not about Sam. It's other stuff.

COOPER: Ok. Ram, we're gonna head out for a burger. You hungry, Woody? Good. Ram, you want I should bring you back something?

RAMOS: Burger'd be good.

COOPER: Come on Woody. There's a food truck outside that burns good meat.

RAMOS: You know that guy's spitting in your food, right? And he's got, like, health violations and stuff?

COOPER: Well, you can't control everything. Tastes good anyway. Let's go, Woody.

They made their way down to the truck and grabbed a seat at a nearby table after picking up their food.

COOPER: You see spit anywhere in that?

WOODY: I don't see anything, Coop.

COOPER: You sure?

WOODY: Yeah.

COOPER: Let me know if ya do. So, Ramos can be an asshole. But you know that, right?

WOODY: Yes. I know that. We don't get along. But you know that though, right?

COOPER: And knowing he'd be here, you still came down to talk to me.

WOODY: I told him I'd be coming by, so he wouldn't be surprised. I wanted to speak to you personally.

COOPER: You didn't want to just call?

WOODY: I prefer face to face conversation. And my phone broke.

COOPER: Talk to me then. You have my attention.

WOODY: You remember you asked me to tell you if I heard about anything? Like about copper wire and stuff?

COOPER: I do remember. You hear something?

WOODY: Yeah. I did. I got told it, actually. I was at Pedro's last night, with a guy I know. We was drinkin', and I said I could use some cash, and he said he knew of a job that paid it.

COOPER: Who was this you were talkin' to?

WOODY: Just a guy I know. I see him around. But he said he could get me in, cause he knew I could drive a forklift, and a truck, and was good with machines. So I said ok. And then, he starts to tell me what it is. Some guys, they are delivering loads of random shit to the docks, to be exported out of the country.

COOPER: That's not uncommon. They taking this stuff to the ports in Jacksonville?

WOODY: No sir. That's what I thought at first, but they are having people drive the containers directly to the port in Savannah. Some to Charleston, but mostly Savannah. Some even to the rail depot in Atlanta, if they need to. New York, even.

COOPER: So, you might be driving a container all the way to Atlanta? Or New York? Sounds like good pay. I wouldn't want to fuck that up for you.

WOODY: Yeah, but here's what caught my attention. I asked what was being shipped. He said junk, and I said ok, what kind of junk, and he said, like metal and shit. So, I asked him, what kind of metal? Like crushed cars, that kind of stuff? And he said some of it, yeah. But there's also some spools of copper that are heading out. And that sometimes, we'd have to do some loading on the containers from a warehouse. But Coop, I heard copper wire, and I thought about what you said. Sounded like that might be interesting for you, maybe. You think?

COOPER: Yes, Woody. That is extremely interesting. Very. I appreciate you bringing this to me. I can appreciate how nervous you might be doing that.

WOODY: You said you needed that, Coop, and I wanted to help. I don't want you thinking bad about me.

COOPER: I don't think all bad about you, Woody.

WOODY: Yeah, you do. 'Cause me and Sam didn't work out; 'cause I'm not around for Ally. I may not show up a lot, but I'm not a bad person, Coop. I want you to know that.

COOPER: Sam can take care of herself, Woody. I love her, but I'm not worried for her. But Ally, she's a special girl, Woody. She needs a dad.

WOODY: I know. Are they doing ok?

COOPER: They are fine, son. Actually, Captain's taking them out for lunch today. He likes to treat the girls with stuff like that. Woody, did your friend happen to mention where this stuff was shipping out to? India? China?

WOODY: Oh! Yeah, he said someplace down South, and it sounded weird. The Yucatan Peninsula. Not really sure where that is. Is that in Cuba?

COOPER: I don't think so. But I'll find out. Woody, I have to ask you - this guy you were paling around with - does he know our relationship? Does he know I'm a detective?

WOODY: Hell no. I don't spread that word around. Plus, he's just come into town. From Mexico, so he don't know who I am.

COOPER: He's in from Mexico? Why?

WOODY: Work. Like everybody else. You ain't gonna try and give him a hard time about being an alien and all, are you? He's a good guy.

COOPER: No. I'm not. I wanted to know who you were talking to, though. He give you any idea where this warehouse of theirs is? The one where'd you be loading containers?

WOODY: Yeah. It's not really a warehouse; more like an abandoned strip mall. It's right over there, off of Tallyrand Road? Next to some condos that were foreclosed on - fucking government. Putting us all out of our homes, man. Hey, you gotta get Ramos a burger before you go back up, right?

COOPER: Yeah, thanks for reminding me. Why'd you do that?

WOODY: Can I spit in it before you take it to him?

Coop walked back in to the office and threw a burger onto Ramos's desk.

"So?" Ramos asked.

COOP (feigning a sorrowful face): Well… I don't know how to say this, Ram, but… I guess Woody grew some balls and asked Sam to marry him. They eloped last night, did the courthouse thing. Ally was the ring girl. He says he's ready to take care of the family. And I'm sorry, but he spit in your burger, man. I couldn't stop him.

RAMOS: The fuck, Coop!

COOPER: Just pullin' your dick, son.

RAMOS: Which part?

COOPER: Which part you think, genius? You know where about the Yucatan Peninsula is?

RAMOS: Yeah. What the fuck? Mexico, man.

COOPER: Mexico?

RAMOS: Yep. Southern tip, just before you hit Central America. Next to Quintana Roo. I always liked that name.

COOPER: Seems like I've heard about that place before.

Ramos remained quiet while he saw Coop running facts and possibilities through his mind.

COOPER: You up for going out tonight?

RAMOS: Tonight? It's Friday. I've got things to do. Can we do this tomorrow?

COOPER: Yes, we can. Might be better actually. Give me a chance to go over some things.

RAMOS: Want me to call Captain?

COOPER: No, not now. I want to see some things, first. But listen here… this conversation I had with Woody was interesting.

RAMOS: Tell me it. But first, tell me he and Sam didn't hook up.

COOPER: You serious? I was kidding.

RAMOS: But did he spit in my sandwich?

COOPER: You think I'd let him do that?

RAMOS: No, of course not. But did he?

COOPER: You should trust me more.

RAMOS: You're not answering the question.

COOPER: You're being ridiculous. I gotta pee, we'll talk when I get back.

RAMOS: Coop!

Cooper walked out to achieve his immediate goal of hydrating the men's urinal, and Ramos began picking through the sandwich with a pencil, searching for a dubious glob that would catch his attention. After a minute he said fuck it, shrugged, and ate it anyway.

CHAPTER **16**

THE PECULARITIES OF SUCCESS

"**D**on't cuss around my child, please." Sam chided The Captain. And to put a hammer on the point, Ally looked up from her ice cream and said, "No bad words, Cap. That's very important."

Captain looked at Ally, who now was working to use her ice cream as a beard. "Ya know, for a three year old, you sure are smart. You tryin to tell me what to do?"

"Yep."

"What do you know about things, anyway?"

"I know I'm a princess. A beautiful one. And, I've got a beard like you, see?"

"You sure do, Sweety." Captain looked at Sam and raised his eyebrows. "I've got plenty of wipes," she said. "Got it covered."

Captain looked back at Ally. "Kid, ice cream is supposed to go in your belly. Why do you always put it on your face?"

"Because that's how I roll," was her straight answer.

"Well I got nothing for that," said Captain, looking back at Sam. "Your dad's fine" he said, continuing their earlier conversation. "You know how he is. After your mom died, he had to redefine himself. Everyone has to do that, but he *really* had to. Your mom was his anchor. She was the Beauty to his Beast. He had to learn how to function without that in his life. And sometimes he goes through spells where he has to work that out again."

"Sometimes I wish he'd just start drinking again."

"No, you don't."

"Yeah. But devil you know kind of thing; At least I knew what was coming. With this… seems that whatever it is just builds and builds inside of him, and he finally goes off for a few days, and when he comes back… he's normal. And really great. And focused. And then a few months later, it starts over."

"Ok. So, you know his pattern. There, you know the devil. You can work with that."

"Not so much anymore."

"You mean like, he's back and forth a lot? Erratic?"

"No, but he's different. Consistently different."

"Dangerous? Hard to be around?"

"No. Really, no. Just… different. He's comfortable with it, and he's a great granddad, as always…"

"Granddad's silly!" Ally yelled out.

"Is there anything we say that she doesn't hear?" Captain asked Sam.

"Nope. I got good ears." Ally answered. "Granddad's my Big Bear! Rooooaaaarrrr!"

"Stop being so cute, kid! I'm melting over here." Captain leaned across the table and kissed the top of her head. "I love you, girl."

"Love you, Cap." she replied.

Captain looked at Sam. "Don't worry about your dad. Thing is, he works in… cycles. Just the way he is, yeah? He's ok. Best man on my force, always has been. I brought him on board, you know."

Sam knew. She'd heard all the stories. The Captain and Cooper Happenstance had gained a certain amount of fame years back, fighting against the Calhoon family in the mountains of North Georgia.

"I've got Ramos looking out for him. It's ok."

"Oh, great. Ramos. You get them both a matching pair of dark sunglasses, Cap?"

"What?"

"It's the blind leading the blind! Ramos is just as bad. I don't know how you ever thought of putting those two together."

Captain laughed. "They're a good team. And I'll tell ya… besides my good looks, do you know what my true skill is?"

"Your modesty?"

"Heh. No, never that."

"What's wrong with having some modesty?" Sam goaded him. "Everyone's gotta have some kind of moral fiber, some kind of discretion about them."

"Ally, could you please go and grab me three of those chocolate chip cookies from the counter?" Captain asked, handing the little girl five dollars. "And make sure they're fresh! Not any of them old ones, ya hear?"
"Got it, the fresh ones!" she answered. When Captain saw she was talking to the lady at the counter, he leaned close to Sam and lowered his voice.

"Listen up. I'm giving ya pearls here, kid. Fuck Modesty. Got that? *Fuck* modesty. It's useless, and potentially detrimental to a person's psyche. It doesn't tell a good story. It's not interesting. And contrary to the understood social "niceties" of our culture, it does *not* create a kind of subtle respect from, nor fucking Kudos out of, an attentive crowd. Among other things, modesty will hold you hostage with what don't really exist, things that you created, and only you can remove."

Sam was used to these lectures from the Captain, he'd been doing that her whole life. The Captain joked around, but he was very serious whenever he spoke. He didn't waste words.

"No modesty. Understood." she said.

"Huzzah!" he replied and sat back in his chair, as Ally came running back with, at least, half a dozen cookies. "What about my change?" he asked her.

"No change." she answered.

"Three cookies did not cost five dollars. Where is the rest of the money?"

"See, these are your three cookies," Ally explained, "and these here are my cookies." She held up another bag, filled with the aforementioned baked goods.

"Where'd all that come from?" he asked her.

"From your money. I had more of it, and I had to spend it. Because that's what you do with money!"

The Captain chuckled and leaned toward her. "You rapscallion." He looked at Sam. "She's got our number, this one."

He sat back and continued on his points. "What I'm sayin' is, my talent has always been to… Find *other* talent, put it together, and make things work. I can delegate that talent to achieve great results. And that's what your dad is, and what, believe it or not, Ramos is; talent. They are unique individuals and they work well together. You wouldn't think so at first, but it's true. You realize how many cases we've put to bed? How many issues we actually solve?"

"Twenty-three," Ally called out. "Twenty-three cases. And I've got twenty-three cookies, see?"

"I *do* see, honey. You count real good," to Ally, and then to Sam, "So many cases, Sam. Scooby Doo ain't got nothin' on us! They work well together, and what's more, they keep each other safe - in their own way. It's better to have them together, where I can see them, than to have them running around on their own."

"Ramos is just a very odd person."

"Ramos is sweet on you, Sam."

"I know. He's not shy about that. It would infuriate dad, so that would be fun."

"Your dad is more understanding than you think. Sometimes too understanding. Especially when it comes to a certain bone head that won't be named at this table, that doesn't show up much."

"What's a bone head?" Ally asked, as she pulled chocolate chips out of the cookies and lined them up on the table.

"Hey honey," Captain asked her, "How's your dad doing? Didn't you and he go to a movie?"

"Yeah! We did. You know what?"

"What?"

"My daddy wrestles elephants. And he rescues bears."

"Seriously?" Sam asked "Everything is cool with dad?"

"Not just cool; he's ice cold. Cool as a cucumber. These two guys, Ram and Coop... see, they're the same side of two different coins. That's why I put them together; for balance."

"And you don't think it's dangerous."

"I mean sure, there's a certain element of danger there... any amount of greatness comes with danger. But it also comes with security. Folks don't mess with them. They cut through problems without emotion and don't get tangled up in unnecessary conflict. That keeps them safe."

"Then, I'll just... trust you, then."

"Huzzah, kid."

CHAPTER **17**

DANA'S PIES: RECIPES REVEALED!

"It was night, and Cooper strode purposefully up to the well-kept mobile home up ahead. The little gravel path was lined with short palm trees. He knocked on the door and swung his jacket over his shoulder. He imagined it would be a good night.

Dana answered with a smile and a glass of wine in her hand. She had on a little sundress that didn't even come close to her knees. She smelled amazing.

Cooper grinned. "I know it's a bit late, but is that pie of yours still fresh by any chance?"

Dana smiled and opened the door wide for him. "How long it take you to come up with that line?"

"Long time," Coop admitted. "But I got it done."

Dana stood up and gave him a light kiss on the mouth, then looked him over, patting his chest and squeezing his arms. "You look fine, honey."

"I feel fine, lady."

"Good." she said and led him into the living room, in front of a large couch.

Sitting there were two young men, very good looking and very strong. Both were drinking beer and smoking cigarettes.

Dana walked over and sat between them.

"This here," she began, "is Mallard. And this *here* is Grouper. I was introduced to them a couple days ago, and I thought that you all would like to meet. They are your kind of boys, Coop."

He nodded and addressed them. "Stand up, both of you. Please."

They stood and each did their best to act as tough as they were big. Coop looked each one of them hard in the face. He felt their abs and had them flex their biceps.

Dana waited silently on the couch while Coop completed his analysis of the young men. Her eyes were big and round. She was anxious for the results, because this was a test for her. Coop would let her know if she had done well or not.

Eventually he told the boys to sit back down, then walked away and found a corner of the room to look at. His lips were pursed, his face was thoughtful, and Dana wasn't falling for his coyness. She walked over to him and whispered excitedly, "Oh I just love this part! You lookin' them up and down. Feelin' them up. Acting as if you don't like what you see."

"You don't know that I like them," Coop replied tersely.

"Oh, I know. You can play all you want, but these are some healthy boys. You want 'em or not?"

Coop turned back around to face the young scrappers on the couch.

"Tell me, fellas. Those names of yours. They farm animals, or what?"

The one named Mallard spoke up. "Those are our initiation names, man. We just pledged a first-class national biking community. Probably the biggest honor of our life. You see our hogs out front?"

Coop worked to keep any derision off his face at the mention of those boys being initiated into a so-called "biker gang." It used to carry more weight, but these days it was akin to pledging a fraternity back in the 80's, when people actually gave a shit about that kind of thing.

But Coop knew the young man was speaking his truth. He obviously believed that joining up with these bikers was a noble thing to do. And hell, why not? Coop thought. A man's gotta believe in something, or else he's just dull. This bike club of theirs was as good as anything else that was out there, probably.

"I saw your bikes," Coop confirmed. "You understand why you're here, fellas?"

Now Grouper chimed in. "Hells yeah, we do. We'll give you what you want, long as the money's there. It's what we do, actually. Kind of our thing. Are *you* up for it though?"

As soon as Grouper asked the question, he knew it was ridiculous. This guy was up for it, there was no question.

Cooper turned around and nodded. Dana walked over, and he handed her the coat he had folded over his arm, along with a pre-counted wad of money.

"They'll do fine, Dana. Good work. But, are they it? Only two?"

"These are the main course, Coop." she replied. "But the usual fillers are out back, if you want 'em for desert. Feeling ornery tonight, honey?"

"A bit," he admitted. "We'll see how it goes. These two will do for a start."

"Thought they might. They're big ones, and scrappy. Lean. Now come on, boys! I get to be in the middle of this, lucky me! I love being in charge of big husky men. Let's get those clothes off of you. There, that's right. Oh my, you are strong. Boys, these here are my assistants, Honey and Lulu. They're gonna help y'all get to know one another tonight."

Cooper took his time, worked methodically taking off his shoes and socks first, then his shirt. The other men did the same, as Dana is collected all the clothes and organized them on different shelves. The men stripped down to their briefs and Dana began to massage their shoulders, one at a time.

"You boys want some more drinks to calm down?" She went and fetched libations. Two more beers for the hired boys, and a glass of sweet tea for Coop. They all stared at each other, sizing up what they'd be wresting around with before too long.

Two other ladies of the house, Honey and Lulu, walked over and began rubbing Mallard and Grouper's shoulders with oil. Dana did the same with Cooper. This continued until the ladies were satisfied that their men were stretched, relaxed and ready to play.

Dana raised excited hands. "Ok! I'd say we're about ready! Put your drinks down, I'll get them later. Follow me! Your dreams await you beyond this door, gentlemen."

They follow her down a dark hallway, with soft red lights. She opened a door at the end of it. "It's magic time, boys."

Honey and Lulu both pull out 8mm cameras and began to record the oiled men.

Grouper asked, "You tape this? I thought you said no cell phones or cameras could come in. For privacy and stuff."

Dana replied, "Oh honey, we tape these on film. We like to watch later, it helps to boil the blood. These are always in my possession. No one else will ever have them."

Now with the cameras rolling, Honey and Lulu followed the men through the door. They walked towards a bed with many fluffed pillows and shaggy blankets, and then past it and out a back door from the far side of the bedroom.

This took them outside, towards a copse of trees that shielded any activity behind them from the front of the property.

Honey and Lulu began hooting and yelling. Dana and Coop remained calm, but their eyes were lit with energy. Grouper and Mallard began to show signs of unease, but to their credit were able to keep a cool composure.

They trod through the silent, thick forest of trees and shrubbery, then abruptly emerged onto a field of dirt, where there were small fires made around a circle that was obviously used as an arena.

Hundreds of men and women screamed, cheered, jeered, and wailed at the incoming contestants, as music that was deep, dark, and electric pounded the air.

There were large screens stationed in four corners of the auditorium, if it could be called that, all depicting previous fights that had been taped and edited with those 8mm cameras the girls had begun using earlier. There was a Grindhouse feel to those films, and that worked well for this setup; but Coop figured that, knowing Dana, that was not on purpose. Those films were what they were and weren't edited to look rougher than they were meant to be.

Dana walked up a steep wooden platform and commandeered a microphone. All the music and noise from the films immediately ceased. "The warriors have been anointed and the arena has been prepared! None of these men will use jewelry, chains, or weapons of any kind. This battle is fought only with flesh and bone!"

All three men walk out into the arena.

Mallard asked, "I won a coin toss earlier, so I guess I'll be going first?"

Cooper nodded. "That'd be fine, son. If I'm still standing after twenty minutes, then your buddy will come in for me. Sound Ok?"

Mallard smiled. "Sure, man. Let me know when you've have enough. I trained MMA style for almost eighteen months. I don't want to hurt you too bad."

Coop grinned. "Ok. Thanks for that, really."

Coop walked out into the middle of the arena, and Mallard followed him. Grouper stayed behind and waited his time to be called into the ring. *If I get into the ring*, Grouper thought. *Depends on how bad Mallard puts it to him.*

Dana once again lifted the microphone and declared, "Warriors of the Night! Begin your battle on my count. And - NOW!"

Mallard immediately charged in, he liked to start fast. Coop, on the other hand, walked toward Mallard with an easy gate. Mallard was quick. Because of this, he was used to taking the initiative in fights early, to gain his momentum. He began to land blows all over Coop, anywhere he could place them. His goal was to throw as many punches as possible in a tornado-style offense to try and achieve two things. One, this immediate barrage of power would possibly off set his opponent, and two, it gave him the chance to search out weak spots to focus on later.

It was a tiring way to begin a fight and he knew it was risky to drain himself of energy early on. To counteract this, he relied on a strong method of defense that allowed him to parry his opponent's attacks while he rested, got his strength back, and constructed the stratagem for his next counter move.

As expected, after a few minutes of high level attack Mallard slowed down and began to switch his fighting style to one of defense instead of offense. It was a smart way to fight.

And Coop started to laugh. He couldn't help it.

"I can't tell what's worse," he chided Mallard. "How weak you punch, or how bad your pussy smells. Both are serious problems. Are you aware you have issues? Or are you too busy suckin' your biker boys' cocks?"

Mallard charged at him again, this time not taking it as easy. And for a few minutes, the scene was a hardcore battle between the two men, both landing and taking hard blows, both getting bloodied up. Eventually though - Cooper began to tenderize him. First the ribs, then the hands, finally the face.

"Were ya able to find those weak spots you was lookin' for, newbie?" Coop goaded. "Did ya have it all planned out in your head how to fight me? How's that goin' for ya?"

Grouper was surprised at the ferocity of this man, but not overwhelmed. He had immediately seen that Cooper fought seriously, and was conditioned for peak performance. He supposed it was good for him that Mallard had gone in first; maybe it slowed the guy down some. Then Grouper laughed at himself for having thought that, because that dude wasn't worn down in the slightest! He obviously lived for this shit. *Well, fuck it*, thought Grouper. *Worst that can happen is I go in there and take a beating. No big deal, I still get paid. I'll heal.*

With that settled in his mind, he turned his attention back to the current blood fest before him and the fate of his newly-pledged riding partner.

Mallard went down and he was a bloody mess. He hit the ground and didn't move but for a couple of shallow breaths. Grouper got ready to be called in.

But Coop didn't wait for Grouper to come in. Rather, he jumped on top of Mallard and continued to reign fists down upon him. Mallard's face was becoming unrecognizable.

Instinctively, Grouper ran over and yelled, "Hey! He's fuckin' down, man!"

Coop did not respond, and so Grouper grabbed him from the back so as to drag him off of Mallard. Immediately, Coop snapped his head back into Grouper's face, forcing him away. Then the battle continued as Grouper realized he was now facing this man alone, while Mallard might be dead just feet away from them.

Coop came at him directly and with no hesitation. Grouper saw him approach and was awed. He saw a creature from his nightmares born into the flesh. And he realized, as he stared into the creature's horrific eyes, that he looked at Grouper, not as an adversary in a combat arena, but as a meal, nothing more than a living piece of meat, like beef cattle, that needed to be slaughtered.

Grouper became desperate then, and he walked past his still, broken friend to the nearest fire blaze and pulled out of it a stout, burning log.

Dana hollered out, "Only skin and bones in this fight boy! Put that down."

But Grouper wouldn't hear her. He looked at the body of his friend lying juicy on the ground and he knew his only chance of surviving was to bring Coop down, and permanently. Damn the rules; he planned on leaving that contest alive.

Coop spoke calmly to him. "Only blood and bones, son. That's the rule. Let me show you."

Coop walked over to Mallard's now useless body, put a foot down into his armpit and grabbed the adjoining arm. And then he pulled, until Mallard's left arm squelched off his body. With no other pretense, Coop and Grouper began battling each other with the flaming log and the borrowed arm. That portion of the evening was entertaining, but not as dramatic as one would expect. Eventually, the flaming log split apart and the arm just kind of disintegrated. Both weapons were tossed aside, and Coop began his final assault. He pounded the young man's face unrecognizable. The finishing blow was to Grouper's nose, which got crunched up inside his head. The body hit the ground.

Cooper threw his hands up in the air and howled victory.

Then Dana saw opportunity for more contest. She hollered over to the crowd of ruffians nearby that had been watching the fight.

"Now!" she cried, "Now! You all can take him now, together! $200 to every man here that goes in to fight and comes out alive! All of you at once, now, go for him!"

Coop turned around toward the oncoming horde of men, smiled, and readied himself for battle once again.

He looked up at Dana and winked at her. These were the pies she served, and they were fucking great.

She always gave him what he needed. Of course, he paid well for it, too.

What came next was similar to the fate of the men Coop and Ramos had faced earlier that week, at the party in the foreclosed house. Bones crunched, and carnage thrived on a massive scale. He left eleven more men dead before he was done that night.

Coop walked away, fires behind him, the dirt arena covered in bodies. Some of those bodies were already being dragged off to a previously unforeseen pit that would soon be covered in dirt.

Any one spectator still around stayed well away from Coop. He was more animal than man then, and his eyes glowed an unmistakably feral red. Folks could claim it was the glare from the fires that reflected from the dark pupils, but they'd know it was a lie.

Only Dana could approach him now. She stood directly in front of him.

"You did well, man-wolf. Your victories are a 'Lucky 13' tonight; your wolf was strong. But now it's time for him to sleep. I want the man back now. Come with me. Come on now, come with me."

Coop, or really, the 'Wolf', covered in blood and brains, followed her to a small wading pool around the corner, behind yet more trees. She shrugged off her loose gown, offering all her flesh to him. He had lost his modicum of clothing in the arena long before, and his sex was hard and willing at once. He took her there inside the small pool, tasting every inch of her skin and filling every viable orifice of hers with all of him. He thrust his final orgasmic stroke some time later while she was bent forward over the edge of the pool. Although weakened by that ordeal herself, she felt his member pull back out of her and he almost collapsed onto the ground.

She held him up with strength she hid inside her delicious curves and bathed him, and washed him clean of the battle, and their love making.

Then she led him inside to the rear bedroom of the house they had been through earlier, and he fell onto the bed naked, asleep immediately. She snuggled in next to him and stroked his hair.

THE WOLF, A BUTCHER, HIS DEMON, AND THEIR MASTER

In the morning, Coop awoke before the sun and found her still asleep, her breasts splayed out for him while she lay on her back.

He ran his hands down her belly, and then gently spread her legs so he could begin kissing the inside of her thighs. She awoke with a sigh, and when he had teased her outer lips with his tongue enough, she grabbed his hair and pushed his face deep into her, and he knew then to enter her with his tongue and fingers, for her pleasure.

Then, with her satisfaction on his mouth, he pushed up and sunk himself into her, and wrapped his arms around her while her legs encircled his back.

The sun rose, and Coop got up to dress. He kissed Dana, and walked out happily, a new man. Reborn.

CHAPTER **18**

BLOOD TEST RESULTS

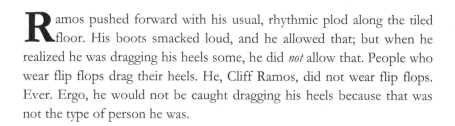

R amos pushed forward with his usual, rhythmic plod along the tiled floor. His boots smacked loud, and he allowed that; but when he realized he was dragging his heels some, he did *not* allow that. People who wear flip flops drag their heels. He, Cliff Ramos, did not wear flip flops. Ever. Ergo, he would not be caught dragging his heels because that was not the type of person he was.

This is no criticism against flip-floppers, he chided himself. He'd been meditating, most recently, on remembering that he was not in competition with everyone else; that he was surrounded by his brothers and sisters; and that he would not judge others on their choices, because many of the choices people made for themselves stemmed from who they were as an individual, while many other choices made came from that much sought-after connection that we all share with humanity.

Ramos was concerned with the "connecting to humanity as a whole" thing. If someone made the purposeful choice of wearing flip flops, that was their prerogative. This was obviously a singular choice, made only for themselves, and had nothing to do with any similarities that they shared with Ramos as a connected, verdant organism of humanity.

This was what Ramos had issues with, and that was a big focus for him during meditation. Early on he found, especially after his father died (was killed), that he relied on snap and harsh judgements of others to determine their worth, and what threat or advantage they offered him. But he did want that connection, that membership card, of society that said he would never be alone.

But it was difficult to be a part of a group, or get close to anyone, without first attaching himself so greatly as to try and siphon every ounce of soul from the opposing party. He wanted to know them, feel them, understand them, make them part of him. This quickly led to being ostracized from any group or person once they realized they were being drained, sometimes literally.

To compensate, Ramos began making rules for himself. These Rules allowed him to assess a situation or person from a removed state. From this state, he could make his determinations about that person and then decide how to proceed in a relationship with them, if at all.

This worked well, as far as societal interactions were concerned. He was able to function well within the clicks and clacks of human dalliances and political activities, so long as he detached himself firmly enough so as to see others as "THEMS," and himself as "A ME."

He became an expert at reading folks; he knew what people would do and why they would do it. Poker was a joke, at least in his immediate peer group, and it was extremely rare – so rare it bordered on mythos – that he met anyone he couldn't get a handle on, someone who kept themselves in check so well that even Ramos couldn't unlock their psyche with one look.

Coop was one of those people, at first. But he and Coop shared such an immense bond, one so large that it was inevitable that they both would come to understand each other quite well.

The Captain, he was the great stone altar of reverence and awe. No one got above the Captain; he controlled every atom of every space he moved into. He was an immense being. Ramos immediately accepted him as a mentor, a father figure, and from that tutelage, he was able to begin understanding the cost of his observed alienation from others. He realized his loneliness and strove to overcome it.

The Captain put into words what Ramos had been thinking and feeling: "When *you* look at other people, Ram, what you see is sheep – fucking sheep. And you are not the shepherd. Hell no. But you're not the wolf, either, and that's what I think that YOU think you are (as an aside, he cocked his head and said in a lowered voice that if he wanted to see the wolf, he need look no further than his own partner)."

He continued, "What you do, Ram, is you walk among the sheep as a sheep, then you go hunt with the wolves as a wolf, and then you come back and drink wine with the shepherd, as a shepherd. But you are not any *one* of these things. You are connected to them, and you know this, but you have trouble being a part of the world around you without forcing it to your will, or devouring it with your curiosity, or destroying it by your need to be a part of it.

"I would think it's like being alone on the deck of a swimming pool."

Captain went on, "Nobody's swimming and the water is calm. This is peaceful to you. You like what you see, and you don't want to just *see* the calm water, you want to experience it, to *be* it. So you jump into it, eager to know this peace, to be a part of this peace. But… that calm you so loved is broken. It couldn't exist with you in it. You realize this, and lay still, and the water smooths out, but not entirely. You act as the water, and it smooths out more. You achieve *some* of the calm you had noticed before, but the best you can do is to be a liar, a tourist; you can no more be the water than the water could be you. And this upsets you."

Ramos looked at Captain with large eyes. He probably didn't blink for a long time, because he suddenly had to rock his head back and shut them tight to regain moisture. The Captain knew he spoke true, and Ramos didn't have to tell him that.

Ramos opened his eyes and asked the obvious: "Then what am I?"

As to this question, Captain had quick, deep thoughts. He'd stayed awake some nights with them. All of which he kept away from Ramos. He sifted through them and chose the bullet points to present.

He answered succinctly, "Something wonderful, boy. I don't know what it is, exactly, but I know it's a fuckin' good thing. But I *will* tell you that you are human, that you are a healthy person, and that you have a meaningful place in this world. Never doubt that." This would seem an obvious statement to most others, but to Ramos it was an illumination. "We just need to figure out the best *way* that you fit in. Because you are different, and that's a great thing!"

From that conversation, Ramos began the practice of expanding his mind and working to unlock his atomic cell numbers. Religion was an obvious go-to, and Buddhism clicked more neatly than others, so he went with that. Meditation also proved a powerful tool. Over the years, his meditations had produced incredible realizations and allowed him to achieve physical goals he'd never thought possible.

In fact, one aspect of his growth was the realization that all people are connected to each other, and that there was a single organism that was "humanity." Ultimately, that was how he was able to recognize that he was related to everyone else. And because he was related to everyone else, he shouldn't judge them too harshly on decisions that were just stupid.

Like, for instance, wearing flip flops. He'd just consider people with that personality trait the same way he'd consider that one smelly uncle he loved; by affectionately avoiding them whenever possible.

He also came to terms with the idea that people, albeit connected to the greater whole, also had their own identity, their own part to play in the large scheme of things, and that was their individualism. This individualistic nature is what gave people their identities, as it were, and this nature is what Ramos decided that if he couldn't judge them on it, then he could most certainly decide if he agreed with that course of action or not. This is what allowed him to be a good detective. He didn't hold grudges against suspects, rather he treated them as a case.

But he did hold grudges in his personal life; truth be told, he *indulged* himself that. And those grudges were beautiful.

His crisp gait brought him up to one of the many flat, hollow doors that segregated the building's rooms. This one said "Forensics." He pushed through and stopped. There he found James, a lab tech that he used to occasionally speed up the results-finding process. He was whiny, deprecatingly sarcastic, and made others feel uncomfortable within seconds of meeting him.

James was tall and unshaven, with long gray hair, and thick glasses. He was sitting slouched on a rolling plastic chair and pushing stuff around a plate on his desk with chopsticks. When Ramos came in, his eyes looked up, but the rest of him did not. This was his greeting. Ramos had come to realize this was an acknowledgement, the way James said "hello."

"Hello sir!" Ramos greeted enthusiastically, to show he was happy to see him. James would act like his exuberance was annoying, but Ramos knew he appreciated it. No one greeted him that way. "I got your message. The results come in?"

"Would I have texted you otherwise?"

"No." replied Ramos. He could see why people were easily offended by James. But then, most people were fucking sheep, and never saw past their shit covered noses to the brown blade of grass they were working to ingest. James was asking, honestly perplexed why he would have sent Cliff a message if the results they were speaking of hadn't come in. He had no sense of tact.

"But still, you asked?" James queried (he never "asked" anything... he queried; never "saw" anything, but observed it).

"Yes. I did."

"Would you mind explaining why?"

"As an introduction; a way of beginning conversation. I get bored with basic social protocol. I like to change the tactics of my intrapersonal interactions." Ramos had thought that up on the way over to see James. He was proud it.

"Ah. Thank you for explaining." said James, and went back to moving things around on the plate in front of him with chop sticks.

"That sushi?" asked Ramos.

"No. Why do you assume that it's sushi?"

"Because you're using chopsticks and it looks like raw meat. So, I assumed sushi. I'm a detective, James. I like to play these little games with myself."

"Ah. Again, thank you."

"If it's not sushi, then what is that you're eating?"

"I'm not eating this, detective. My dinner is over there," pointing vaguely over his shoulder.

Looking over in the general direction referenced, Ramos saw a half-eaten sandwich falling off of a napkin that was placed precariously on the top of a large round mound that was slumped under a white sheet. Ramos assumed, correctly, that this was the latest deceased project to be rolled in here for James's examination. For all of James's idiosyncrasies and disdain for clichés, he played the part of the "sloppy, sandwich eating police coroner" really well.

I bet he watches Bones and acts out different parts, Ramos thought. Probably writes down lines and practices them in the mirror. Figures that's the way he's supposed to act around other people.

"But you were right about the meat part," James continued. "This is what I scraped out of that person's colon earlier today. Really, it's fascinating."

"Ah. And the chopsticks?"

"Like you, I guess… bypassing standard operating procedure to alleviate boredom. Ha! Guess we are somewhat similar specimens, you and I."

Ramos ignored the attempt at familiarity.

"May I see the results, James?"

"You want to do that now?"

"Yes please."

James walked over to a small stack of files, picked one, and handed it to Ramos who read it immediately.

"My God," Ramos asked him. "This is correct? These two blood samples are related?"

An expression that Cooper would have instantly recognized - and then immediately questioned – emerged from within the eyes of Ramos. It mirrored his process of deep thought and concentration; complicated type stuff. James didn't know about any of that, but he did see that his visitor's pupils had dilated, and… was that red?

Realizing that James was staring, Ramos asked, "Here's a riddle for ya, J (he found James receptive when he used little nicknames for him): When is a door *not* a door?

"Ah! You fancy yourself a Gunslinger, do ya? Jesting with Blane the Mono? Well, I accept your challenge, and thank-ee, sai!" James responded, and he thumped his chest three times.

This confusing narrative from James created an enigma for Ramos, so he completed his internal reverie and focused hard on the gibberish this other man was speaking.

"I'm not following you, James."

"I thought we were doing Dark Tower? Stephen King?"

Ramos shook his head, but James kept guessing. When his social anxieties peaked, the result was to keep speaking, repeat himself, and create a non-answerable loop.

"Blane the Mono, in route to Topeka, The Wastelands? Roland the Gunslinger?"

Then Ramos understood; not the exact reference that was being made, but that James was quoting some line from some book. Something he may have remembered from high school? He saw James's expression become more frenzied, more afraid at not finding a way out of this social quagmire, and decided to alleviate his proverbial pickle.

"Stephen King, got it! The Gunslinger. Good one, J. Your brain works quick, I can't keep up with you."

James's alleviated reaction was instant. "I had just re-read the series last month, so, ya know… I had it fresh on the brain. You probably hadn't read them in years, huh?"

Ramos had never read them. But, he *did* once have an English teacher in high school that was a Stephen King sycophant that had – not unsuccessfully - tried to use King's myriad library of characters to help her students relate with the actual, very aged literature they were studying at the time. Ramos didn't remember much about the literature, but he sure remembered staring at the loose cleavage of that hard working, very well-endowed teacher and how he never missed a class of hers.

"Been a while, for sure." Ramos uttered.

"The answer to your riddle, Gunslinger," James continued with renewed creativity, "is a jar. When is a door not a door? When it's ajar!"

To himself, Ramos thought: Fuckin-A, *ajar*. This door got blown wide open, baby.

To his well-read cohort standing in front of him, he said: "I appreciate all your help, James. And, I know this is a given with a guy like you, but I'm counting on your discretion in this matter. This was a personal favor for me - and as of now, I owe you one."

"Ah, you're welcome," James answered, trying to be cool about it but secretly crying tears of happiness on the inside. "Not a big thing. Of course this is just between us, it goes no further. I would hope you know that's an absolute."

"You are a scholar and a gentleman, sir." Ramos responded, stroking it a bit more. He was in a good mood, and he wanted to ensure James's silence – but in a way that would leave him *alive and useful* for future scientific queries. "I know my trust in you is well placed."

It was like working with a dog, he thought. I'm giving him treats. If he had a tail, it'd be wagging!

"Seriously, glad I could help. We're friends, it's what I do for a friend. You owe me nothing."

"Even with friends, James, there are debts. Friendship itself is a debt. Don't take this lightly. Listen: having a man like me owe you a favor is a good thing. You ken?"

James removed the admiration from his eyes long enough to appreciate the gravity of what Ramos had told him. And he realized that having Ramos owe him a favor would *indeed* be one hell of a good thing.

"I ken. Thanks."

Ramos nodded. Then he clamped his hand onto James's shoulder, gave a "We are men. We do men things!" type of squeeze and planned on walking out of there before the testosterone wore off and the conversation had a chance to pick up again.

But, he wasn't quick enough.

"How about this," James said with some serious puppy dog eyes at work, "I've got two tickets to the new Space Dinosaur movie that just came out. I pre-ordered them. Usually I use the second seat to hold all the drinks and stuff, but ya know what? I'd like to have a buddy go with me instead. So, you wanna go? I've already got your ticket."

"Ah… no. I mean, not now. For sure we'll do it, though."

James was immediately sorry he had mentioned it and his face turned red from embarrassment. Ramos realized he had spoken too harshly.

"Wait," Ramos asked, "Did you say you *had* the second ticket? It's not already sold out?"

"Oh yeah! I got the ticket ready to go, man. It's hot in my pocket." James' face returned to a normal shade of pale and hope returned to his eyes.

"Then Hells-yeah! Yes, I'd love to go. It'll be fun. I'm in a great mood right now, and you are a big reason for that. So yes, I'll go. It got great reviews, I think I heard?" He'd heard no such thing.

"Well – I don't listen to critics, they're a bunch of snobs. They don't know good entertainment. For them, it's all about sales and marketing, about who pays them the most. Ya know? It's corporate bullshit, one percent type stuff. They panned it, saying the special effects were outdated. But they are SUPPOSED to be outdated, man! It's sci-fi low-budget art."

"Yeah." Ramos said. "Fuck those guys."

"Great! I'll get there super early and make sure we get front row seats. And, I personally know the kid who runs the projector; he'll let us catch another movie for free. Or, maybe we'll just see Space Dinosaur a second time. Really man, you'll enjoy this. Space Dinosaur was this underground comic thing back in the early 80's ok, and it really IS a solid critique on the Reagan administration during the space race. Like, here we are in space, and look, we're still pulling the same old shit... trying to blow each other up, ya know? Nothing's changed. AND, this is the one where the Space Dinosaur travels to the planet of the Topless Tiaras, this group of scorned princesses that were all younger sisters to the older princess, but never became queens, and now they are battle amazons who no longer wear clothes to show off their independence!"

Ramos smiled. He couldn't help it. He just hoped that James didn't take it the wrong way.

"Sounds good. I'm really looking forward to it, James. Where's it playing at?"

"The Gorgon Theatre, downtown. You know it?"

"I know it. They serve beer, right?"

"Cliff…it's basically a bar that happens to have a movie theater in it. The movies were more of an afterthought when they opened. So yeah, they sell beer."

Would the world stop doing Ramos favors today? He hoped the hell not!

Ramos said, "Ok, I'll meet you there. You got the tickets, so you have to let me buy drinks. No arguing, I insist."

James shrugged. He was still blowing loads in his pants from Cliff agreeing to his guy's night out.

Ramos continued, "James, I'd like to ask you one more favor. Do you have any of the samples left that I had given you? Specifically, the one of the child?"

James was nodding before the question was done.

"Enough to run another test? JUST to be 1000% sure?" Ramos pushed.

"Cliff, it's impossible to be more than 100% on any definitive substance when not accounting for change in said matter, but… yeah, I'll take care of that. I'll send you the results later tonight, although I'm sure they'll be the same."

"Yes. Please do that. This is a delicate matter, and I want to be super, super-confident of the results. I am very eager to confirm those results. I'll be running around tonight, so just email me, or text me. You've got my number."

"Yeah I do!" James agreed. "Will do, buddy. Will do! Can't wait for that movie!"

"Me either - Buddy. See you then."

Ramos performed an exaggerated about-face, and marched - almost skipped - out of the laboratory. James went back to the colon excrement on his plate, grinning as he made a smiley face out of it with his chop sticks.

Ramos had just agreed to the most ridiculous man date of his life, and he would have agreed to a million more of them to get the results that he held in his hands at that very moment. Like a dismayed hunter that had finally regained a lost trail, he strode forward with the greatest weapon a man can wield – purpose.

CHAPTER 19

GIFTS

There's something to be said about a McDonald's breakfast - two things, really.

First, it speaks to some of the best mornings (and this is a relative thing) that people wake up to. The full breakfast platters contain everything a sane person wants to have shooting out of their small intestine thirty minutes after ingestion: sugar, carbs, protein, cheese, bread, butter, fat, and grease; taste, fucking taste! And this food is colorful, it's a day spa getaway for the retinas, it's an aesthetic happy ending. Even the smell is addictive. Finally, it sets a perfect table – it has all the appropriate shapes. That's not *real* food being served, everyone knows that, but it looks too good when it's portioned perfectly on the breakfast nook to care about that.

Second, for every extreme good, there's an extreme bad. In this case, the bad is that there's five pounds of nature-killing, garbage dump filling, Styrofoam packaging holding maybe one pound of China-processed, animal torturing, heart destroying, asshole ripping, questionable food (actually, there's no question – it's not food; it's an acid trip for your taste buds).

And the people putting this food together are acne-ridden, dirty-handed, spitty, snotty, smelly, and rude teenagers; fucking teenagers who could give a SHIT about your edible happiness that morning. It becomes tiring for them to try and *not* spit into every glop of eggs they pour into a to-go bag for some asshole wondering why it's taking so long to serve up the colored, melted plastic that their asshole kids are going to eat in a few minutes.

It's a yin for every yang, a balance for every beam, a pregnancy for every couple using the pull-out method as protection.

Conclusion; fuck it. This is America, Jack (oh, your name ain't Jack? Fuck you, go back to whatever country you came from, you commie asshole). It looks good, we gonna eat it!

Ramos walked up to Sam's house that next morning with a perfectly square and sturdy brown bag containing all the aforementioned American goodness that a family deserves. Ally slammed into his leg on the front porch and he stiffly walked into the house with her still hanging on.

He saw Sam leaning against the wall, her arms folded, her legs crossed, and her eyebrows up. Her t-shirt barely covered her navel, her panties did nothing but outline her sex. He could smell her early morning musk.

"Got breakfast!" Ramos shouted.

"You are obnoxious and loud." Sam responded.

"Yes ma'am." said Ramos. "Ally, put this on the table please?"

Ally grabbed the food and took it over to the table. Ramos walked over and kissed the neck he'd love to devour; he let his fingers brush the small of Sam's back where could feel her cheeks begin to part. "I done gone huntin', woman. I broughts the food."

"May I ask why?" Sam purred.

"No. You may not. I'm a man, it's what I do. That cannot be questioned. It's in the Bible somewhere."

"Are you bringing blasphemy into my house, sir?"

"Quite possibly. Assuredly. Get your sweet ass to the table, woman!" Ramos demanded in his worst John Wayne impersonation.

Sam laughed and pushed him away. "Be right back. Ally, you're in charge. Don't let him act up!"

Ally held up a large wooden spoon from a drawer. "I'm in charge! You behave, got it?"

"I got it." agreed Ramos. He walked over and picked her up and slung her over his shoulders. Her hair smelled perfect and he knew he'd die before he'd ever let anything happen to her or allow himself to be separated from her any longer.

He sat down at the table and placed the giggling child on his lap. She snuggled into the crook of his arm and she showed him how she liked to cut up her pancakes.

"How do you like to cut yours up?" she asked him.

"'Lotta syrup." he answered back.

"No, weirdo, how do you want to cut your pancakes?"

"Lotta syrup."

"That's not what I asked."

"But that's the answer! Put a 'lotta syrup on them pancakes, kid."

Sam came back out to the table, unfortunately wearing boxers and a loose long-sleeved shirt. Ramos got up, still holding Ally, and said "Hold on, we have to pull your chair out for you!"

He held Ally out and she grabbed Sam's chair. Ramos pulled, and the chair came out.

"Well that *is* some fine service, thank you both." replied Sam with her hand on her chest and sat down.

The conversation was funny, the food was good, and the discarded packaging all fit back neatly into the large brown bag it came in. The brown bag was then pushed into the garbage can and waited to be shoved into a land-fill where its contents would last for the next one thousand years.

After, Ally was thrown into the bath. She showed Ramos how she lined up her princess dolls, so they'd be able to get their hair washed and nails done. He heard her splashing and singing as he walked out down the hallway.

Sam wasn't in the living room when he returned. He turned and found her back in the bedroom. She was on her bed, propped back up on her elbows; the boxers and long sleeves were on the floor; her under shirt was pulled up to just below her nipples, and her legs her were open so that her panties were just a little askew.

Ramos motioned backward with his thumb. "Trust me, she'll be in that bath for an hour." Sam said, answering Ramos's unasked question.

"We won't need even close to that!" he said and walked over to her.

He bent down, and she raised her hips, but hadn't needed to. With one hand, Ramos ripped the panties off her waist, leaving a small red mark. He began to drop to his knees, and bury his lips between her legs, but she sat up and made him stay where he was.

She undid his belt, and palmed his member, watching it grow and moisten in her hand. Ramos sighed as she took him into her mouth and wrapped her fingers around his groin.

She finished him off in less than a minute, and at first, he was ashamed of that. But he looked at her and saw that she meant for it to happen.

He lay in bed next to her and they kissed, giggled, and listened for any sign that would indicate Ally was leaving the bathroom.

"All that for a McDonald's breakfast? What do I get for Panera's?"

"I wanted to be the one to satisfy you. The first time, to set things on the right path. I want you to be so happy with me, Cliff."

"I've never been happier, Sam. Never. All that came before, it's gone - doesn't exist. All I want in life are you and Ally."

She just looked at him. He continued.

"You *never* need to worry about me being happy with you. You are my woman. There is no other. You always have been. And Ally is my child, Sam, and you two are my family - my tribe."

"We can talk later, Cliff. I know you love Ally. And she loves you."

Ramos rolled her over onto her back and made sure she was looking directly at him.

"You look very serious," she said, amused.

"I am serious."

"I can tell," she said and laughed.

"Hey. Goofball. This is my serious face, see? This means I'm not kidding around. 'Kay?"

Sam winked her eye and gave him a thumbs-up.

"Okay, so you're laughing, that's fine. But here it goes: I want you to know... that I know. This is my family, Sam, you and Ally, and I know that I have emotional *and* physical rights to this claim."

Sam stopped laughing.

"I know, beyond any doubt, that she is my daughter. I know that, and I know that you are to be my wife."

Sam did not talk. She couldn't.

Ramos continued. "It's ok, honey. It's ok. I don't know for sure why you kept it from me, but think I may have an idea. And I know that none of that matters. I'm here now, we all are, and it's time. I will give you all of me. I will give you all of anyone that you ask of me. I will give you gifts and we will love each other."

Sam smiled, but remained silent. "You going to talk?" he asked.

She slapped him across the face. "I honestly thought you'd figure it out a long time ago. What the fuck? You been busy?"

"You know, kind of." was his reply. "How about you? What you been up to?"

"How'd ya do it?" she asked.

"Do what?"

"You got some kind of DNA test done. You got fucking blood samples, didn't you?"

Ramos rolled back and stretched out. "I just took a guess, is all. Actually, I was kidding around. I can't believe it… she's really my daughter? Wow. Crazy shit."

"Where'd ya get them from?"

"Of all the things we could be talking about right now, this is SO not what's important…"

"I'm changing doctors. Ally is changing doctors."

"Why? You love Dr. West. He's known her since she was born!"

"Dr. West is great! And I'm pissed that we can't see him anymore!"

"Why?"

"Because I can't trust him! Not if he's giving you information about my child."

"He didn't give me any information. Or samples. Don't leave Dr. West. Promise me, Sam."

She nodded and kept thinking. He watched her smile, seeing if she could figure it out.

Her eyes got wide. "Oh… Cliff. Tell me you didn't go into my bathroom and get…"

"Yep!"

"You got a used tampon? Ew!"

"Had to. Otherwise, I'd have had to draw blood."

She thought about that. And nodded. "Makes sense. That's what I would have done. What about Ally?"

"Come on. You can figure that one out."

And she did. She thought about all the play time that had together, and about all the science experiments they'd done, and all the things they'd built.

One thing Ally had loved the most was the microscope. They'd went outside and found anything they could that could be put on a slide and analyzed.

And what's the one thing that Ally would have insisted they look at? Ramos could have mentioned it, probably he did, but Ally would have demanded they do it once it was in her head.

"You both pricked your fingers, didn't you? So you could look at it with the microscope."

Ramos put his fist up in the air, knuckles toward Sam, and she raised her own fist to bump his. "Boo-yah!" he said. "She loved that, by the way. She kept asking what else we could cut off ourselves to analyze."

Sam laughed. "Probably that was why she was so intent on smashing bugs to put on slides."

"Probably."

Sam looked at him. "I love you."

"And I you, my lady."

She reached over then to stroke him again. He rose quickly, and she pushed him back and mounted him. He was deep inside her, with her knees were tucked tightly into his ribs.

Breathless, she spoke to him. "Cliff. I'm so sorry."

"Don't be, baby. I understand. I'm back now."

She increased her rhythm, adding to the intensity. "You have to understand about Woody, Cliff."

"We're not talking about this now." he said, grabbing her hips.

"We are." Sam replied, driving him into her. "Woody was safe. And you scared me. I loved you, always loved you, but you scared me. The only man I couldn't control completely was you. I understood you. And you saw me, and no one ever had. I'd never let them see me. No one would accept it. But you did accept it."

She saw that Ramos was close to an end and slowed down. He caught his breath, and she said "I could carve him out like I wanted to, just like we needed him to be, but he broke. He wasn't strong. Fuck, he'll never be the same, Cliff. Shit! What do I do about Woody?"

"There is nothing *to* do." Ramos grunted. He was still hard, but his attention was focused on this now.

"He'll not be bothering *anybody*, Sam. We explain to Ally that I'm her dad, and Woody was her uncle. And that I had to go away for a while and couldn't be around, so Woody stepped in because he loved her. That's it."

"And then?"

"And then he fucking disappears, woman. He's gone."

"Like how?"

"It doesn't matter how! It just matters that he *will*."

Sam began moving her hips again, and Ramos allowed himself to be led.

"Ally loves Woody, Cliff. We can do that, say he's her uncle, just what you said. But you can't drive him away for good. She still needs him to come around, he's good for her. And it's my fault he's even here, Cliff. My fault. I fucking lured him, and I broke him, and now he's lost. I feel bad about that."

"No. You don't." said Ramos. And he was right.

She turned her head, made a flippant gesture with her chin. "I should, though."

"No. You shouldn't." Ramos said flatly.

"Regardless of your feelings for Woody, you listen to me. He has to be around. Not a lot, but enough so she can see him."

"Ally is fine." said Ramos. "She could care less about him. She knows he's nothing to her, and up to this point, she's had every reason to think he's her dad and she still doesn't care. She's smart, she knows who her people are. She does not need Woody at all, she's done with him. Why are you fighting me on this? Let me make us a family, dammit!"

Sam increased her thrusts, and Ramos became unable to talk. There were not many ways to stop the course of action Cliff Ramos decided upon, the man was a tank. But she knew that syphoning away his sexual desires was an effective, albeit brief, option.

"You're going to marry me." she said, sitting up and placing her hands on his legs.

"Yes! Gods, yes!" he cried back.

"I'm going to be your wife." she continued.

"Yes!"

"And you're going to give me a wedding present, darling. The bride deserves a gift, equal to the ones I'll be giving you for years to come!"

No answer from Ramos, he had little breath.

She reached behind her and leaned towards him some to lift up. They were both sweaty, so finding lubrication was easy; she used it to maneuver fingers up into Ramos's backside, slowly pushing in through tight walls. His reaction was instant. First a tight squeeze, then a forced relaxation, to allow for the welcome intrusion.

"A present for your wife, agreed? Anything I want!"

"Fuck yes, anything you want, my love!" he moaned, and then could no longer talk. He arched as he came into her, his eyes rolled into the back of his head. Sam continued to ride him, and to pull every drop of energy she could from him. A man such as Cliff Ramos was verdant and had an infinite amount of vitality. It could be drained, surely, but that lasted only a short time.

He slowly pulled his mind back to himself and blinked his eyes. And he noticed that he was still inside her, and that her hand was still plunged into him.

"You're not done, sir." She grabbed his throat and continued to ride him. "It's my turn."

He remained hard, and she bore down on him thoroughly. His oxygen began to ebb and his sight dimmed, and he thought this would be a great way to kick out and so welcomed the experience, and then he felt her hand relax from his throat and her warm juices flow down from her around his waist.

She removed her hand from his ass and lay on him, feeling him retract from within her.

Just then, they heard a sing-song voice yell out "Moooommmmmyyy! I need a towel please!"

Sam yelled back "Don't you have the two I gave you earlier?"

"Yes ma'am, but they are very wet!"

"Why are they wet?"

"Because I put them in the bath. Duh!"

"Don't you "duh" your mother, chicken butt!" Ramos called out.

"Can I please get a towel?"

The newly re-connected lovers climbed out of bed and hastily threw clothes on.

For the next few hours, they behaved as any normal family would. They took a walk in the trails near the house, they played games, and they read books.

Later, they were curled up on the couch, watching the last of some Disney movie, and Ally was passed out with her head on his lap.

Ramos was drowsy as well, but he looked over at Sam before sleep could claim him. "I'm excited to hear what you want for a wedding present, my love. Please make it a challenge."

"I promise." she yawned back.

"But so you know… I've already given you one gift, Sam. What you said to me earlier: I thought you might have called me out on it by now? The gift I gave you, I sent it to you in a nice, puzzle piece box. Similar to the puzzles you would do when you were a kid, like you told me about."

Sam studied his pupils, his eyelashes, as her gears turned around this new fact.

And then her gears clicked on the obvious, but up till now unseen, truth. She smacked him lightly on the shoulder and laughed.

"Cliff Ramos. I thought so! I mean, I wondered. You are so bad! Seriously, you did all that for me? That was so nice, for real. You're sweet."

"So, you liked it! Seriously, I was trying so hard to surprise you, but was so scared it'd all fall apart. Took me a week to put that thing together, but I knew it'd be worth it."

Sam rolled her eyes. "That woman was *such* a bitch. Do you know I gave her plenty of opportunities to put me up into management? To give me a cut of her little enterprise that she had going? I even tried to seduce her; and she was too vain to let even *that* happen."

She might have told Ramos she had ridden to work with the coffee mug still on the car's roof, from the glib tone of his response.

"Really? You did that? Ha! Too funny."

"I know! I tried, I really did. Actually, I was beginning to think of how to end her on my own, but... surprise! You took care of it for me!"

Ramos put up spirit fingers. "Surprise! I'm so glad you're happy. That's all I ever wanted. And I want you to have me in your life."

"You are Ally's father, and you will be my husband. You've paid your price... you left me, and I had to punish you. But you stayed around, and now, you have me. And your daughter."

"I love you, Sam."

"I love you, Cliff. Please hear me, though. Hear me well. You want me, and Ally, and this life – everything comes in threes. You suffered via exile; that's one. You unburdened me by taking away a pain in my life and making it yours, that's two. The final and third gift, Cliff, is you leaving Woody alone, and in our lives."

"After everything, *this* is your ultimatum for our family to become real? This is the only way?"

"Not the only way, no. I can understand your feelings against him. To your credit, I don't know if I'd be able to show that kind of restraint if the situation were reversed. But that's what I'm asking from you now, to make our daughter happy. And to help me remember that I *do* still have a thread of humanity left in me. And to serve as a reminder to you – never leave me again. Ever."

Ramos nodded his head and averted his eyes down to the sleeping princess, his Ally. He and Sam's fingers played with each other across the couch.

"I can't answer you on this now, Sam. What you ask is… I can't even begin to think of walking away from it. There is a cancer within our family's territory and it needs to be cut out. I can cut it out, I have that power. Don't you want me to remove this thing that is not good for our pack?"

Sam gave him puppy dog eyes. "Woody is not a cancer, Cliff."

"Then it's like asking me to fly. I'd try, but I have no ability to do it. I would fail."

"But you WOULD *try*. That's what's important. And I know you, dude, better than anyone. I know that if I truly asked you to fly, you'd likely find a way to do it. You are strong, and determined, and extremely goal oriented. I respect those things."

"*Only* those things?" he teased.

"Well, and your cock. Obviously."

"Obviously."

"This third requirement - swear to me that this is the end of it. Swear to me there are no more stipulations to cross or grudges to bear."

"I swear, baby. I swear. We are well spoke on this." She told him.

"We *are* well spoken. I swear that your final gift will be given to you. I will let Woody be, for as long as you allow."

"As long as I allow? I wasn't putting time limits on this thing. This just *is*."

He was stubborn. "For as long as you allow, it will be."

She recognized the futility in arguing semantics. "Fine. Yes. Thank you, I accept."

"You are welcome, dear heart. I would *also* have you hear me on something."

"I will hear you."

"Never again, Sam. We are a tribe now, an entity. For better or worse, it's us and no other. Never again will you separate me from my family."

"I understand."

"I hope you do, Sam. I also hope you realize that I will never again allow myself to be away from Ally. Whatever choices I have to make, they will be to ensure that she is always with me. I accept your punishments and I accept your forgiveness. I need you to accept that I am now a part of your world, forever more, and in Ally's; always in Ally's. She is my daughter and I am her father."

Sam had already known this would be a provision of their healing. She was letting Ramos have his daughter, he now had access to his soul offspring. Ally *was* the offspring of Cliff's soul, and of hers. Never was a child more a lush product of its two parents. Although Sam admitted that of the two, Ally favored Ramos. She had Sam's logical perspective and grasp of her position in the world, but she was utterly dynamic as Cliff was, and even more determined than he to finish anything she started. Her brain worked on different levels of reality that Sam could only guess at, very similar to how she imagined Cliff's mind operated.

The two of them together were sentimental, occult. Macabre? Was that the word?

Sam also knew that Cliff spoke true when he said he'd never be apart from Ally again. It scared her to realize that if he had to make a choice between her and Ally, he'd choose Ally. If Sam tried to take Ally away from him… then she would make an enemy of Cliff Ramos. Likely, she would not survive that.

This scared, and excited, her. What's more, it earned respect by her. With the only exceptions being her father, and possibly the Captain, Ramos was the strongest man she'd ever met. The only man that was her equal, if not her better.

Her father was more than strong, though. He was a Force. He was a force that was transient, but couldn't control where it went. He needed outside help to decide where in life to go and just how best to get there. When her mom was killed, her father lost his guiding light. She was the Beauty that soothed the Beast, she was the balm to his burn. Without her, he was truly lost. Coop needed not only a guide, but also a firm hand to ensure his obedience. It was primal and it was raw.

She could give something like that to Cliff, in fact she had earlier that day. She could do anything to Cliff and he'd be able to endure. Whatever torture she put to him, he'd take it and say thank you. They were two parts of the same soul. They were a being.

But Ally was his offspring, his legacy. Not just by blood – that was almost inconsequential. Anyone with any heightened sense of being knew that. She was his creation of the soul, of the spirit, of the demon, of the wolf, of the joke he made of the world.

He could no more part from her than from his own head.

The only thing Sam could ever do to jeopardize their coming together, and shit, her *life*, was to make any kind of move to take Ally away from Cliff again.

Even her father would understand that. He hadn't approved of her dealing with Cliff as she had, but he accepted it. He understood it, even if he didn't approve of it.

She understood perfectly what Cliff was telling her. He would forgive and allow her almost anything in this world. He would provide her anything that she asked; but if she ever worked to place Ally out of his reach, her life would become forfeit.

Yes, she thought. That is the word; *forfeit*. She saw in him this unwavering fact now in his mind, his body, and his soul, and it made her feel warm, and right.

"I understand completely," she told him. "On my life, I understand."

He nodded and kissed the fingers on her hand one by one, and then lay his head onto her arm and fell asleep. She looked at her family, laying with her on the couch.

This was her Tribe; This was her Pack.

CHAPTER *20*

THE NEW LEATHER BOOK

That night, Ramos went out. He was no longer required to explain his schedule with Sam, although he still would.

He went to his home in the woods and changed into his darker, heavy soled boots that he used for hiking and dense wood outings, along with black denim jeans and a matching t-shirt. He clipped a side bag over his shoulder that contained several tools and walked out into the copse of trees that bordered his house. This lead to a hidden path only Ramos knew of, and he followed it to a dark, open expanse of wilderness that no one but him ever crossed through.

He used no flashlight, although he had one in his pack. He didn't need one. The moon was bright, just a few days to full, and it cast more than enough light to give him the scant bearings he needed to move confidently in the brush.

About a mile in, he came upon a running stream. He followed it south until he found a small dam he had made years ago. Here, the water piled together to make a small pool before continuing on its way over the far rock edge.

To his left was the small wooden hut he had built, and to the side of that was an adobe structure he'd been creating for the last few months. The hut was nice, and private. It stood in front of, and had its back against, a large earthen mound. This allowed for ample protection from the elements, and a sense of stability. Ramos liked to imagine that this mound might be a Native American burial site, an old and forgotten piece of history. He had remained vigilant as he built the hut's foundation, but unfortunately had never found evidence of old bones being placed there.

He dug a large tunnel into the bottom of the mound, and then opened up the area once further inside. This wasn't the original plan, but he had inadvertently found himself modeling his earthen house after what he'd read a hobbit's home would be like. Find a hill, bury into it, shore it up, be safe.

After he had dug out an area almost ten feet by ten feet inside the dirt, he shored it up with beams and brick. He dug out ventilation shafts and installed a fire place.

After that framework was complete, he built the aforementioned wooden hut in front of the large earthen mound's entrance. The back wall that connected to the hut would be a false one and would only open when Ramos plied the hidden latch. The purpose of that was to hide the mound's inner room. This was to be his sanctuary, his hidden hobbit hole in the ground. If hunters were ever to stumble across the shack, they'd take it for nothing more than just what it looked like. They'd have no way of getting inside the earth behind the wooden walls, nor would they even suspect that was possible.

No hunters or vagabonds or rangers had come along in the years Ramos had built up the mound area. That wasn't too surprising, this was his private land deeded to him by his father, but there was always the chance that folks could stray.

His adobe structure was a squat, sturdy thing with a rounded shape. It was a kiln that he had made from the mud, water, and char of the surrounding area, and he was amazed at how useful it had become. He blazed scorching fires inside of it and was able to melt, bend, and shape other metals – particularly his knives.

With these fires he was also able to dry and harden the sheets of mud and char he created within handmade wooden molds. These he used as shingles to build small roofs around and on top of the hut.

The Mound, as he called it, was his place to meditate, to think, to work, and to create what was important to him. His leather books were all created here. One day he'd allow Sam and Ally into his sanctuary, but that was far off.

Now, the kiln was cold and dormant; the small adobe roof that covered it had some small spiders dangling from it, waiting for food. These would go away once the fire was relit and the smoke became thick.

Ramos entered the front door of the hut and stood inside the dark room, smelling the treated cedar planks and listening for any signs of intrusion. The land outside gave away nothing except for the steady flow of the stream.

Convinced he was by himself, he pulled the latch that opened the inner wall. He stepped through it to the inner dome under the mound. There was a large wooden table in the middle of the room, with tools and various clamps on top of it.

This was where he had spent hours designing the box that was sent to Brenda. That bitch had been making Sam's life hell, and she deserved much worse than what she got.

The trick had been getting the box into her without using a courier service or going there himself. Ultimately, he knew he had two choices: either go in at night and bypass any security that was there, or pay someone to deliver it quickly, get out, and when they returned to Ramos for the rest of payment, he would make sure they disappeared.

Probably, he thought, choice number two would be the best option, but then he'd have to research very carefully who he felt comfortable carving up at the end of the job. That research could take time he didn't have. This left him with the first option; he'd have to go in himself.

Ramos had no problem with option one, he'd broken into plenty of buildings without ever being detected. But it still left him with the issue of placing himself at the point of murder, and this he could NOT risk.

He didn't feel that he had a choice, though. To make sure the job was done properly, it could only be him.

And then, his mind began to work. He did some quick research on Sam's company, her office in particular, and found that it was currently hiring. This interested him.

Finally, after an enormous amount of research, he figured out exactly how to get Brenda's package to her, with no detection.

Alphonso Shaw was his answer. The kid ran a back-street shop that Ramos bought many of his blades from. Some were imported from Japan, some Alphonso made himself. He was not a mason by trade, but he was talented and liked to experiment with various alloys. He used all current technology to forge new and better knives, swords, and various other lethal instruments. He wasn't yet able to make the really prime weaponry from scratch, but he was excellent at repairing existing blades that Ramos brought him.

Shaw was about the same age as Ramos, and usually an interesting guy to be around. Ramos limited his time with him, though, because the kid was a talker; he never shut up. He only stopped speaking when he was repairing knives, which in that case, you couldn't take him out of his self-induced trance.

But socially, he was a burgeoning little hipster. He had once bragged to Ramos about studying as a Mixologist. Ramos told him that he didn't want to hear about that fanboy fancy drink shit, and Alphonso had just laughed and then began to explain the fine art of creating libations to him anyway. It hadn't fazed him one bit that Ramos had no interest in having that conversation.

Ramos knew other things about him as well. Some of those things Alphonso had told him in confidence (always a bad idea!), and the others Ramos found out on his own.

Although Alphonso had a knack for making and repairing weapons, his *real* talent, his calling in life, was that he could always locate the most incredible weaponry and make sure it made its way to the highest paying market. Other dealers would shake their heads at certain requests, or just come up empty handed after a half-hearted attempt. But Alphonso had *always* gotten Ramos what he had asked him for, no matter how rare or how costly the order. The kid just always found a way.

This is what had peaked Ramos' interest in Alphonso. How did this kid always find such valuable weaponry for sale when other dealers could not? "I have contacts in Japan," Alphonso explained once to Ramos, "that make sure I have access to any products my clientele require."

"Fascinating. How'd you manage that?" Ramos asked.

"I'm half Japanese, dude. I'm genetically linked in."

"That's very convenient." replied Ramos.

"It is." agreed Alphonso.

Another time, Ramos was in Alphonso's back-room looking through stacks of inventory that had just arrived, when he overheard the young proprietor with one of the local toughs that was looking for a brand of butterfly knife not available on the open market any longer. "I've got you covered, man." Alphonso soothed his customer, "I can get that for you. It'll be tough, but I can handle it. Ya know - that's a very interesting choice of blade you're looking for; very specialized. I can tell you know your shit."

The young hooligan didn't know a damn thing, Ramos knew by looking at him, and most likely so could Alphonso.

But stale bread always tastes better with butter, yes sir it does.

The hooligan might have begun to get an idea that Alphonso was piling it on, because he began asking questions. "How do you know you can get it? Have you looked for them before? Why ain't you got any here?"

Good questions, all of them.

Ramos stayed hidden behind boxes and leaned over to hear how Alphonso would handle this guy. This shit always made him laugh.

"Dude, I'm black. I'm from the streets. I've got connections from Harlem that grant me access to any specialized weapon my customers are asking for. I haven't failed yet, my brotha'. I'll get you your blade, and I'll be discreet about it."

"Half now, half on delivery." the tough said.

"No… actually, you pay in full ahead of time. Before delivery."

"In full, all up front?"

"Plus, a thirty percent finder's fee, and a twenty percent delivery fee, and a fifty percent discretion fee."

"That's like double the price!" the young tough exclaimed.

"No, it's not." Alphonso explained. "It's not double anything. The price is what it is. I was breaking down the specifics for you, because I thought you might appreciate that. My brotha."

You just lost that sale, Ramos had thought. But, he'd been wrong - big time. Alphonso's new customer pulled out wads of cash and handed over the full asking price to seal the deal.

"You got one week," he said to Shaw, in a weak attempt to save face.

"I got as long as it takes, man. I'll let you know."

"If you fuck me on this kid, I will find you and I will pull your tongue out of your wise fucking mouth."

Alphonso was still holding the newly acquired wad of cash out in front of him, he'd never put it in his pocket. He raised it back toward the prideful man in an obvious show of refusal. "Take this back," he said. "I don't want it. Fuck you and your shitty attitude. I've never screwed any one, ever, and I've never taken money that didn't belong to me. As far as I'm concerned, this is still your money. We have no deal on the table. I am too damn busy making money with other people that are way more polite and so much easier to deal with than you are, and I will not waste my time worrying about you and your sissy fucking time line. I assume you heard about me from someone, and that someone probably told you I was dependable. And that's why you're here. But you obviously don't trust what you've heard before, or what I've said to you tonight, so you need to take this money back and be quick on your way outta here. Go look on eBay, or maybe Amazon. I hear they got a good selection. And free shipping, if you're a Prime member, so it's a win for you."

Ramos admired the kid's spunk.

As it turns out, Ramos knew the guy Alphonso was talking to. His name was Buster, and he was always involved in some kind shit or another. Not a huge threat, but he had a temper. He was known for being paranoid, and accusing people of talking behind his back. Ramos had run into him a few times, but nothing serious ever came of it.

But he was curious to see how Buster would react after being spoken to so harshly. Ramos decided that he'd step in, if necessary. He continued to wait.

Fortunately, he hadn't had to intervene. Buster backed down. "Alright man. Just don't fuck me. Bitches be trying to pull that shit, and I ain't got time for that, ya' hear?"

Alphonso, to his credit, didn't make things worse for the man. He nodded, pocketed the cash and said, "I'll let you know when I've got it. It may take a few weeks, or maybe I get lucky and call you in a few days. And so you know, B, if I can't find the blade you want, you get every cent back. You hear that? I don't like people knowing I couldn't get something for them. But if that does happen, then I can at least make sure they don't lose any money. I got you."

Buster left, and Ramos walked out from behind the boxes. "You got huevos of iron, man." he told Alphonso. "Good job not letting that guy scare you."

Alphonso looked back at him, eyebrows up. "You kiddin' me? I almost pissed my britches. Fuck me. I hate confrontation."

"I wouldn't have guessed that."

"Dude... that guy's a pussy, but all it takes is one pussy with a gun on a bad day with something to prove, and I'm eatin' dirt."

Ramos nodded. The kid was smart. "You able to get what he wants? Sounded like it was rare."

"Yeah, I'll find it. Shit, finding it's the easy part. *Getting* it, that's usually where it can get challenging."

"How so?" Ramos asked, but Alphonso waved him off. Ramos let it go, but was now legitimately curious as to how "lil Alfy" ran his business.

So, he watched him to learn more about how he acquired his special goods.

Alphonso was good at finding out where the knives were that he was looking for with some fairly basic web search, and then "procuring" them by practicing the old, and honorable, art of Breaking and Entering.

If he needed a knife from a pawn shop, or a sword from a museum, or rare ninja throwing stars from a private collection, he would simply go and... get them. He could bypass alarms, pick locks, and usually be out of the building in under two minutes.

Ramos followed him the next night, presumably while he was on the search for Buster's knife. He'd done his own quick research also, from his office, and found that within the city limits, there were three of the knives he was looking for. Two were in pawn shops, that was no surprise, but the third was someplace that Ramos hadn't immediately thought about - in his own police lock up! He had been, literally, three floors above what Alphonso was going to attempt to steal and risk his life for.

Without thinking through the "why" of it, Ramos walked down to where the confiscated weapons were stored and had the knife in his hands in less than five minutes.

He had planned on going straight to Alphonso that evening, but changed his mind. He'd get Alphonso owing him favors eventually, but he'd decided to follow him first, and see if he could tell how good he really was at getting his hands on merchandise.

Alphonso drove to a pawn shop East of town, in a rural area. The sun was down and Ramos had to be careful that his headlights didn't rat him out. There were some old cars and trucks in the lawn of the pawn shop (hinting that they sold old car parts as well), tacky as shit lawn furniture all over the place, and containers that showed they were agents of a metal recycling center; this dude was an entrepreneur!

The show began well enough: Alphonso parked behind some trees, stayed quiet for a bit, and then walked straight towards the front door of the small shop. He had a brown bag in his hand. When two large canines suddenly came running at him, he opened the bag, reached inside, and pulled out gobs of hamburger meat to throw at the dogs. Sure as shit, they stopped in their tracks and began to inhale the raw burgers.

Alphonso wasn't greedy with it; he gave them a lot more, taking care to stay well away from the slack of their leashes. Ramos would have thought he'd have saved more for when he was walking out of the shop, but Alphonso had given the dogs everything he had brought, and then pocketed the empty brown bag.

But Ramos saw later that there hadn't been any need for extra hamburger meat during Alphonso's retreat. It had been laced with copious amounts of canine valium, and the dogs immediately began to feel the effects of it. "It's not enough to kill 'em, ya understand, I'm an animal lover." Alphonso explained, "but it's sure more than enough to knock 'em on their ass till sunup!"

Dogs done and snoring, he had made his way to the side of the building and with a few quick hops, had scrambled up the wall like a fucking cat and was on the roof in seconds. There was a TV dish up there along with lots of other wires and metal shit that Ramos assumed had to do with the alarm system.

Alphonso made quick work of whatever he needed to do and got back down the same way he'd gone up. He went to the front door and reached into his back pocket for a specific tool - and then reached into his other back pocket, and then into every other pocket he had on him. Shaking his head, he went back to his car and began searching through it. Then he got out, cursed, and stamped his feet (all very quietly, of course). Resigned to another course of action, he looked at the dogs still sleeping on the ground, pulled the brown meat bag out of his pocket and, after returning to the front of the shop, used it as a glove to punch in the glass of the front door.

No alarm went off, and he quickly disappeared into the dark store.

Then Ramos heard a rustling, and a loud succession of farts, come from the dormant truck sitting in the corner. An old man crawled out the door and pulled a shotgun from out behind him. The sound of glass breaking had caused this guy to wake up. He saw his dogs snoring side by side and, furious, he stumbled into the store.

Ramos put his hand on the steering wheel and laid on the horn. Neither of them would know who was doing it, or why, but the old man would look back and Alphonso would wake the fuck up to the danger he was now in.

A shot was fired, more glass broke, and the yelling began. The sounds of a scuffle were clear. Then Alphonso ran out of the store and into the woods, and Ramos saw he'd also managed to get a hold of the old man's shotgun, which he was holding very tight in both hands as he raced for safety. After a minute the crotchety old man busted out the entrance, cussing up a storm and holding his hand to his head where Alphonso must have whacked him. He just sat down there on the porch, staring at the dogs that had failed him that night. Empty whiskey bottles were still falling out of the old truck the man had crawled out of, and the sound of the dog's snores became very rhythmic, and more audible, as the minutes passed. The old man didn't move for a long time, and then just slumped over towards the nearest part of ground that'd catch him so he could escape the horrid reality he called life, if only for a few unsatisfying hours.

Ramos had stayed put until he was sure his car wouldn't be seen driving off; he had though, seen Alphonso's car start up down the road and peel away, and he followed in that direction.

He had walked in later to Alphonso's warehouse and found him laying on a dirty sofa with a pack of ice cold peas over his eyes.

"The fuck happened to you?" asked Ramos.

Alphonso jumped and asked what Ramos was doing there.

"Just checking in," answered Ramos, "to see if you got anything I'd want."

"Nothin' right now, man."

Alphonso began rubbing his head and Ramos asked if he was alright. "I'm fine. Had too much caffeine earlier, and I've been trying to cut back. That shit's crazy addictive."

"I understand." said Ramos, sitting down beside him. "Caffeine'll do that to ya. And, by the way, so will being shot at by a redneck who is drunk as piss and walks around with an illegal sawed off shotgun at night."

Although Alphonso stared blankly at him, Ramos could tell his brain was working on a smart-ass comment, but nothing happened. Ramos smiled. "Did you at least get the knife?"

He saw the young man's expression turn from anxiety to dismay and that was answer enough. So, he pulled the knife procured from the police lock up out of his jacket and handed it over. Then Ramos explained where he got it, and how he'd followed him.

"What about the police report from the break in?" Alphonso asked.

"I'll bury it, if one even shows up. But I truly doubt that the owner of that fine, upstanding business wants police around. He's better off to let it lie."

"And what do you want from me?" asked Alphonso.

"Information, when you have it. Also knives, the best you can get. You know what I like."

"And if I ever don't have what you want?"

"Then your sparkling personality will have to suffice."

Alphonso inspected the blade Ramos had given him to make sure it was genuine. "You gonna get smacked for takin' this outta lock up?"

"Nah. It wasn't a part of any big investigation; it just disappeared."

That wasn't exactly true, thought Ramos... there'd been paperwork done, and promises made, and favors owed. Nothing *really* disappears out of a police weapons lockup, it all has a trail. But as far was Alphonso was concerned, Ramos had tapped into his monthly allotment of police magic and made the sought-after knife simply vanish from custody. "Now you can call that asshole and tell him you landed his shiv." Ramos continued.

"How much a cut do you want?" Alphonso asked.

"I must not be making myself clear, Alf," Ramos pointed out, enjoying how Alphonso flinched at being called "Alf", "I don't want a cut, or a percentage from your sales. I'm not hitting on you. I'm not making you an informant. There is no contract in play, implied or otherwise, and no secret deal. Simply, I like to know good people who practice in various useful trades. So to be clear: I don't – want – a cut. Please take the blade, with my compliments."

"For this to work," replied Alphonso seriously, "you will never call me Alf again. That is not negotiable."

"I'm calling you Alf. Or, maybe Alfie. Or, whatever the fuck I want, because I can." Then Ramos flashed his winning smile that would have won awards if only there were competition for such things. He liked to do that after making a threat, or an ultimatum.

Alphonso drew a hard line then with Ramos. "No fucking way. I won't allow it."

But unfortunately for Alphonso, from then on, he would be known as Alf to Ramos.

"Why'd you have to say you weren't hitting on me?" Alf asked.

"I was making a point, dill-weed. That I wasn't looking to profit from you, not literally or otherwise." Ramos answered.

"I got that. But you could've explained everything without derogatorily alluding to the fact that I'm not an attractive man, dude."

"You *want* me to hit on you Alf?"

"Hell no! I'm straight. And don't call me Alf."

"Ok then. Alf."

"It's just that a man tries hard to look good, right? It doesn't feel good to be rejected. You didn't have to put that part in there, it's like you had to say it to put me in my subordinate place, ya understand? But since you felt like that needed to be said, then I must have needed to know it, right?"

Before answering, Ramos took an exaggerated breath and pretended he was thinking real hard about Alf's logic.

"Tell ya what," he said magnanimously, "I'll let you blow me, if you want. I just hate that I hurt you with my insensitive words and rash statements; I need to think more before I speak. So, to make you feel better about yourself, to alleviate any rejection you felt from me - I'll let you put me in your mouth. I know you're straight and all, but this would just be a guy to guy thing, an understanding between two bros. This will show the level of trust, you see, that I have in you. No thanks are needed, I know you appreciate it. You. Are. Welcome."

"Fuck no, man! I ain't dustin' my knees for you!" Alf hollered out.

"See, now *I'm* the one feeling rejected. What's the problem? I don't mind telling you, Alf, my penis… it's nice. I have perfected the man-scape, and everything is perfectly proportioned. I'm not kidding, it's a work of pure fucking genius. I don't let just anyone get a taste, only the special few. Consider yourself lucky."

"No."

"For real?"

"No."

"Come on."

"No."

"I feel like you want to, but are just embarrassed to tell me."

"Dude… NO!"

Ramos continued his badgering. "Hey man, I'm not gay either! For real! I'm a get-along kind of guy, I prefer to foster good relationships over bad ones. I avoid bad confrontation when I can. What I'm telling you is, I've got a wonderful, extremely pleasant, penis. I can tell you that confidently. And so you don't feel that I'm rejecting you as a man, I want you to dine on my schlong, Alfie. It's my gift to you, and I hope you enjoy it."

Regardless of the fact that Alf had no intention of ever mouth-riding Cliff's meat bone, he had nevertheless been impressed by Ramos's confidence in the matter.

"For real, it's that good?" he asked.

"It is that good, Alf. It is a wonderfully amazing penis. It's like, Boogie Nights amazing."

Alphonso, now Alf to Ramos, looked down as if he was considering the idea, but then said, "Nah. I'm good, man. I see that you're sincere. So I appreciate that, and I know you accept me as a man. We're on point."

Ramos felt he deserved a fucking Oscar for not crying out laugh-tears through his butt hole right then. He smiled warmly and said, "Well good. I'm glad. But you'll let me know if we need to have a talk again, right? You won't hold that shit inside?"

Later, Ramos approached Alf with the job of getting his special box undetected into Brenda's office. He had set Alf up for an interview so he'd be expected at the office. The idea was to have Alf get into the building in the early morning, wearing a generic maintenance suit to mitigate unwanted attention. He'd get the box onto Brenda's desk, change into interview clothes in a nearby bathroom, then stroll confidently back in at 8:00 am for his interview.

Being able to use Alf solved a number of issues for Ramos. First, and most important, Ramos didn't have to be there. Second, the job got done competently. And third, Alf could make sure that no one except Brenda was hurt. If Alf suspected, even a little bit, that anyone would have messed with that box before Brenda did, he was to quickly intervene. Ramos may have been vicious, but he wasn't heartless. He didn't kill without reason.

"Why would I have to do something? What's in the box?"

Alphonso got no answer and tried to decipher the intent stare Ramos was giving him. It wasn't menace, or irritation; it wasn't a lie. It was... madness. It was a question, like your best friend inviting you with him to plug a grenade in your ass and eat lollipops while you both waited for it to blow up. Why would anyone ever ask you to do that? Who would even think about that? It wasn't even a *little* bit funny.

What that look said to Alphonso was: *Why in the hell would you ask that? Does it add any value to our conversation? And would you really want to know the answer?*

No. Alphonso realized he did *not* want to know the answer. Also, he realized something else; that even though Ramos was not threatening him, he felt scared. He was fearful; not of the job, or what could happen to this "Brenda" chick, but because he suspected that were he to know the real reasons behind Cliff Ramos' actions, his own view of reality would be distorted, and made impure. This terrified him because he instinctively knew that being on a similar plane of reality that Cliff Ramos thrived on was NOT a good thing.

He also didn't like to think of what the consequences would be if Ramos were ever disappointed in him.

So, Alphonso changed his question. "What if I *do* have to do something?" he asked, emphasizing the "what's" and omitting the "why's" from the existing conversation. "What do I do then?"

"I'm leaving that to you, Mr. Alphonso Shaw." answered Ramos, using the kid's full name. "You have a talent for the gab - use it. I believe you are very capable of talking yourself into, and out of, most all situations."

"You think I talk too much?"

"I think you're perfect for this job. And actually... there'll be a girl at the front desk, a real pretty one that keeps to herself. Talk to her as much as you can. The more she's focused on you, the less she'll be wondering about what's up in her boss's office."

Alphonso smiled. "I got you! You need my *smooth*, huh. I get it." he said, completely serious. "I'll go in like Bond, but like the black bond, that Idris

Elba should have been. Or like a Bruce Lee bond. I'll make her swoon, so I've got control of the situation. I got you, man."

Ramos smiled and nodded, knowing that Sam would instantly hate this guy once he opened his mouth.

"You understand me perfectly, sir."

"Ok. Chicks dig the mixed thing, ya know. Shouldn't be too hard. If I can get her number, think I should take her out after, to make sure we're in the clear? Follow up on the mission and all that?"

"If you can get her number? Sure, do that. Good idea. Use your inner Elba/Lee James Bond and get what additional information you can from her." *It just keeps getting better*, thought Ramos.

Ramos had played off Alf's Bond example, certain that the Fates were on his side then, because his new accomplice here had no idea about the affinity he and Sam had for Bond, but here he was, talking about it. That was a good sign, showing that all his intricate plans were aligned with the cosmic flow of the universe, and the validity of his actions became more assured as he continued to explain the cloak-and-dagger details of the operation. Ramos went on to tell about the microphone that would be embedded in the unique package, and that Alphonso could listen to what was being said around the box. "That way," said Ramos, "you'll know if anyone besides Brenda is going to open it. Just put in your headphones while you wait. Act like you're on Facebook or something."

"Facebook? Where the hell you been, man? I'm on Snap Chat. And Twitter. And Instagram."

"I don't give a fuck."

"I didn't think you did."

And it had all worked out.

Here in the woods, Ramos carved out his place of solitude. He made decisions here, planned here, and did his best work here. The first thing he did was to build a small fire. The flames relaxed him and the smell of burning wood kept him alert.

He sat on a wooden chair and closed his eyes, made sure his back was straight, inhaled deeply ten times and began a mantra that he used to gain focus. Ramos stayed under for only fifteen minutes. Usually though, he'd meditate for close to an hour and completely feel as if his brain had undergone a wildly successful reboot. When he first began years ago, he had to stay under for longer time periods if he was to realize any effects on his consciousness. It had been difficult for him to remain alert and to keep his mind from wandering, and this was disconcerting. The point of meditation was to intentionally plant yourself in the-here-and-now, to control your thoughts from going where they pleased, and to force them to only recognize the present mind.

It was hard for him. Maybe he just wasn't able to do it? His fear that he was too disconnected from the human packs of the world to achieve any kind of mental alertness surpassed mild concern and became a certified phobia.

Then he found mentors, via Buddhist priests, mind counselors. He learned that the battle of focusing one's thoughts was the sole purpose of meditation. That was the exercise. Ramos hadn't been doing it wrong, he just hadn't conceptually understood that the struggle of focusing *was* the entire premise behind meditation.

Once he understood this, he viewed it as a skill to learn, a challenge to beat, a goal to achieve. At first he used apps on his phone that provided guided sessions. As he progressed, he was able to discard the help from guided learning and instead only use some form of white noise to help him concentrate (he preferred "babbling brook" or "soft rain"). Eventually, he hadn't needed to use headphones, or any type of artificial help, at all. He could bring himself under without having to completely block his mind from the world - which was, of course, the idea; to find legitimate focus while still accepting, and even participating in, the world around him.

Mistakes were made early on, like the decision to lie in bed during a meditation session. This put him to sleep, and that was not helpful when a person was working to achieve a state of alertness. In other cases, he'd used meditation to help him sleep and that worked well, but the problem was that his body began to think that "Med time" (as he called it) was "Sleep time" - even when he was sitting up, he got drowsy. So, he disconnected the two ideas, and never put himself under while in bed or while trying to sleep. The Med's specific function centered around being alert. Sleeping was not the desired goal.

Eventually, he began to attain a deeper understanding of the skill. He could stay under for hours at a time if he chose to. Now though, he was proficient at the exercise and was able to go under in seconds to achieve his desired focus.

"The Reboot" was his name for it. A systematic cleanse of the mind; organizing of the tools in his garage; getting his desk in order. Presently, he completed a normal "reboot" in about ten minutes, whereas before it took the lion's share of two hours. This was a necessity for him now. It was as important as any physical exercise he did.

His eyes slowly came open, and he sat looking into the fire. This was his favorite part, just when he came back up and the exploding electrons in the flames connected to the racing atoms in his own brain.

Outside now, he stripped off his shirt and stood in the dark next to the adobe kiln he'd constructed. As organic as he tried to keep it, there were modifications made to it. The fires he torched inside the foundry got hot enough to bake mud and char to create roofing materials and tools, but when he had needed heat in excess of one thousand degrees to begin melting softer metals such as aluminum and tin, the baked adobe wasn't cutting it. It cracked and, what's worse, if molten aluminum were spilled onto it, the surface would explode because of the stored oxygen still inside.

He needed more resilient material, and so he used a simple mixture of Plaster of Paris and sand to create a mold that bordered the inside of the foundry, and then he shored up the inside with plates of steel. As long as he wasn't trying to melt anything stronger than aluminum, that would work nicely. The steel plates would hold up against the heat.

For stronger projects, where he needed to melt and forge steel, he kept it simple: a hole in the ground for the kiln. The soil was a perfect container, and with an added vent hole on the side for a large amount of forced air, he could create heat reaching almost three thousand degrees.

He stretched out his limbs and went back inside to his fire, and to the project of his immediate attention.

Deep into his hillside hideout, on the left wall there stood an old wooden chest with drawers. Ramos pulled one of these drawers and it rolled out smooth with no noise. Inside rested five of his blades with worn handles and gruesome memories.

In a smaller drawer sat an oiled rag bundled around a whetstone, and he used this stone to sharpen every one of his knives until they could have, each one of them, split the atoms in the air around him.

He walked home an hour later, but went directly to his car. He was on a set track and in his mind, there were obvious steps to take. He drove out to the edge of a wooded area and parked in front of a fence with a sign in front of it explaining that this was private property. It was early evening, still some light out but not much. Most of the trees were blocking it anyway.

He was dressed in a tight black t-shirt with matching jeans, and in that light even the brown leather of his boots and belt melded into the darkness approaching.

THE WOLF, A BUTCHER, HIS DEMON, AND THEIR MASTER

The knives were strapped securely on his back, each in a spot he could instantly pull from: Two at his shoulder blades pointing down, two behind his kidneys pointing up, and the last resting on the back of his belt. He could make them appear like a fucking magician.

Looking down at his phone, he checked the location of the GPS signal he was tracking and saw that his target was less than a mile in front of him, deep into the dark woods ahead. He'd put a tag on his prey weeks ago in various spots within his clothes, but he assumed the ones that he was picking up were the ones attached to the person's boots.

He lunged into the bush not at a run, but rather a steady walk. Twisting an ankle was a shit-ass thing to happen, so better to avoid that entirely.

He thought about having Coop here with him, that it would have been fucking boss seeing the man work at tracking prey. He had told Ramos once that he didn't hunt, because he didn't have to. But Ramos suspected that, if put on a path, Coop would lumber through these trees like a great wolf that smelled his dinner from miles off. He wouldn't need any GPS tag, either.

But this was not Coop's party. It was his, and he was not a wolf. He thought of himself, at times, as a demon joker; methodical, but playful. Like now with a slight grin, easily pushing away branches and going on toward his purpose. Ramos did use a GPS tag, because why not? It was available, it was easy, and it worked. This wasn't sport for him, it was vengeance. It was purpose. The end justified the means.

His steps didn't stagger; they stepped the same length each time and with the same force. He plodded along patiently when finally, he saw what he was after. It was Woody, of course, spraying green markers on trees that he meant to drive spikes into afterwards.

He watched Woody and saw that he wasn't wearing the hiking boots Ramos had put the tracker tile on. Rather, he had his back pack with him, the one he had in the car when Coop and Ramos had picked him up the last time.

A person being watched will eventually begin to feel it, especially if the proximity to the person watching them is close. Woody began to look around, putting his ear to the night to confirm any sounds. He didn't hear Ramos, but he could feel him, and he was getting uneasy. Listening to his instincts, which kick into a higher than normal gear out in the deep forest, Woody bent and put his supplies back in his bag.

As he stood up to leave, Ramos stepped out of the trees like the demon he most certainly was, and Woody caught the yellow spark in his eyes before he saw anything else.

To Woody's credit, he didn't cry out or scream in fear. He simply ran, without hesitation. He ran, simply because that was the smart thing to do.

Ramos walked at first, then increased his pace to run after him. Woody still had his bag with him, and he flung it back over his head toward Ramos, and it damn near hit him. Woody didn't turn around, and he never began to yell. That would only use up the breath he needed to make his escape to safety. He nimbly jumped from rock to rock, and avoided holes that he had marked earlier.

Ramos had underestimated Woody's ability to travel in the wild. Woody was at home here, and Ramos was thinking that he shouldn't have waited to apprehend him. He was thinking that this chase needed to end quickly because Woody was much more agile out here than he'd thought he'd be. If this went on for too long, he'd lose him for sure.

And then Woody took a quick lunge to his right and for a second, he was lost into a copse of trees. Ramos plunged in after him, and after two quick steps almost fell into a deep hole made some time ago by a tractor that was now sitting idle.

His arms swung wide and his feet slipped, but he was able to throw his top weight backwards so he landed on his butt not inches from where he would have taken a plunge into the black pit.

And that was all the time Woody needed to step out from the shadows he was hiding in and fling himself towards Ramos, who had just managed to get to his knees. Since his hand was on the ground already, Ramos flung a wad of dirt at his previous prey/now attacker, and that was fortunate for him, because Woody had charged in with the intention of spraying him in the face with the can of paint he'd been using earlier.

Good idea, thought Ramos grudgingly; *blinding your opponent makes them much easier to kill.*

Woody had taken advantage of the dark terrain and used surprise to turn Ramos' attack back around on him. Moving quickly was the only way to put the situation back to rights. The clump of dirt that Ramos threw blurred Woody's vision for a half second, but he still managed to spray Ramos on the side of the face with the paint.

Ramos rolled to his side, planted his feet and lunged up at Woody who had turned to face him. Woody was clever, but Ramos was much, much faster. He knocked the can from Woody's hand and reached to grab his neck, seeing only the blood he ached to spill.

And then his chest flared in pain; so much so that instead of continuing his attack for Woody's neck, he chose to grab his shoulder instead, so he could just knock him back and away.

Ramos looked down and saw a bloody gash across his belly and chest peeking out from beneath the ripped shirt. Woody was backing away from him, and Ramos saw that he held a sharp spike in his hand, which he had used to rake Ramos across the front. Had Woody lunged at him with any more accuracy, any more ferocity, that spike could have driven well into his belly.

And that idea infuriated Ramos more than the gash on his chest ever would. He had underplayed and underestimated his opponent, terribly, and he wouldn't do it again.

In fact, he'd even gained an unexpected respect for Woody that night. Too bad for Woody though, that Ramos' respect hadn't come about much earlier in their lives.

Woody, again allowing his instincts to take over, began to run. Ramos couldn't let him disappear again, but he also wasn't going to crash into the woods that Woody was so familiar with. Without even having to think, Ramos released a blade from its holster and sent it flying; his aim was true. It stuck fast in Woody's shoulder blade and stunned him enough so that he immediately felt the ground come up to meet his face.

Ramos approached quickly, kicked him in the ribs, and then hauled him up against the nearest tree, letting him stand on his own for a second while breathing heavy.

Up to this point, neither man had said a word. They had only acted immediately, each toward their own purpose. Woody spoke first because now was the time for words, but really even these were unnecessary.

"Stay the fuck away you crazy asshole!"

"No, Boogles. You and I have a reckoning to complete. Now."

"My name is Woody. You lame fuck."

"Your *name* is no longer of any consequence."

Woody lunged again, but Ramos easily stepped aside from the spike and smoothly brought his fist into his opponent's abdomen. It caused Woody to immediately lose breath and topple over, but – to Ramos' increasing astonishment – robotically popped up and launched an immediate counter attack. He meant to tackle Ramos, to get him back on the ground, but Ramos was now on his feet and perfectly focused, and so would be extremely difficult to compromise. Ramos reflexively brought his knee up to meet Woody's nose as he came near, and it exploded like a water balloon. Woody went down and was basically dead weight as Ramos wrapped a hand around his throat and lifted him back up against the tree once more.

This time, Ramos didn't let go. He kept his left hand on Woody's throat and squeezed to cut off his air supply. A new blade appeared in his right hand, as a scythe would in Death's. Woody saw this and although he was barely conscious, he still fought to wield his spike against the enemy, against his eminent death. Ramos smiled, and nodded. He let him hold on to the spike, out of respect for the battle he waged for his life. He was happy Woody fought well at the end - not every man could.

Ramos spoke to him, not unfriendly. "Don't you pass out on me, Woody. Look at me. Right at me. I need to know I have your attention, boy. Do I have your attention? I'm letting up on your throat a bit. There."

Woody gasped for air but remained still due to the deadly instrument pointed directly at his throat.

Ramos continued, "I've always respected you, Woody. If your body was as big as your heart, then man, we would have all been in trouble! You never backed away from a fight. I admire that. You were a *fighter*. But here's where you messed up; you always jumped into a fight, but you never learned how to *win* one. You could take a beating, but you could never *give* one. At some point, you are no longer considered a fighter because losing is all you do. That makes you a loser, and a fool, and an asset to no one. And now, Woody, you've messed with me, and I am also a fighter. I've lost plenty, but I've won so much more. And as time passes, I lose less."

With difficulty, Woody stood straight. "Please. Please stop."

Ramos shook his head soberly. "It's too late for that."

"No, I mean... stop talking. *Please,* stop talking. Your voice makes me want to throw up."

"For real?" Ramos asked incredulously.

"Did you practice that shit in a mirror before you came out here tonight? You're pathetic."

Ramos couldn't help but laugh. "Ha! Good for you. Sarcastic to the end. I'll admit I can ramble when a ramble is called for."

"A *ramble?*" Woody sneered. "I spit better haikus out of my ass, written in cursive, than the paltry shit you come up with while standing on your soapbox. Been listening to it for years, dude. It's terrible."

If Woody's words were irksome, it didn't show; Cliff's face was reliably resolute and impassionate as he continued talking to his adversary. "Possibly that carries some truth Woody, but you need to hear this. See, I'm doing you a favor. Not every man gets to die knowing WHY he lost his life. Most people are too self-absorbed to realize the truth of these things. Death doesn't come down and explain his reasoning to the souls he takes – he just takes them. It's his choice and anyone with an opinion can go fuck themselves. But you get to see your killer and understand your fate, and that is a rare honor. So, you're welcome for that."

Ramos stopped talking to allow for the sarcasm he was sure would spew from Woody's mouth after that last comment, but again Woody surprised him. He'd kept his tongue still and his emotions in check.

Ramos continued, "You chose to fight me, man, and that's fine. I respect that. But now I finish the fight. I will have my prize. You've held this tiger by the tail for too long. You infected my *pack*, my *brood*, my *people*, and it's my job to end the infestation."

"With Sam, I – I didn't have a choice, Cliff."

"I know that, Woody. I do, and I've come to terms with that. I am a man of honor, and pride. I am a man of Pack, you see, so I need you to know that I take no pleasure in what I'm about to do. I'm fighting my basic instincts on this, and I *never* do that. But it must be done, because it's the right thing to do."

Woody had a second to process those last words, and he let out a moan as Ramos pulled his knife back high over his head and brought it down toward him in one smooth, powerful, and most final ultimatum.

The woods went quiet as wrongs were put to rights and individuals merged into Packs.

The fire sighed, and roared, and laughed as it ate more bits of scrap meat that Ramos threw at it in the underbelly of the secret hill. He'd been working hours that night. The wound across his chest probably needed some attention, but at this point, there was so much blood on him that he couldn't have found where his cuts ended and the other, not his, blood began. He carved into the meat, drained blood into buckets, and deftly sheared skin off of the body in front of him. He then took that pelt to a set of clamps along a square frame and hung it to tan by the fire.

There were bone fragments and meat bits still on the table, but ultimately, he had used all that he had acquired. That was a point of pride for him. He raked the offal from the table into a steel bucket and scrubbed the table down with a course sponge and water.

Outside, he stripped naked and cleaned himself thoroughly in the stream. Except for his boots, he threw all his clothes, along with the offal, into the now red-hot fire stoked inside his adobe furnace. He laid on the ground in the dark night and watched the cosmos tower above him. He fell asleep, naked as a babe in the woods, and he awoke later, amused, to a throbbing hard on. This didn't surprise him; the night air had done that to him before. But he knew for certain that the tanning from earlier was the cause for this particular uprising. He obliged his pulsing member, stroking it gently and then rougher, and quicker, as the mood required.

It didn't take long. His belly felt the warm rain of his release, and he kept his hand moving for a while longer to make sure that all potential pleasure was exploited.

He lay there breathing hard and his body dared to fall asleep on him. But he pulled himself off the ground and walked back over to the stream to wash again.

He felt renewed, freshened. His manhood was limp, but still held the girth of its raucous statement to the world. It was proud, Ramos knew, and so was he. Good work had been done that night, and more still needed to be done.

Back inside his den, he pulled on a fresh pair of jeans, careful not to allow the zipper a chance to play its always rueful joke. Then he sat back at the old wooden table and began to work on his craft, his love.

He had fine stationary in a neat pile, waxed thread and a sewing-all, wood glue, craft glue, shears, and other tools to help him to create a new notebook that he would cherish, as he had all his others. The others looked on him then, from their shelves in his lair, as he put together another one of them. The other notebooks, the pack of words created from Ramos's mind, stood tall and legion around the wooden shelves in that private, fire-lit, and creative den that was the sanctuary of Cliff Ramos.

CHAPTER **21**

THE PAPER MACHET HOUSE

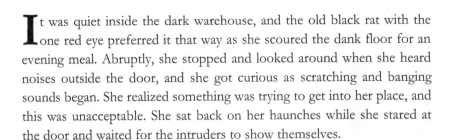

It was quiet inside the dark warehouse, and the old black rat with the one red eye preferred it that way as she scoured the dank floor for an evening meal. Abruptly, she stopped and looked around when she heard noises outside the door, and she got curious as scratching and banging sounds began. She realized something was trying to get into her place, and this was unacceptable. She sat back on her haunches while she stared at the door and waited for the intruders to show themselves.

When they did, she would politely ask them to get the fuck out. Or, maybe these intruders would do well for her dinner, if they weren't too big and didn't cause too much trouble about being eaten.

She was the oldest and meanest rat of this territory; for years, she had fought every other animal that had come in and tried to claim the land.

Her scars were wicked, and her tail was gnawed, and sometimes she forgot she only had one eye until she was startled by some object on her left (her missing eye side), and it would make her laugh. This was her land, her legacy. She had birthed what seemed like hundreds of babies here (some of which she had eaten as newborns, some others she had had to fight off and kill for dominance as they came into their prime), and she would never leave.

There were times, though, when she would have feelings that were alien to her. Not often, just every now and again, when she'd think about all her babies and how most of them had either left, died, or had been killed, she'd feel a peculiar ache in her stomach, even though she knew she wasn't hungry.

She could never understand the idea that maybe she hadn't *had* to push away her entire pack over the course of her long life. Some had to go, of course, and there always had to be a leader of a pack - and *she* was the leader of this pack, so she fought to keep that right. And she won that right. Time and again, she won it. But did all of them have to go?

She had become respected as a warrior and was unopposed as a leader. Times were good, and she ruled without question.

And then, times weren't so good. Her legitimized ruling state should have been enough, but it hadn't been, had it? She could never rest. She always had to crush any other member of her pack that could be a potential threat to her.

And the pups, the newborns, and of course the weak and ailing would be eaten - they always were. But she went the extra step, at times, to eat not only the weak babes, but also the babes of opposing and promising blood-lines to ensure that only *her* lineage would survive.

The fighting became brutal, and if she had known the idea of it, she would have called those times by their true names: Anarchy. Chaos.

Other Rats rose up as War Lords too, with their own following of able warriors. Some prospered and some perished. Old Grandma had her own clan of stout killers, and over the years, they were able to defeat all those who rebelled against them.

She used all of her cunning and fighting resources to win. Promises were made, and alliances were formed with some clans in order to defeat others. Then in a grand act of deceit, her brood would turn on their allies and wipe them out, leaving none of the opposition alive.

Eventually, there remained only two recognizable factions of Rats: those strong few who ruled, and bullied, and dominated all they could, and those many others that were weak and allowed themselves to be bullied, ruled over, and dominated so they could be fed the very little nourishment that Old Grandma siphoned to them.

Eventually the weak died out, and the strong ones of her clan, instead of rising against her, just left. Together, they might very well have defeated her, but it wasn't worth it to them. They'd just take off and leave her to the kingdom she had forged.

She saw some of them, at times. She saw the families they made and the broods they grew. And these sightings are what gave her the awkward pain in her belly, and morose thoughts in her head, that she could not understand.

However, these thoughts were quick and usually stopped not long after they had begun, and her abdominal pains were an irritation that she barely noticed. Her memory was not built to store regret, or the past, or things she couldn't change, and this allowed her to never dwell on the consequences of her actions.

It was just that every once in a while she wondered why, after having grown such a large following, she was now alone everyday with no company except for the other Rats she saw in the small pools of water on the floor. She'd look into the pools while drinking, and she'd spy another

Rat under the water also having a drink. Those Rats seemed familiar to her and so she accepted them as they appeared, but she'd usually leave their meetings irritated because she had the idea that maybe she was being mocked.

She cocked her head toward the noises outside as they continued and listened as an incredulous Cooper asked a grinning Ramos, "How do you just *happen* to have some in your car?"

"It's not a lot, Coop. A small amount."

"Not a …? That's like a terrorist saying he only has a "small amount" of a nuclear device. Where'd you get it from?"

"From nowhere, man!"

"Fuck you say?"

"Nothing, right? Ok, I was down in the labs yesterday evening talking to James, and I *happened* to go by the armory on my way out. Stephanie was working. She – "

"The armory? That's on a different floor. It's not on your way out."

"Can I continue? You wanna hear this? Okay, well Stephanie was working and she let me in. See, I happened to notice earlier this month that the amount of C-4 that was physically there in holding was *more* than what was recorded on file. Not by much see, just a little, but still different. So, I took some of it that was, technically, not even there."

Coop smirked, "You stole C-4 out of the police station's armory. "

"Coop…"

"You hear how that sounds, right?"

"No, Coop. Listen to me. I balanced out their books. I walked away with material that *technically didn't exist!* I did nothing wrong. And actually - I was very altruistic. Because when audit time came around, and good 'ole Stephanie had to account for the incorrect documentation of a very volatile substance, she could have gotten into a heap of trouble. Now, she won't have any issues at all. I could have saved her job, Coop, and she'll never know it. Some would say that makes me a very benevolent man."

"I have nothing to say to that."

"Probably for the best," Ramos agreed. "But I'm ok with her not knowing. I don't need the award when I do something nice for someone else, just me knowing is enough. I… SHIT! RUN!!"

The old red-eyed grandma rat jerked when one of the creatures outside yelled, and she inched forward, curious to see why. Then her animal instinct kicked in and she knew better than to argue when it said to get out of there, and quick. She turned to run, but the explosion still caught her. The doors and surrounding mortar were blown open with a tremendous clash of titans, and the Old Grandma was hurled roughly into a pile of rocks. She lay there, stunned, as more cement, rocks, and rebar landed around and on top of her, covering her completely.

Cooper walked in first, keeping his sight up to spot debris that was still coming down. Ramos followed, glancing off in the opposite direction from Coop to get an instant topography of their new surroundings.

Guns were drawn, pointed down. Both waited for an alarm to ring or for shouts to warn of their intrusion, but nothing happened. All they heard was the sound of very old dust settling in all new places.

They moved forward slowly in unison, waiting for the scale of the warehouse to wrap itself around their brains. Then to his right, Ramos noticed a small pile of cinder blocks, rebar, and dirt begin to shift apart, and he jerked his head back as a small head only seen in nightmares pushed itself up and out of the newly fallen debris. The body attached to the head was gnarled and scarred, and all together the thing measured almost three feet in length. The claws were more like talons; the teeth were better described as serrated knives protruding from a Great White's mouth. Its face leered at Ramos with a hatred that was acrid. One eye was shut permanently from scar tissue caused by the earlier removal of said eye, but the other eye – that was what Ramos truly saw and immediately intuited. He knew he had never seen a truer physical example, a live specimen, of a demon that had crawled out of hell and had taken this new form on Earth.

This thing looked at Ramos with its remaining red eye, and had any *man* looked at him that way, he'd have shot him dead on sight from an uncontrollable instinct to survive.

"Holy Fuck, Coop. Oh, look at this fuckin thing!" Ramos hadn't backed up any more, he was intrigued now. He had never seen a goblin in the flesh. He'd always known they were there, had sensed they were around, but up till now, he hadn't been able to say he'd come into direct contact with one.

Now he had, and he was fascinated. He wondered, did he feel kinship? Did he understand this thing?

It was possible. But this thing looking at him, it wanted his balls in its mouth, so it could shred them into moist sinews of meat, and then feast on his Adam's apple while he was still alive and choking.

This thing was pure hate and ugliness.

And Ramos sensed that a connection with this nasty creature might not be out of the realm of possibility. That thought made him sick, but he realized the potential truth behind it.

He also realized that if this thing felt any resemblance toward him whatsoever, it made no difference. The demon in front of him would kill and eat its own kind, he was immediately sure of that.

THE WOLF, A BUTCHER, HIS DEMON, AND THEIR MASTER

This gremlin had no Pack, it was never able to be with others. Ramos knew that it was contemplating an attack. It was hurt and old, but it could be fast. However, Ramos was faster. If it came for him, which now he hoped it would, he'd grab it around the wind pipe and begin to dig his hands inside the puterid flesh of the creature as he stared into its one eye and felt the spit from its open, hungry mouth, snarling at him not an inch away from his own neck.

He'd look it in the eye and tell it to return to the hell that it came from. He wanted it to know that it was Cliff Ramos that had sent it back there.

He prayed that the hell-sent grotesque beast in front of him would attack, and right then. He wanted it dead with its blood on his hands.

The giant rat moved its back legs, positioning itself for an attack, and Ramos smiled.

And then, the rat stopped moving. It stood perfectly still, petrified, as Cooper turned towards it for the first time. He looked down upon the abomination not with fear, or astonishment, but – as prey.

Old Grandma might have sensed a possible victory in Ramos; she smelled burnt ash on him as she did on herself, and she had dined on kinds such as that throughout her entire life. But this new creature intrigued her. She looked up at it with awe and immediately knew it was her superior. Not just in size, for that meant nothing to her, but in an animal hierarchy that was born of the cosmos. Attacking this new predator would be an insult to it, and a dishonor to her. Also she feared, for the first time in her long life, the type of pain that could be caused by one such as this.

The thing she looked at was strong and she could tell it was well nourished. She suspected, rightly, that it belonged to a healthy and verdant Pack. Its eyes burned a dark, maroon-like red as opposed to her brighter crimson hue. It bore into her soul with the boredom of a child picking an apple from a tree, taking a quick bite, and then throwing the now dead fruit aside.

Old Grandma lowered her head and relaxed her legs to release the tension of the planned attack that was now dissipating from her memory. She had no wish to be a meal for this creature tonight, and she allowed her challenge to fall away.

The two men watched as the red-eyed monster sunk back into the dark and listened as the claws (talons) limped away over the newly fallen cement and debris of the warehouse.

"I've never seen one this close before." Ramos said first.

Cooper sniffed with disgust. "Fucking rodents."

"You get the size for that thing?"

"Still a rodent. I've forgotten it already. Come on."

Ramos nodded and followed.

Coop said to him, "Ok. Well, good job on the door - but that was *all* the C-4 you took, right? You don't have anymore?"

"Are we talking about this now? We just blew a huge door off of a warehouse, made all sorts of noise while trying to find evidence of illegal copper-exporting bandits, and you're concerned about the police station paperwork?"

"We ARE talking about this later, Ram."

They began to search the warehouse. Ramos ran the beam of his flash light over a nearby crate, and asked Coop, "Did you say Boogles was gonna meet us here?"

"I did." Coop answered.

"And that he was going to bring a key?"

"Yes. I said that, too."

"And he didn't show up."

"I don't know where he got to. He's probably out spiking trees. Or fucking squirrels." He shrugged.

"That guy, I'm tellin' ya - never around when you need him. Good thing I brought my own key, huh?"

Coop ignored the poke for affirmation. He asked, "What were you doing talking to James in Forensics? Didn't think you two'd run in the same circles."

"I needed information."

"About what? That burn box in the mail?"

"Yes."

"Really? I thought we had that covered for now."

"We do. I went to James because I wanted to be discrete. I had some tests done. You know that rash I told you about?"

"Nope."

"I've got a rash, and I was concerned that it was contagious."

"Was it?"

"Not a lot."

"See, there's that "'not a lot'" again. I don't like hearing that from you. Is it *some* contagious?"

"I got cream for it. Don't worry."

"I'm sure you have cream, jerk off. What with all those loose guys you go out with?"

"Escorts. They're called escorts, Coop. And some of them are very nice. Paying their way through college and shit. Like you do on weekends? Except you don't go to college anymore, so… what's the deal?"

Coop shook his head. "Horny. Can't help it. Tell me what you're up to, Ram."

"Okay, so I *did* go to inquire more about the box Coop, I was serious about that. But there was some other stuff James was looking at for me - stuff that needed to be discrete. I'll tell you about it later, I promise."

Cooper nodded and accepted the answer. "Look there! Trucks."

They walked deeper into the warehouse where a number of empty trucks were backed up against the docks and recently arrived crates were stacked and awaiting their chance to be loaded.

"Let's get into those crates." ordered Coop.

Ramos pulled open the lid on the nearest box and exclaimed, "Oh shit! Boogles was right. Look at all this copper! There's lots of money here, Coop. He wasn't kidding."

Inside the crates were ingots of pure copper, stacked neatly into tight rows. Ramos looked up. "Here's the missing copper, man. And they've already melted it down into bars for easy export. There's no way to trace this shit now, there's no markings or identifiable tags left. Basically, it's new material."

"They could track it by the missing material reports, and shipment orders, maybe?"

"Maybe. But probably not. Either way, this is mucho suspicious enough to make sure that it gets held up for a while and seriously investigated. I mean you'd have to think this is some kind of probable cause, yeah?"

Cooper shrugged. "I can make anything probable cause."

"There's at least three truckloads of this here now. All the boxes look similar, and I bet they're all full like this one is."

Cooper nodded in agreement. He swung his flash light around the loading bay and gestured over to another section of the vast working area.

"Over there, see? More boxes, but they don't look like these ones with copper. They're longer, flatter."

Ramos replaced the lid of the box holding the copper, and they walked over to the new cache of crates. Ramos handed Coop his flashlight and pried open another lid with a steel bar he found on the ground. They stared at the contents of that crate with a fixed awareness and an understanding that shit just got real. Both men felt the adrenaline of impending action in the near future.

Automatic weapons lay in rows beneath them. They were packed in Styrofoam and wrapped in oiled cloths for protection. Coop set his light on the ledge of the crate and slowly lifted one of the arms out of the box, then expertly unwrapped the oiled lining so he could inspect the gleaming rifle that now sat in his hands.

"Looks brand new." he reported, "I don't believe it's ever been fired. No serial numbers, of course. But I also don't see any signs of where the serial numbers used to be before they removed them. This looks as if it was made without an identity. That, sir, is very interesting."

"Looks almost like a toy." said Ramos.

"How do you mean?"

"Just that. It's like, what I'd expect to find on the weapons aisle at a toy store. Looks too perfect, too shiny – almost as if it's not even real."

"It's real." Coop replaced the weapon in the crate and closed it up. "It's very fucking real. But I agree, it seems different. These aren't like other AK's I've known – the smell is different."

They gave the warehouse another once over to make certain nothing was missed, then allowed their feet to echo in the massive darkness as they made their way back to enlarged doorway they'd blown out earlier upon entering the loading station.

Cooper gave no thought to the one red eye watching them as they left; Ramos, before walking out, turned his head back and smiled. *Fuck You*, he thought.

Once outside the warehouse, Coop gave his assessment. "This is a big deal, Ram. We're talking export of weapons now. We're in to bigger shit than we thought."

"You think Captain'll shit for not talking to him up front?"

"Yes. But he'll get over it once he sees what this is. I'll call him now."

Ramos stopped him. "Hold up. What's over there?"

"Ah, old condos I think. Foreclosed, like every other place around here. Those buildings have always been behind here, same owner as the warehouse, I think."

"There's lights on. And cars out front one of the units. And the gate leading to it from here is open."

"Well. If that's not an invitation, I'm an asshole."

Cooper put away his phone and they walked down a dark path towards the building that seemed to have activity inside it. They found the basement and shone their lights into the small windows. Inside, they saw jack-hammers, boxes, and a big hole in the cement ground.

Ramos flipped out a small blade and quickly sliced through the window's small lock. They jumped inside the basement of the condo and landed soundlessly on the floor.

A large metal locker was sitting there; Coop pulled the handle and found that it wasn't locked.

Inside the locker were large stacks of cash, all protectively wrapped in cellophane.

"Safe's got dust on it." Ramos said, "And it's all beat up. I'd bet your balls that they dug that thing out of the hole in the floor."

"Yeah… How much money you think that is?"

"Shit. Couple mil, probably? Maybe they just dug this up so they could ship it out along with the guns."

"That, or they want it to buy more guns. Good set up, here. Condos in the back, warehouse up front. Easy access to and from. Fucking perfect operation."

"Well not *that* perfect – we're here."

"True. They'll be irritated with that. Let's check upstairs, see if anyone's around."

Their guns were out, but at this point they made no attempt to muffle their footsteps. They assumed their presence was already known, and they expected a fight. If that was the case, they preferred to just get on with it.

They emerged into a living room area. Coop walked through the door while straightening his tie, and Ramos checked his gun to confirm it was fully loaded. He knew it was, he just liked to check. The room they were in was fully furnished. It had couches, TV's, tables, everything; it looked normal. It looked like what every other living room in America looked like.

But it was wrong, they felt that immediately. Coop walked over and pushed the TV aside, and it fell to the floor with no sound at all. Ramos kicked the coffee table and found it hollow.

"What the fuck, Coop. None of this stuff is real. Were those guns in the warehouse real?"

"*Those* were real weapons, for a fact. But this stuff... I don't know what this is."

"I think I know."

Ramos holstered his weapon and walked over to a machine that looked like an oversized copier. He bent to look it over, but was interrupted when the front door slammed open. Coop and Ramos immediately assumed that men were crashing through the front door to apprehend them, but realized the door was kicked open by a heavy foot simply to achieve a quick opening. Three guys walked in, and each one of them carried heavy, clear boxes over their shoulders containing some kind of dark liquid.

At first, none of the men noticed the intruders. They were too busy trying to keep the heavy, uneven containers they were schlepping into the building from spilling over, and then getting them safely onto the ground before they could relax.

Eventually, after all the dark boxes were on the ground and the men had a chance to stretch their backs, they looked around to finally see Coop and Ramos, who were standing quietly to the side and watching the hard working gents go about their laborious job.

The two factions looked each other over, and none of them seemed all that surprised to find this new wrinkle that had emerged into their reality.

Ramos, ever the social butterfly, was the first to break the silence.

"We were gonna see if y'all needed any help with those, but… looks like you've got it handled. So we'll just hang back here out of your way."

The last guy to walk in grinned and said, "Fuck me." He walked back to the door, held out his hand, and yelled, "Hey, hold up. Stay out there. We got a thing in here."

Then, still smiling, he looked over at Cooper. "Shit's cool, right? All this?" He waved his hand around the room motioning to the faux-furniture the detectives had been discussing earlier.

"To be honest, friend, this is creepy. I'm not sure what to make of it."

"Okay, I can understand that, seeing how you just walked in here, but once you get past that… I mean, we were just practicing with these, but if you're going to be working somewhere for a long time, you want to be comfortable, right? So, we at least created the *illusion* of comfort, anyway. We're proud of it; we really tapped into our creative natures."

"Sure," Cooper went on, while Ramos was nodding amiably to their hosts, "Good for you! Way to go fellas, job well done. I could immediately tell you guys were the creative types. But hey, before I ask you to bore me with all the fascinating details of your artistic achievements, could I first ask you to just pretend that I understand anything I see here in this room? It's only because I'm feeling that we'd be stuck discussing it for quite a while, since it's so damn interesting, and I'd rather we move on from that point, just for now, and onto a more relevant topic."

The man raised his eyebrows and Coop took this a sign to continue. "Tell me this, if you don't mind: What's the deal with downstairs, and all that digging?"

"You found that, huh? Figures."

"Right? It's a fucking mess down there. We couldn't help but be a little put off by it."

The group's speaker cocked his head and narrowed his gaze. "You really don't know what this is? That stupid look of yours isn't you just playin' with us?"

"I mean, I have a guess…"

"Sure, of course you do. You're a smart enough guy, you figure things out. Honestly though, I find it kinda' hysterical that you two have no idea what this operation is. I don't really know if I believe that or not, but really, it's irrelevant. See, regardless of what you assholes do or don't know, it's obvious that you don't know everything, and that sucks for you."

"Is that a fact?" asked Coop.

"Oh yeah, it's a fact. Cuz' see I *do* know what's going on here. I know about the entire operation, along with everyone involved. And I know other things, like, who YOU two are, and exactly WHO you work for. And most importantly, I know this puts you in a very precarious position just now."

"I think you know shit, hombre." Ramos chimed in, and then winked at Coop to assure him he had his back on this.

The man looked at Ramos, and then back at Cooper, who shrugged and said, "Please continue."

"What I want you to understand, detectives, is that the easiest way to make sure this little impromptu meeting does NOT turn into a volatile situation, is to have you look inside that large duffel bag over there in the corner. Go ahead, open it up. Nothing's gonna happen."

"And who are you?"

"Manny. You can call me Manny. It's what my friends call me."

Cooper stayed where he was and kept his eyes on the three men in front of him. Ramos went over to inspect the bag and wasn't surprised to find it loaded with heaps of hard cash. He looked up at Coop, and nodded his confirmation.

The guy calling himself Manny continued, "Since you came in from downstairs, I know you saw our trunk of money. Sorry boys, I can't offer that to you, it's spoken for. What I can do, though, is gift you with this bag. Not as much as downstairs, obviously, but it's a lot. People have retired on less."

"Understood. We take this bag of money, and then what? I want to be clear about your intentions."

"You walk out of here, and no one has to go home dead tonight. I know how you two can leave a room when you're done with it, and I'm telling you that there's no cause for that now. Okay? You take that bag, walk out, and give what's in it to whoever you need to, or keep it for yourselves, whatever. You can even call this place in for a bust come morning, and we'll leave behind some product so that it rates as a good find."

He paused, and lowered his voice before continuing. "But the deal, Mr. Cooper Happenstance, is that you and Mr. Clifford Ramos take that bag, and you just fucking leave. After that, my crew'll be gone in under two hours, completely, and you won't be seeing us again - ever. Everyone lives, and everyone is happy. The End."

Coop replied in his even tone, "Um-hm. So when you come across two random guys all up in your business, you always just offer them a bag full of money to politely go away?"

"Well no, of course. Usually, we'd just throw you in that hole we got downstairs, and then after we'd paved over you with cement, we'd laugh and wonder how two dumb fucks like you managed to find your way in here at all."

"Sure, I get that." Coop agreed.

"Here's the problem, though: you all are not *just two guys*. We know who you are, and we respect you, if you can believe that. We respect you, and what's more, we respect mightily the man you call your Captain. This is a unique case - we'd never insult the prized warriors of a venerated War Lord. Rather, we'd be honored to pay tribute to show our humility and respect, and hope that we can all go about our lives, much richer, much happier, and much less dead."

Cooper nodded with sincere appreciation. "You sir, are an orator. You communicate well and precise. I say in truth, that is a lost skill."

"Thank you, I agree. I've been speaking with Toast Masters for almost ten years! I'm telling you, everyone should do this. It is an asset for anyone. Better communication is the key for a productive life, and I'm glad you appreciate that fact."

"Most certainly I do, Manny. Tell me though, if you would, who's still outside?"

"No one you're going to meet, Mr. Happenstance."

"Again, direct and to the point, I appreciate that. Well then, tell me something else, if you can: What's all that mess there in the boxes - some kind of liquid?"

THE WOLF, A BUTCHER, HIS DEMON, AND THEIR MASTER

Manny laughed, and held up his hands. "Come on, Mr. Happenstance. You're putting me in a position where civility is becoming hard to maintain."

Before Cooper could reply, Ramos spoke up. "I know what it is, Coop. It's ink."

Cooper didn't immediately understand Ramos' explanation, but acted as if he did by nodding and smiling contentedly at Manny.

Looking over and on behind Cooper, Manny said, "Ramos, I heard you were a smart guy! Top marks for you, son. Now guys, I hate to be rude, but I do expect an answer. I've offered you all a kind of olive branch here, and you either need to take it, or... or don't."

Cooper never took his eyes off Manny, but spoke to Ramos. "What d'ya think?"

"It's a lot of money, Coop. He speaks true."

"You doubted my word?" asked Manny.

Cooper walked over and looked into the bag, and whistled. "Of course you spoke true, Manny, I knew you would. Your word is good with us. Fuck's sake, how much is in there?"

Manny looked up and began to think, "Ah, I don't know exactly, but give or take a hundred g's, it measures up to approximately... I don't know, what do you guess it measures up to, Greg?"

Another man behind Manny, with biceps bigger than most people's thighs, shrugged. "It's a shitload, Manny. Roundabouts, ya know."

"Yeah, that sounds right." Manny looked back to Cooper. "Approximately, Mr. Happenstance, it's a shitload. A shitload of money is in that bag, and even when split two ways, each half is still a shitload. I believe the numbers hold up well in that math."

"Fuckin' A Manny, I've always wondered what a shitload of money looks like. So, thank you for this."

"You're welcome."

"Now, tell me, Manny – and I promise this'll be my last question… how much money is in that safe we saw downstairs? And to keep the math easy, just round it out in terms of shitloads, say, so we're talking apples to fucking apricots here."

Manny continued to smile, but his tone revealed an obvious displeasure. "I've already explained to you how that money is not available for me to bargain with."

"Okay, we got that!" Ramos interrupted. "But dude – there is a bona fide *mountain* of money sitting just down those stairs, and it's ours to take! It has to be worth at least five shitloads to you for us to leave it alone."

Manny glared at Ramos. "Don't you mock me, boy! I've given you a generous and honorable offer, and you are using it to insult me."

"No, you misunderstand me." Ramos continued. "It's like this: If we had come in through the front door like you all did, and *only* seen this bag with the shitload of money in it and nothing else to compare it to, then yeah, we'd have been really impressed with it! But you have to remember, Manny, that we came in through the basement window, so we've already seen the huge case of money stacked downstairs - and that simply dwarfs what's in this duffle bag. Hard to believe, I know, but it's true. It's all about a man's point of view, really. You can't fault us for using basic economics, and the theory of human perspective, to prefer the larger of the two fortunes. That's just science."

Manny's patience was finally at an end. "That box downstairs, gentlemen, contains money that isn't mine to lose, and it isn't yours to take. And neither is the money in that bag, or your lives for that matter, if you don't leave here now. I'm trying very hard to keep things under control tonight;

but if I'm going to be honest here, I'm thinking that we've all talked way too much already."

"Damn. I was enjoying listening to him talk, Coop. He's got a gift."

"Me too, kid. Oh well."

The tension in the room with the fake furniture congealed into a nice, thick pomade that any real hipster would've been proud to smooth his hair down with. Manny's crew realized that things had become serious, and so began to size Cooper and Ramos up for weaknesses. They began to mentally blueprint how to systematically rip these two men apart quick and with the least amount of mess; but of course, they didn't realize how Ramos and Cooper had already gotten their bead on Manny and his men, and had long ago finalized what their next five moves would be in this altercation. Manny's men, in other words, were dead men.

Cooper remained perfectly still. Ramos fingered a knife he had settled onto his back. And to show that fate still had a sharp sense of irony, it chose that moment for permitting a fiery spray of bullets to begin tearing through all the windows, doors, and walls, ultimately shredding the room and everything in it. All the men moved to find cover, but there wasn't any. Ramos was getting sliced with flying debris, but even with his reality being dismantled around him, he still had the instinct to forgo the blade and pull his revolver. When bullets were cutting through the air, he needed a weapon that also used bullets. That way, when the crime scene was later inspected, it wouldn't be circumspect when the men he killed had multiple craters in their bodies stemming from the various lethal calibers Ramos had injected into them. That could be blamed on the swarm of killing metal now coming through the windows.

Greg, the one with the enormous biceps, pulled out his gun and leveled it at Ramos, then let loose three potentially lethal rounds. Ramos fell to the ground avoiding the bullets meant for him and shot upwards, firing twice. He landed one bullet in Greg's throat and another in his chest. Then for complete assurance, because Greg was a big dude, Ramos exploded his kneecaps with the remaining ammunition in his revolver.

Meanwhile, Cooper broke the neck of the un-named third man not a second after the windows burst in with shrapnel. Then he looked over to Manny and saw he was clumsily trying to work the pin out of a grenade – so Cooper threw the broken corpse at him to delay the activation of the weapon.

Ramos jumped up, reloaded his weapon, and began firing wildly outside of the front door to try and hit anything responsible for shredding the room they were in. Cooper, unfortunately, had not deterred Manny from pulling the pin out of the explosive. The pin had fallen to the floor, and the bomb was live. But Cooper *had* been able to at least reach Manny while he still held the explosive, and so he slammed him against the wall with his shoulder while also wrapping his hands around Manny's one hand holding the weapon. Cooper used all his strength to ensure that Manny couldn't release the bomb, or even move his arm to cause a reaction.

"You get a visual?" he asked Ramos.

"No, dammit!" yelled Ramos as he stood up and listened to the sound of a car speeding away. He walked over to Coop, and Manny spat out, "You should have taken the money, you dumb fucks."

Ramos ignored him; he had read the situation immediately, and began to look around for the pin on the floor while Coop held Manny still. He found it quickly and without a word came over to put a bullet in Manny's head. The body fell back, but the hand Coop held never budged. It stayed perfectly still while Ramos carefully pushed the pin back into the grenade.

With the weapon immobilized, they carefully laid it on the floor and slowly rolled Manny's body onto the top of it, followed by Greg, and then finally the never-named third guy. They hoped that would be enough padding if the thing still decided to blow.

Ramos said "Fuck. What now? I didn't see who was driving that car. I didn't even see the car."

"Not important." answered Coop. "We'll leave Manny and his grenade here, for now. I need you to go and get the smaller truck we saw at the loading dock and bring it here."

Ramos saw the plans immediately form in Coop's head. "We going shopping?"

"Yep. We'll load up all the guns from the warehouse into the truck before we leave, and also that case from downstairs. And the duffle bag, of course."

"What about the copper?"

"Leave it there. We'll deal with it another time."

An hour later, with the guns and cash in the truck, Ramos pulled up outside the front of the condo. He waited a minute, and then saw Cooper backing out of the door. He was pouring gasoline down the steps. When the gas can was empty, he tossed it back through the open door and stood up to stretch his back. A cigar appeared in his hand and he lit it deliberately, letting the smoke curl around him. Ramos patiently watched this routine, laughing to himself. Cooper took five long minutes to enjoy his cigar, and Ramos, to his credit, said not a word during that meditative period – but he laughed hysterically as Coop threw the cigar's hot stub into the trail of still wet gasoline he'd created.

Flames were immediately born. They quickly multiplied and greedily ate their way back up the stone steps of the front porch and into the condo itself. Ramos watched as a large, gradual bonfire emerged from the building, until finally a large explosion boomed from the inside causing the fire to increase exponentially in size within seconds.

Cooper walked to the truck and settled into the passenger seat. He reached into his pocket and placed the pin of the grenade down onto the dash board.

"Fire's good," said Coop, "but it gets positively beautiful after it burns down the stand that was holding up a live grenade from hitting the floor."

"That is sick! I love it. But honestly, I would have thought there would have been a bigger…"

And the condo blew hellfire a second time, much bigger and much louder than the first round of explosions. Random shit rained down on the truck and smoke filled the air, and the two crazed men watching it all happen began to howl and scream and laugh hysterically at what the Gods had allowed them to create that night.

Through the course of the night, they had escaped a rain storm of bullets, found enough weapons to supply an army, uncovered a fortune in money, gone to battle and killed their adversaries, and finally had built the mightiest of bonfires so the Gods could see them and recognize the power that they had superiorly wielded. They were victorious. They were conquerors.

They jumped out of the truck and up to the fiery hell spewing from the destroyed building, and they began to dance, and sing, and howl up at the sky as they created poems about their adventures and sang odes to the deities that stood with them during the slaughter of their enemies.

From atop the warehouse in the back, the demons that lived inside Old Grandma looked upon the two figures howling and dancing by the fire, and they knew they were fortunate to have avoided the mighty wrath of these two that so easily brought death to those they met.

And another pair of eyes, as well, watched the two men (if they could still be called men) revel in their destruction, and marveled at the paranormal-like scene she was witnessing.

Ramos kept yelling "Burn, baby, burn!" and would have continued on until morning had Cooper not pulled him aside.

"Tell me. You know what that thing was in there that we just burned down?"

Ramos wiped his face of tears and worked to control his laughter and hysteria. Somehow he managed to center his brain back to a point where he could converse with his partner. "That was a 3-D Printer, I'm sure of it," said Ramos. "And that stuff those guys were carrying, that had to be the plastic ink. Actually, it kind of sucks we blew it up. It's cool shit."

"And what does a 3-D Printer do, exactly?"

"I guess... it makes things."

"What things?"

"Anything. Everything. You program it with instructions on how to build something, just give it the specs. Then you add that fluid, which turns into a sort of plastic when it hardens; and then you hit the start button - instant "whatever". This is one of the biggest technical advancements of the day; I saw on YouTube where a guy made a whistle with a printer like that."

"It could also make couches, and TV's, and stuff? Like inside?"

"Of course. Theoretically, it can make anything, or any part of anything."

"Like weapons? Could it make guns, you think? Like the ones in the back of this truck?"

Ramos nodded. Cooper continued to talk.

"OK. Take me back to my car. Then follow me, I've got a place we can stash the truck for now. When we get there, we'll check to make sure there's no GPS trackers on it, and then double back here for your car. Then I'll make the call. The Captain is going to Fuckin A shit his pants."

The two merchants of death drove off to stow away their newfound riches, and the lady that had perceived a shred of their true nature finally got a hold of herself enough to bring the phone up to her ear and make an urgent call.

"It's Rosa. Some serious shit just went down, man. Those two guys showed up days earlier than we expected. What happened? What you think? We lost this entire set up - ALL of it. Manny's gone, and Greg. And that other guy - I don't remember his name."

"No, don't call the Captain yet," continued Rosa. "I *know* who these guys are now. I can get to them. One of them has a daughter that worked with the real estate blond I knew. She and her kid live close to here. Give me four guys and we'll go see them tonight. Then we bargain their lives to get our shit back. But we don't call the Captain yet, not until we take care of our own business. He needs to see we can clean up the mess."

She hung up the phone and thought to herself: *I am going to personally rip the balls off of them, with my own fucking hands. Fuck what the Captain says, they are dead men.*

CHAPTER **22**

MID MORNING WHISKEY

It was morning and the two men were driving through dimly lit dirt roads that would them directly to The Old Dog's Wet Fart. Cooper pointed ahead.

"This is it, up here. Go ahead and pull in."

"Where the hell you find this place?" asked Ramos. "I don't think this road is even on the GPS."

"I know some people; they recommended it to me. It's out of the way and I like it."

"Out of the way? Who would recommend a place like this? Did you find it on Trip Advisor?"

"No."

"Yelp?"

"I don't know what a Yelp is."

"I – know! Zagat. That's been around longer, you probably use that one." Ramos pulled out his cell phone. "Let me see what the Zagat review is on this place."

"Ram, focus. Put that up, we're going inside."

"No, Coop, I'm serious. You *have* to look at this kind of thing. When people like something, they want to let other people know about it, so they get credit for "discovering" it first; but if something's bad, they want to let people know about that as well, so they get credit for letting people know what to stay away from. If we are going to be putting their food in our bodies, we need to know what kind of establishment this is. People don't lie about this stuff and I don't mess around with where I get my food from."

"Why are you fucking with me right now?"

"Why are you *making* it so easy for me to fuck with you right now?"

Coop sighed. "Dana told me about this place a while back. Her baby sister runs it - name's Sadie. It's a locals' place, but folks who get lost tend to show up, too."

"If Dana's sister runs this place, I'm in. And speaking of Dana: you ever get those pies your ordered?"

Coop turned his head away. "I got 'em."

"And?"

"They were delicious."

They fell out of the car. They were beaten and torn and bruised, but in good spirits. Ramos followed Coop inside and appreciated the heavy wood that built the place, and the barrels being used for tables, and the wicker chairs along the walls.

To their left was the large bar of the house, and that's where they sat, with Ramos on Coop's right.

After a moment, Sadie walked up to them.

"Coop, good to have ya. Dana told me you'd be up this way."

"Yep."

"And who's this?" asked Sadie with her thumb toward Ramos, "He good company?"

"He's a pain in my ass, Sadie, but he makes good company. This is my partner, Cliff Ramos. Ramos, Sadie. She keeps the place."

"Ramos?" she said, "Really? Sounds like a Mexican Chuck Norris."

"Sweet. I *love* Chuck Norris. Hi, I'm Cliff."

"Pleasure, Cliff. Nice to have ya. But I'll call ya Ramos. Cliff is boring."

"What! "'Cliff'" doesn't sound like action star material to you?"

"Cliff sounds like an over-weight Cheers background extra to me, Ramos. Not an 80's action hero."

Ramos looked at Cooper with mock exasperation. He turned back to Sadie.

"19-*80*'s action hero? Sadie, my new and ignorant friend - that's like saying Aerosmith was *only* a band from the 70's, but in truth they were rocking new, and relevant, material well into the 2000's. Chuck Norris helped define, albeit over saturate, the 80's action genre, sure, but he also, in my opinion, made a much stronger name for himself in the last 20 years."

Sadie nodded. "OK. You're more a Texas Ranger guy, not so much a Missing in Action guy. I dig it."

"Sadie, Chuck Norris headlined that show for eight years, '93 to '01, and he's STILL making movies. He's a living cliché that everyone loves. That guy is cool as shit. His early stuff is good, but his later stuff is even more impressive. He had serious lasting power. His movies today are just as good, if not better, than his earlier ones. That's what I like."

Sadie looked at Coop. "This every day for you?"

"Yep."

"Right on. Finally, someone who knows something about something."

Cooper disregarded the huge grin that spread across the face of his partner.

"Thanks much, Sadie. Coop, I like her. Good call on this place."

Still ignoring Ramos, Coop asked Sadie "His knowledge of Chuck Norris qualifies him as somebody who knows something?"

She shrugged. "Sure. Hey, heard you were at my sister's the other night. She ok?"

"Yeah, she's good. You haven't seen her?"

"Not lately. Steve's been throwing out some hot dishes here, and it's all we can do to keep people fed."

"Steve that new cook I heard about?"

"He's good. Throws something different on the menu every day. You give him half an apple and a raccoon's ass, he'll whip up the best something or other you've ever had. I tell ya true."

"The MacGyver of culinary creation, huh?" added Ramos.

"Yup."

"Is Raccoon's Ass in season now?"

"Not sure, I'll have to check. Actually, if you could do me a favor – go and look there in mirror and let me know the answer to that."

"See Ramos?" Coop laughed. "I like it here the place has class."

"With a capital "'K'", honey" Sadie agreed. "So, what can I do ya for?"

"Milk - if you got it, and whatever's cookin' hot now."

"We got milk. Almond milk ok? Homemade, for real."

"Dammit, no. I said milk, Sadie, not nuts. Why the fuck can't you serve just regular milk? Milk is milk, not nuts."

"Because I've got almond trees out there and they crossbreed. So, I get almonds. And it takes very little effort, or land, or resources, or time, or money, to sustain those trees. And do you know how much it takes to sustain a fucking cow?"

"I have no clue."

"Fucking right, you don't. Dude, it's two acres for every pair of cows. Ramos, you know how expensive cows are to maintain?"

"To quote a recent acquaintance of mine… probably a shitload."

"Damn right! Very expensive. So tell me, Ramos, which is healthier? The carbs in cow milk, or the protein in almond milk?"

"I'm gonna say protein."

"Correct again. And Ramos, do you know how much milk we like to use here for our recipes?"

"Like, a little less than a shitload?"

"Correct. And Ramos, last question - simple economics; wouldn't it make sense to use the product that comes in an almost unlimited supply, is sustainable, tastes good, and is cheaper to produce?"

"Hold on, Sadie. I majored in English and Russian literature in college. I didn't get into those supposedly factual "'math'" (using air quotes with fingers) classes. All those numbers, and common-sensicals, that somehow "'equal'" (using air quotes with fingers) something? No way, I can't answer that - not without a very capable abacus."

"Smart ass. I've done the hard math, and the answer, no surprise, is that almond milk is the smarter way to go. We make it right here, and it is a very sustainable resource. So that's what we have, Coop."

"Fine. The almond milk is fine. Just both of you, shut up."

"You sure? 'Cause you didn't seem too sure a minute ago."

"I said FINE. I'll take the damn nut milk."

"You want chocolate in that?"

"Yes please." He looked at Ramos who could not even begin to control his grin. "Keep it zipped, Chuck Norris."

"K'. But you did say 'nut milk'."

Cooper ignored him and spoke to Sadie. "What's on the burner today?"

"Oh!" she came back, with wide eyes, "You'll like it! This is, like, brunch now, so we've got eggs benedict, plated with steak tartare and served with a side of hollandaise sauce. It's fuckin' good."

"Steak tartare?" asked Ramos. "You serve that here?"

"Did I spit when I spoke?"

"And Eggs Benedict?"

"I'm beginning to think you don't listen well."

"You think right." Coop said.

Ramos continued, "Ma'am, I will have the steak tartars, please and thank you."

"You got it. And to drink?"

"Can I get a Mimosa with that?"

"A Mimosa?"

"A Mimosa, yes. Champagne mixed with orange juice, maybe spritzed with a few crushed blueberries? Really goes well with brunch."

"Oh, right - I know what a Mimosa is." Sadie smacked her forehead. "My bad. What I *meant* to say was: Sorry, no, we don't serve that weak-ass shit here. And also, do not ever ask for that pansy kind of drink here again".

"You're difficult to work with, Sadie. But hey, I'm used to working with difficult people, so I can roll with it... What *are* my drink options? I'm thinking a strong house red could go well with the steak?"

"Whiskey."

"Sorry?"

"Whiskey. It's a type of bourbon, distilled brown liquor." Sadie explained.

"Got it. My bad, what I *meant* to ask was: Anything else to drink here besides whiskey?"

"Nothing else. We distill it here on site. That's what we serve."

"But Coop, he's getting milk!"

"You want milk?" she tried to help, but not really.

"No, for fuck's sake. Whiskey, please."

"Excellent choices, gentlemen. I'll be right back."

Sadie left, and Ramos looked at Coop.

"So… there actually *is* a dog on the porch that farts, Coop. I saw it. And this shit-hole place deep in the woods serves premium distilled whiskey and steak tartare, and grows almonds for milk on property."

"Yeah."

Coop said nothing else on the subject. Ramos was thinking he had stumbled into his own private Shang-ri La, but since Coop wasn't elaborating, he dropped it.

"I called Captain, had a talk. Told him…" Coop began, but got cut off.

"Coop! Holy shit! Do you see him? That guy right there?"

Coop looked around, using all his senses to find any immediate threats, but he found none.

"I only see the cook." he answered.

"Yes! Him! You know who that is?"

"He's the cook."

Sadie returned with their drinks and Ramos yelled at her, "Sadie! The cook, what's his name?"

"Steve?" she shrugged.

"Steve N. Lamar?"

"He just goes by Steve, usually."

Ramos punched Coop in the arm, irritating him as the almond milk he was drinking began to slosh in the cup. "Coop! That guy, he won Iron Chef, like twice! He owns restaurants. He has entire shelves in the grocery store that carry only his specialty recipe sauces. The guy is a celebrity. He's a world class cook!"

Coop checked out the average looking guy at the end of the bar; he was sipping a small glass of wine and had a dirty rag over his shoulder. His back was against the stained wood and he was going over a list of recipes for the week. He didn't seem like a celebrity to Coop.

"We haven't had the food yet, Ram. Little soon to say how good he is, ain't it?"

"He's good, Coop."

"You had his stuff before?"

"No..."

"Then you don't know."

"No. I don't."

"That's ok. I'm sure he's pretty good."

Ramos would not, *could* not, let it alone. "Sadie, how the HELL did Steve N. Lamar get here?"

"He just showed up one day. Said he got lost, so I gave him directions back to the highway. He sat down here at the bar, and drank our whiskey... and stayed. He asked if he could cook here, and I asked if he had any experience, and he said he had some, so I said ok, go cook me a burger. And he did, and it was fuckin' good. So, I said, ok, you can cook here."

"That's it? He got lost?"

"People around here are either born local, or they got lost. And most people that get lost here end up staying. Steve's one of them."

"Well," said Ramos, "Fuck me. I have never awaited a meal with such ferocity. Can't wait. And by the by, this whiskey is great. I've never had better."

"I know you haven't. Thanks, though." She walked off and said, "Hey Steve, ya got another fan over here!" Steve looked up, smiled and nodded. And Coop, still unimpressed with Ramos's discovery, continued to disseminate information to him.

"As I was saying... I called Captain. Told him everything."

"Everything? How much of everything..."

"Not everything, Ram; I only perused the main points."

"What'd he say? Did he start yelling?"

"No, he was calm. But with Cap, I never know. I didn't get into details, I just gave him the cliff notes and told him where we are. That's it."

"What's the next move?"

"To wait here. Eat the 'eggs Benedectine', or whatever. He knows this place; be here in a few hours."

"Captain knows about this place?"

"Said he did, so I guess he does."

"Ok." Then, "Damn, Steve N. Lamar - go figure. That guy disappeared from TV, just left and didn't come back. No one knew why. Guess we know, now. Funny where people end up."

They settled in at the bar and enjoyed their drinks. This was the first time that things became quiet, and they let it stay that way. Even Ramos shut up and watched Steve in the kitchen as he prepared their meal. Coop sat and appreciated the breeze flowing from the fan.

They noticed, but did not concern themselves, with the men beginning to walk in and sit among the tables surrounding them. At first, they came in first one at a time, then as a pair, and then one again, until the room was filled up with close to fifteen new guys.

Coop and Ramos allowed their minds to listen to what their senses where telling them; Coop began to smell the air as its odor changed noticeably. Sadie also raised her head and became aware of the guests.

One last man walked in, and all the ones who had previously arrived stopped their idle chatter and looked to him for direction.

This last man, he walked straight to the bar and directly towards Cooper. He held a flip phone in his hand, already visible so it wouldn't look like he was reaching into his pocket for anything. He laid this phone down in the space between where Cooper was resting his elbows.

At this point, Cooper had recognized the shift in reality and had adapted to it; the phone man sensed this and was a little put off that his well-planned surprise approach hadn't caused more unease from the intended targets.

Coop looked up at the man. "Excuse me, friend. What the shit is this?"

No messing around, Coop immediately became the aggressor.

Phone Guy had figured on an immediate, and harsh, response and so wasn't put off script. "That's your phone, man." he answered. "You must have dropped it. I picked it up for you. You're welcome."

Coop remained silent.

"'Thank you' is what folks usually say when that happens."

"Why do you assume it's mine?" Coop asked.

Phone Guy smiled. He'd been waiting to say the line. He'd practiced it in the mirror. "Because I was told to give this to the pussy at the bar wearing shiny boots. Looks like I found him. Plus, you're about to get a phone call from that there phone real soon, and it's a call you'll want to take. So that's your phone, asshole, and I am doing you a favor by making sure you didn't lose it."

Cooper nodded. He slowly turned his full torso towards the man speaking to him and bore his gaze into the man's head. Lesser men had curdled under that gaze, and shrank away on instinct; Phone Guy was no exception. He took a step back as Coop got his measure.

Ramos hadn't moved at all. He'd been looking at the glasses and mirrors on the bar in front of him, studying the reflections and watching the move of every individual man seated at the tables behind them. As was usually the case, Ramos saw that the men were not immediately ready to attack; they were there to intimidate and wouldn't move unless told to. And as was also usually the case, the men did not see that Ramos *was* ready to attack, immediately, without hesitation, and on his own merit.

Just then, Sadie returned with the aforementioned eggs Benedict and steak tartare. Deliberately moving slowly, she set the ordered plates in front of the two waiting men. No one moved. Cooper continued to stare Phone Guy, and Ramos kept his gaze on the mirror. He did, though, give a nod of thanks to Sadie before she walked away.

Here's a rule every Bad-Ass should know. If you are going to be the guy to break a deep and heavy silence in a very tense situation, then you had better do it well. This is because, generally, the first person to speak wasn't able to take the pressure of the stand-off and couldn't help but speak. He is weak, and he is a loser because he just lost a real-deal game of dominance.

A true Bad-Ass, on the contrary, *can* be the one to break a silence because that person is in complete control of the day and it is obvious to everyone present that when the Bad-Ass speaks, it has nothing to do with the game of wits at hand. The Bad-Ass speaks when he wants to, and never before or after he has spoken.

Cooper Cornelius Happenstance was such a Bad-Ass. He could have recited the Gettysburg Address just then and would still have been considered the dominant presence in the group.

He remained silent though, because he wasn't yet sure if Phone Guy was worth speaking to anymore.

Phone Guy probably sensed this, and – spoiler alert! – spoke first. He lost that battle of men the second he made a sound. He lost, and was shamed, but knew he couldn't stop there. He had to push forward if he was to save any part of his face that was laying on the ground in pieces.

Phone Guy lost by saying, "Your food's here. Looks pretty good, what is that? Damn, smells delicious." He knew that was weak and wished he had rehearsed something better.

Ramos, still looking ahead, replied "It *will* be delicious. And if you've ruined my opportunity to eat it, that's bad for you. Because I will literally... and I'm not saying that figuratively, friend, I mean this for real... I will *literally* slice the skin off your bones, a little at a time, if you make me miss this meal."

Then Ramos turned towards Phone Guy, and said "You're welcome."

Phone Guy didn't reply because he was trying to think of a pithy, witty remark to make up for his previous loss, but Ramos stole the silence and continued speaking. "Because most people, when they are given a warning that allows them to avoid a situation that would cause them great pain and humiliation, say thank you."

Phone Guy was pissed - these two redneck hipster assholes had stolen all his best lines! His reptile brain was thinking about how he'd been robbed of delivering the perfect sinister threats to his victims, and it was ignoring his most basic instincts that were yelling at him to get the fuck out of the flowing river of molten lava he was standing knee deep in with the two killers in front of him.

Just then, Ricky Martin began to sing "Livin' la Vida Loca" from the flip phone on the counter, and the buzz on the wood made that chainsaw-like noise that no one enjoys. Phone Guy exhaled, relieved that the picture of his shit-soaked honor was no longer the visual focus of the surrounding men.

Ramos tapped Coop's back. "Before you answer that, Coop, please remember that our food JUST came out. It's hot and perfect and will cause multiple orgasms inside our mouths. This fucktard needs to wait a damn minute while we experience perfection."

"This is not the time to fuck around, Ram."

"Thing is, Coop? I'm really *not* fucking around. Are these assholes worth missing a meal prepared by a legendary chef?"

"Thanks for that!" Steve called out from the kitchen. "Hope you enjoy!"

Ramos waved to Steve, then raised his eyebrows to Coop expecting an answer.

Coop frowned and said apologetically, "I promise it'll be quick."

Ramos slammed his hand down on the bar. He yelled, "Dammit!" and furiously pointed at Phone Guy, who inadvertently flinched as he began to get viciously, and verbally, assaulted.

"You! You are a mother fucking piece of hairy spunk-juice that your mom wiped off of her hairy ass after I got done ripping the shit out of her, literally, with my ass raping dick! I am going to fuck your world up man, I'm going to change your reality to one only existing in horrendous pain, if I am not eating this incredible meal in relative peace in the next thirty seconds!"

Ricky Martin kept singing, and Cooper held up a hand to try and mitigate his partner from yelling any more, but Ramos only got louder, and more vehement with his words. "You are a *nothing*, and I will NOT allow a NOTHING to interrupt my fucking space! You are below me, and I will use you like I use a door mat, you slug, and then I will fillet your face with my blade so it matches your mothers vagina after I was done shoving my fist into it!"

He went silent, still pointing. One of the men who walked in earlier began to giggle, and another guy wisely shut him up.

Cooper asked, "You done?"

"We'll see, won't we?" he said accusingly to Phone Guy. "I made a promise to you, and I'll be sure to keep it, you slimy, oozing stench of herpes-puss."

"Gross." Coop said and held the phone up to his ear. "Talk. I'm busy."

A snappy, and very pleasant Hispanic voice spoke to him.

"Detective Happenstance? Good morning, my name is Rosa. I hope you are having a pleasant meal?"

"Haven't had a chance to know yet. They make their milk out of almonds, here." Cooper liked to throw shit like that out in a tense situation to potentially distort his adversaries' train of thought. Sometimes it worked.

"Almonds? The nuts?" Rosa asked.

"The same."

"What's wrong with cow milk?"

Cooper was thinking misdirection wasn't going to work with this lady. He was also thinking that he liked her voice and began to fashion an idea of what this Latina looked like. It was an attractive idea. "Something about sustainability… but what are ya gonna do?"

Silence on the phone. Coop looked at Ramos, who had begun tapping his fork on the plate, and pushed the button for speaker phone.

"Well this is awkward. I hate phone silence. Do you?" said Rosa.

"Ha! I really do," Coop answered. "Plus, I'm not much of a talker anyway, and the phone doesn't help. But I know it'll smooth out here in a minute, it always does."

"You are so right, detective, but here's the thing - I don't really have a minute? I am really in a hurry this morning, so I'm just gonna let some people say hello to you now."

Ramos saw that Coop was instantly concerned. He heard the phone being handed over, and another lady's voice came on the line. It was Coop's daughter.

"Daddy? Dad! This BITCH needs her ass KICKED, you understand? Daddy?"

"I'm here Sam. I understand. Are you well?"

"Besides this bitch putting a gun to my head and…"

Rosa grabbed the phone back. "See, I should have led with that. It's a much better conversation starter, right? A powerful intro."

"You just made this very personal, Rosa. Of all the things you could have done to try and get back what I know you want, this was the worst choice. It was stupid, and I hope you understand that you made a terrible mistake. Because you will be dead before the day is out."

"She's got Sam? Fucking BITCH!" Ramos yelled out, and pointed another finger at Phone Guy.

"Please tell that young man you're with to watch his mouth - he's quite rude. And yes, I thought you might feel that way, so I've also brought along… I'm sorry, honey, what's your name again?"

"I'm not talking to you! Stranger Danger!"

Ramos choked, "Ally! Baby Girl, are you ok!"

"RAMOS! HELP! THEY HAVE REALLY BAD BREATH AND THEIR ARMPITS STINK AND THEY'RE UGLY!"

Rosa got back on the line. "OK, boys. It's me. I'm assuming you want me to release them?"

"No." Coop answered. "Keep them there with you."

"Well, that's interesting. Why is that, honey?"

"They are going to watch as I strangle you, Chica. I am going to break the life out of you right in front of them. And they will be glad to see it."

A coldness emanated from Rosa; it came purring out of the phone. "You mean, like how you strangled that little girl years ago at the Viking's house? She was the only one left standing after you had killed everyone else in the room. She was completely helpless, Coop. Still, you went to her, and you put your hands on her neck, and you squeezed. You saw her soul bleed from her eyes, and you watched her die. Are you going to kill me like that? Like you did that young Chica?"

Coop didn't answer and Ramos increased his attention.

Rosa continued, "I saw the tapes, my love. Cameras were all over, of course, and I got to see the whole thing; how you came charging in, like a bull, and broke to pieces every man, woman, and child that was in that place. I was – I *am* - fascinated by it. It was so gallant! The wounded hero coming to avenge his murdered wife. And you did that, bro, big time! I mean, wow! You were a fucking werewolf in there, a real Chupacabra!"

Coop couldn't recall specific details, but rather dull sensory memories. He went back to that now. Ramos began tapping his finger on the bar and allowed Rosa to blow explosive air on an already deadly hot kiln.

"And then you walked to that little girl, Cooper. You must have blamed her for bringing your wife to that place to get killed. And you weren't wrong, she did bring her there to die. So you put your hands on her, and you squeezed until she popped."

Rosa continued, "I said to myself, 'This is a sick man,' and then I finally realized: you are no man, not completely. A true man couldn't kill a child, but a man also couldn't do what you did to the Viking's entire crew – *most* of his crew. Only an animal could have done that. But really, could an animal do that without the sickness of a man's ego?"

She paused to make sure she still had his attention. She did.

"But really, you have to know… she would have never brought your wife there by herself. She wasn't stupid. She only did that because I told her to, Cooper - only because I told her to. I didn't want that bitch wife of yours messing with one of my most hopeful earners. I was going to make a point with her. And I did. But then you came, out of nowhere, and that place burned to the ground. But it wasn't until a few minutes ago did I realize just HOW you got there, and WHY you did. Now, for the first time, I understand that Captain sent you in, using your wife as a tool he knew would allow the monster inside you to run rampant in my house. He was able to disintegrate all of his competition so he could focus on moving his guns. And then you know what he did? He played the fucking hero, getting everyone back together. You didn't get everyone that night, Cooper. You missed me. I should have been slaughtered like the rest, but I didn't come in till later. I was the one that found your mess."

She finished talking. Coop had had enough time to regain his mind. He focused and felt the cool heat of battle joy come over him. Ramos, conversely, was seething and working to get a hold on the situation. Cooper spoke, "I wish you had been there, Rosa."

"I know you do, honey."

"What needs to happen now? What do you want, and how?"

"Simple, Man-wolf. Two things: The truck with all our shit in it, and your life. My men there will follow you to where the truck is now, and when they have it, you will come to this address that I've texted to you. It's a cabin in the woods, very secluded, and perfect for what happens next. You will come to this cabin, and you will see that I let your daughter and granddaughter go. Then, your foul mouthed partner can take them home. You know you can trust him, and I have no cause for his death. And then after he is gone, you will stay behind so I can put a bullet in your fucking brain and bury your filthy body in cement. Isn't that weird? Knowing that in just a couple of hours, you're going to be lying in a brick of dried cement buried into the ground?"

"I *will* bring you the truck, and you *are* welcome to contend for my life, Rosa. I've tried to lose it myself many times, but have never been successful. Maybe you can be, but I doubt it."

"You are too confident in your abilities."

"No. I'm realistic. The truck comes back to you, as do I. Those two girls *will* remain alive. But Rosa, these dipshits you sent here to collect us aren't taking me anywhere. We meet on my terms."

"There's no choice about this, *pendejo*. This is how it will be. I sent those men to bring you here, and it's up to you if you want to disagree with them, but regardless, you *will* be here in two hours, and with my truck. Set your watch. If more than two hours go by, I will begin cutting pieces off of these ladies. The address is in your phone. The clock starts now."

She waited for Coop to reply, and when he didn't, she hung up.

Ramos took the phone and scrolled to the address, then plugged it into his GPS. He looked to make a mental note of the time, and then Phone Guy decided to speak again. "Let's go."

Ramos replied in deadly soft tone, "You heard we're not going with you. Take your joy boys and hit the fuckin' road. We'll be there."

Phone Guy was still smarting from his earlier loss of pride, and he knew that if he was going to salvage any kind of respect from his men from that day, he had to do it now. "We were paid for a job. We're gonna do that job. Let's go."

Scuffling sounds scratched loud as the surrounding men began to get up from their chairs and increased their attention towards the escalating shit storm. Ramos acknowledged the men and thought it was ironic that the problem of having superior numbers on your side is that it puts you into a mindset of safety, and of inaction. These men weren't really expecting to do much today.

But they were wrong, because Ramos wasn't getting the meal he wanted.

He looked at Coop and ruefully shook his head. "You are *such* an asshole. I fucking told you. Do not ever say that I didn't tell you, Coop."

CHAPTER *23*

BAR FIGHT MOVIE SCENE

*F*or the sake of literary creativity, we'll now explore how, if this were a movie, these action scenes would block out on paper.

Cooper stands up and sees Sadie appear from out behind the bar with a shotgun in her hands. She uses it to blow rock salt into Phone Guy's chest and it knocks him backwards onto the floor.

The hands of Ramos flash up under his jacket and two blades appear shining with intensity. Cooper simply drives his fist into the first head he can get a hold of.

What follows is a HUGE, EPIC barroom fight. Blood and brains fly and men get cut open. It would make the old Gods proud to see humans fight so gloriously.

Coop takes on five men at once, and Ramos jumps forward into the melee to ensure he fulfills his promise to Phone Guy. After having to cut around several of his adversaries, Ramos found Phone Guy and sat on top of him while he sliced his face into neat, evenly measured, shreds.

Only two men are left standing when it's all over. Ramos and Cooper are covered in blood, little of which is theirs. They can barely stand, but they are the *only* ones standing. Ramos's blades are dripping red life onto the floor; Cooper's knuckles gleam stark white through the skin that is no longer covering them. He grabs a shirt off one of the dead guys and rips it up to achieve a healthy swatch of material, which he then uses as a bandage over his knuckles. Ramos deftly drops his blades and they stick into the hard wood like they were pulled there by magnets, while the skin that he peeled off of Phone Guy's face and scalp remained hanging in beef jerky-sized chunks from his bloody hands. He wouldn't let them drop away, he'd earned those.

Since standing has become a challenge, they decide to sit back down. Ramos says "Hey, look at that!" and is happy to see his eggs are still good and hot, and not at all ruined from the ill-timed brawl. He slaps his prized hunk of epidermis onto the bar next to his plate and begins to eat savagely.

Sadie begins pulling dead bodies to the side closet so she can dispose of them later. A couple of the *supposedly* dead ones weren't so dead after all, and they got up, grabbed the unconscious Phone Guy - and what remained of his face – to run out the door, just as a local fisherman, who'd lived there all his life, was walking in. His name was Walt. He nodded at Sadie, who nodded back to him, and he went to have a seat in his favorite corner of the bar.

CHAPTER 24

TIME TO DRINK

Ramos asked, "Sadie. Could we please have two whiskeys?"

She brought them over and he said gratefully, "Thanks for that."

"No worries. They're on the house." she shrugged.

"No," Ramos replied, "for the other thing."

She grinned, "That's on the house, too."

Cooper looked at Ramos. "You know I don't drink."

"Today, Wolfman, ya do." That wasn't said in jest, or as a dare, or a demand.

"Yeah..." he agreed and tilted up the cold glass to taste the poison ecstasy on his lips again.

Ramos continued. "We're going straight to the cabin, I got that. I need you to tell me what we're walking into, though. Explain to me what I need to know, and let's go get the girls."

Coop said, "Depends." And he licked his tongue around the lips that were dripping bourbon honey.

"What depends?" asked Ramos.

Cooper asked directly, "Who am I talking to right now?"

"To... me." That was not an answer.

"To you?" Coop challenged. "Or to the 'Butcher'?" He looked down at the slabs of skin that Ramos had placed neatly on the bar while he ate his special eggs. "Because honestly, Bam-Bam, one of them is more useful to me today than the other."

Ramos breathed in heavy gulps of air, and exhaled feeling much better about – well, about life in general. He always did when he could talk straight with his partner about things. "Both," he replied. "You're talking to both. We're one and the same, Wolf. That's the primary difference between you and me... that I embraced my inner acid long ago and made it a part of me. It already was anyway, there was no choice, I just finally took heed of it. I've been trying to explain all this to you. That's what you need to do. Take heed of who you are."

"I do take it. You know that. I let it out when I can."

"That's a band aid. You're constantly building a divide within yourself that should never, ever have existed."

"So, in your narrative, Cooper Happenstance dies and becomes a monster."

"No. No, he…. he emerges. He evolves. He *becomes*."

"It's still a form of death, boy."

"Fuck your pessimism. By that idea… we die every day, every minute. Every time we gain a new memory, we become something we weren't previously. Our skin and our bodies have been growing, aging, and regenerating since birth. That ain't the same skin you had as a kid, man. You don't think with the mind you had twenty years ago, you exist with the consciousness you have *now*. True passion is when you can make your identity a living process, and not the static version of who you are at this minute."

Ramos leaned in close so his words carried all the weight he intended. "So, you tell *me* then… who am I talking to right now?"

Coop turned slowly and got face to face with Ramos. His eyes were fierce, and his words deliberate.

"You told me once that nature ain't pretty, and that you'd made peace with that. I hope that was true. Cause when you're with me, you're gonna experience a LOT of nature."

"Tell me what we are heading into. We both have daughters in there. You hear that? Did you hear what I just said?"

"I heard you."

"That doesn't surprise you."

"No."

"You knew."

"Of course I knew. And I made you earn your way back into her life. Also… you and Sam have similar tastes - the same kind of mental processes. You both have desires that I know you tried to quench together, early on. And I thought maybe, for the good of you both, I could keep those desires apart. I hoped that maybe they'd filter out of her, in time. But that didn't happen. She merged with every part of herself, and is perpetually strong because of it. Ally is the same way… her reality is how she wants it to be, and that is true power. But they're not whole, Cliff. They need you. Woody would have never survived had he really stayed around. And I'm serious about that. Speaking of… have you heard anything from him? I told him to contact you if he ever couldn't get a hold of me."

"No. I haven't seen him." Ramos answered as bluntly as he was able to.

Sadie brought out a bottle of house whiskey and set it on the aged wood of the bar. Coop grabbed it and refilled both glasses. They each drank, and Coop remained quiet. So, as was his nature, Ramos talked.

"Well. I'm glad you see how it all is, now. But while you sat high on your classy fucking morals, friend, you let your personal demons interfere with OUR fucking lives, and that is some serious bull-shit, Coop. You judged and determined our lives, and that's wrong. At some point, we're to have a reckoning about this. You need to know that."

"Point taken. I did what dads do. You'll have to accept it. Y'hear?"

"I did accept it, long ago," Ramos answered. "That's why I'm talking to you about it now, instead of placing a knife into your heart."

Coop raised his glass, once again full. He had to wait patiently for Ramos to meet his toast, though, and after a long minute – which Coop thought of as a bit contrived - the glasses hit and the men drank.

Ramos said, "Tell me who these people are before we go and kill them."

And Coop did.

CHAPTER *25*

NOW AGAIN

THE CABIN

"**O**h, Fuck." said Ramos.

Coop rolled in behind and stopped just beside him. Their reaction was such that they might as well have been looking at a pile of shit that had come to life and started taking lessons to become a leprechaun; instead, they were looking at The Captain, Rosa, and men from Rosa's crew, standing in front of them.

A much-needed silence was allowed to exist for a time until the Captain, who was the most capable and statuesque person in that room, spoke first.

"While this is sinking in fellas, know that both Sam and Ally are on their way back home. They are unharmed. And they will not *be* harmed. Understood?"

He focused his attention pointedly at Rosa; she turned away from his gaze, but he continued his silent inquiry of her until she looked back at him and conceded his point with a nod.

Then the Captain spoke to the detectives. "And you two. Did you just hear me? Do you comprehend the information I gave you just now? Fucking tell me that you heard me say those girls are safe."

Ramos spoke, "I heard you, Captain."

"Good, Cliff, thank you. Cooper, you tell me now - that you understand what I said about those girls being very safe and in no danger."

Coop said nothing; he breathed steadily.

The Captain walked forward and got in his face. Their noses touched and their breath fluctuations intertwined with one another's. He spoke darkly to a dark place, on a gravel road.

"Cooper, you fucking beast. You are a pure breed, very historical. You are the wolf that the dog never should have evolved from. I love you. But I NEED to KNOW that, before we go ANY further, no matter WHERE this goes in the next five minutes, you heard me explain to you that your daughter and granddaughter are safe. This is important, you fuck. Did you hear me? Answer, now!"

The reply was slow, but audible. "I heard you."

Captain stayed in his face, waiting on a more believable confirmation. Ramos leaned over to him.

"Maybe if we could talk to them, Captain. Hear their voices in real time and confirm their safety? I believe that would help."

"Ramos, you meddling demon. Fuck that. You heard my words when I said they were safe, and that is the only word you need. You'll call them later. But not now. Right now, you need to trust me that I made sure of their safety."

Coop nodded his head once in agreement.

The Captain accepted this and spoke. "Ok, good. That's all I needed, my friend!"

He turned away and walked back to his conglomeration of interesting criminal acquaintances standing behind him before continuing his oration.

"Hey! We've got ourselves a real fuck stick of a situation here, huh? We gotta get this sorted out! Now Cooper, I need you to stop staring daggers at Rosa, here. You need to pay attention to *me*. Didn't I tell you two assholes to NOT go anywhere unless I told you to? Well there was a reason for that! Fortunately it all worked out ok, but now, we need to stop the bleeding. Now tell me, first, how did you end up at the condos?"

Again, Ramos spoke. "We followed a lead having to do with the copper wire thefts. That's why we were at the warehouse."

"Yeah. That's material to make quick money. Good for exporting," the Captain explained.

"What is this, Captain? Why are we here? We've followed you blindly, done what you've asked, and now our lives are being threatened because of it. We don't deserve this. We've given you everything."

The Captain nodded, with empathy.

"You are good boys – just so damn naïve, and so mistaken. YOU'VE given ME everything? Really? Had you two fucking sociopaths NOT become cops, you would have become deranged serial killers on the streets. You two have talents, lives, abilities, that few people have. I found you, and put you together, because I knew that otherwise, I'd be letting monsters and demons roam unchecked in my town. You two get results, and in YOUR world, you are sane. Coop, I've known your family for generations. And you, Ramos… I know about your family history as well. And you have no idea, I promise you, of the power your lineage holds; power, and poison. It's rare that one follows without the other. I either had to eliminate both of you when you were younger, or take you in as my own. You probably don't remember Coop, but there was a particular camping trip we went on when you were a teenager, and I'll admit it… you weren't going to come back from it. I was going to end you, because you were a force I didn't know if I could condone in this world."

"You thought me evil." Coop stated this, never questioned it.

"Evil? No. But Powerful? Oh, yes. And with a large potential for sickness, for acid."

"Why am I still alive then?"

"Because, much like a nuclear power plant, I believed that more good than harm would come from your power. And, if I'm being completely honest, I feared what would happen if your blood ever spilled on the ground and got into my city's water. Were you contagious? I had no idea. But I knew I loved you, and I loved your father and your mother. I owed them a great debt, Coop, and I feel I honored that debt when you came back from that camping trip alive. The story is similar with you, Ramos. I owed your family a debt, and so you lived, where otherwise you would not have, and again I feel that your – peculiarities, your demon – is better left inside you than being dispersed back into our world."

The Captain paused to organize his next line of thought. "So, you two came together by me and I have taken care of you. I have guided your actions and used your talents to what I believe is the benefit of everyone we are sworn to protect."

Coop spoke. "Why did we ever deserve your love? We never asked for it. Your protection was never anything but self-serving."

The Captain chuckled. "First, let me say this: You two *never* deserved my love! I should have drowned you fuckers in a mud puddle while you were children. I didn't love you, and I didn't want the extra responsibility. What saved you both was the debt I owed to your parents. I loved and honored your parents, and that is the ONLY reason you two are alive. Over the years, I grew fond of you. I stepped in to the role of mentor and made sure you were well raised."

He continued, "What? Don't believe me Cooper? You don't think I did right by you two? Between you and Ramos, there are bodies all over this state that have been beat to death into a bloody pulp, and ones that have been filleted of their flesh. There are trails that lead to piles of bodies that I kept clean for you two, and I did it out of love. I did it out of respect. And, I did it for the common good - because if you two weren't reined in, there would be a madness in this world that didn't need to be here. So don't you DARE accuse me of being abusive. I've taken care of your messes for years. Of course there are reasons for what I did, Coop, and stories, and explanations that go along with those reasons. None of which are being mentioned today! Just know that I feel that I have debt to both your families, and so I took you both under my wing. You became part of MY Pack. Of MY Clan. I hope that appeases you for the moment, because for now, that's all there is."

The Captain raised his eyebrows daring someone to question him further, so he could verbally anal fuck them sideways.

Instead, Coop turned his attention to Rosa. "Remember that promise I made you earlier? I don't forget things, Chica. You and me got business."

"Captain," she said, deciding to ignore Coop and work with the man in charge, "I know you have feelings for these two, but you need to put three bullets in each of their fucking heads, right now. You said it yourself, they are unsafe. There is no reason they should still be breathing. Here, I will do it for you."

"No, and no. I've made it clear that we are only talking right now. If anyone speaks one more word about who in this room needs to get killed, I will put a bullet into them myself. Back the fuck up, Rosa. And Cooper, cool it. Fucking children, all of you."

"She kidnapped my family, Captain. She meant them harm. People don't live after doing that."

The Captain took a deep breath to remain calm. "Coop, just listen, would you? Here's where we're at. I was more than happy to point you in the direction of the Viking. What happened to your wife was terrible, and showed just how far that organization had strayed from its original purpose. I wanted vengeance for your wife, and you went about it with a righteous fervor that I was incredibly jealous of. There was an advantage in that for me as well; The Viking was moving heavily into the illegal sex and slave trades, and also narcotics. Make your money how you have to, I kept telling him, but keep the kids out of it. I can't and won't ever condone prostitution, especially when most of the girls are underage and illegal. It's sick and perverted."

"We had a falling out, and I laid low. When you went in there and wiped out the entire operation, then I was able to assert my leadership into the organization; a kind of ghost CEO. We'd stick to manufacturing weapons and exporting valuable resources. That is a man's world, those were the decisions made, and that is what allows me to sleep at night."

Ramos said, "The 3-D Printer we saw. You found a way to manufacture assault rifles with it, right? That's what you're exporting."

"Yes. Smart kid. We paid almost half a mil for the machine, but it pays off in a very short period. We used to have to buy the guns from someone first, and then sell them to someone else for more money to make a profit. This is the standard business model of the modern world. Problem is, the more people that are involved in the moving of these guns, the more risk there is of being found out. So, we simply cut out one whole side of the equation - we'd just make our own fucking weapons! No trail, no trace, no nothing. These things never existed to begin with. No one is truly exploiting this technology yet, not to its maximum value. There will be others jumping into the market in the near future, but while we *are* still one of the few players in the game, we're making it count."

"And then, you two FUCKSTICKS walked in there and blew my money-making machine up. And you stole my guns! And you took my millions of dollars! You boys have no fucking clue what you cost me."

Coop shrugged. "I mean, we have an *idea*. It was like, a shitload, right Ram?"

Ramos affected a contemplative look. "Yeah, I'd say about that. Give or take."

The Captain noted their impertinence but continued. "So, first thing's first: where is my fucking truck? The one you packed with the money and guns? The printing machine may be gone for now, but we can still fill the most urgent orders quickly. You'll be showing my associates here exactly where that truck is right now."

"And then?" Cooper asked.

"And then, we figure out a very neat and tidy copacetic situation that all of us will adhere to. I knew it'd come to this sooner or later."

He turned towards Rosa. "I sent these men to that brothel you were running for the express purpose of shutting it down – which they did, famously. I need to know, Rosa, you are no longer trying to build that business into any kind of working company. Prostitution has completely stopped, correct?"

"Yes. Correct. We stay only with arms dealing. You got no more problems from me."

"Good. And do me a favor Rosa – tonight, when I have my dick up your ass and am fucking you mercilessly until you bleed, you keep that in mind.

Remember that I am the boss and that the only reason you are alive is because I like the way you are so easily a holster for my dick. You're good at what you do in business, and I value your skills, but never assume that you are anything other than a whore to me. Any assumption by you to the contrary will result in your head being displayed on my bedpost. I am not talking figuratively."

"I understand."

"I wonder if you do. You have a penance to pay, a big one, and if you behave appropriately tonight, and for many nights after, I might have *only* one or two of my best men have their way with you after I've finished, as opposed to my entire crew. Your choice is to either get dead or to do penance. I don't know which one you'll end up choosing, though, and that'll be interesting."

"That settles nothing between us." Coop said.

"Yes, it does." Captain replied. "Right now, you are going to go with these fine gentlemen and show them where the truck is. Then after that, you're going home to clean up. And Ramos... do you have a date with James in forensics? What the fuck is a Space Dinosaur?"

"A movie, sir."

"You paid a hefty price for the information he got you! He's singing to the office about how you two are best friends now and are having a "'guys night out'". It's really sad. I could have done that for you, boy, but I understand your need for discretion."

"Anyhow, that's the plan. Monday morning, you two are in my office to speak with me about how you are going to reimburse the nearly $1 million worth of property damage you caused in only one night. You aren't going to like most of what you'll do to repay it all, but you'll get over it, and you will do it, and you will make right by me. We'll keep our city safe and continue the business of making money as usual. Understood? Now go."

People began to break off into groups, going about the orders that Captain had meted out. But Coop, using a momentum he had been building deep inside his physical mass, lurched forward and grabbed Rosa by the neck. He slammed her back into a wall so that her skull bounced off it like a bobble-head doll. To their credit, her men reacted quickly and it took about five of them to get Coop's hands off of her. She fell to the ground in shock as Coop immediately put two of his attackers down with broken arms and ribs. Another man came at him pulling a gun but then found he had a blade wedged into his shoulder, complements of Ramos.

Coop found Rosa again, reasserted his grip about her neck and lifted her off of her feet so that she dangled from his massive arm.

"This is what Maria saw when I did this to her. I never make promises I can't keep Rosa. Never."

The Captain bellowed "COOPER! DOWN! She is NOT yours to have! Put her the fuck down!"

Cooper did not let go, and Rosa's face continued to go pale. She began to pee down her legs from the certainty of knowing she was going to be dead in the next few seconds. Coop spoke again, "Your dick in her ass, Cap, as funny as that is to me, in no way compensates for the harm and danger she brought to my family. She will pay penance to me with her life."

"Coop." Ramos spoke softly, standing beside him. He didn't interfere with Coop's handling of Rosa, he only wanted to communicate with the big man. "Wolfman. Let her go. Captain's got this. I know you're focused only on vengeance now, and you're right to be. But you need to let her go, man. She's not yours to have. Her life is spoken for."

Cooper watched Rosa's eyes begin to close, then slowly set her back down on the ground. His hand left her throat and as she slumped away from her attacker, she hoped that her windpipe wasn't crushed.

Tension drained from the room.

Then without questioning how he immediately came to know it, Ramos saw that Coop was not finished collecting his justice. He spied an axe handle in a corner near a small pile of wood and, slowly, moved towards it.

But as he curled his hand around the rough wood of the nearby bludgeon, he saw his partner begin to move and muttered, "Coop, NO…"

Cooper blindly shot back at Rosa, grabbing her by the front of her throat with one massive hand. He was momentarily still, and they locked eyes to create a shared universe only they existed in; a millennium could have passed between them in that long second. Then he closed his hand into a fist so that his fingers were pushed through and into her flesh, and he ripped her throat and Adam's apple right out the front of her neck.

She couldn't scream or breath, and he made sure she saw him drop the remains of her throat onto the ground as he crushed them with his boots. Cooper stepped away, and Rosa fell into the dirt and died.

Coop was just getting started. He ran at the nearest guard that was a threat and hurled him to the ground. Then he elbowed another one's nose as he approached from behind, and turned to raise his heel before crushing the face of the first man he put down.

He heard "Fuck, I'm sorry!" and then felt the first thump of the axe handle as Ramos wielded it against his head. He turned toward his new attacker in such a rage that it left him blind as to who it was he was facing.

Then for the first time, Ramos experienced what other men have faced when Coop was tearing down on them. He felt the weight, and the mass, of the big man and how he could draw it into himself. He recognized Coop's control over the physics of his environment, and how, very literally, time slowed down for him as he become faster, and stronger, and intent on absorbing the lesser-formed life masses around him, who were slower and weaker and no longer deserved to live an independent existence.

Ramos felt the impossibility of escaping the larger being. He was fast, and he had energy, but not enough to pull away from the gravitational force in front of him and escape outward, as the universe itself *had* barely managed to do eons ago when it obtained *just* enough speed to continue spiraling away and escape from being pulled backwards into the singularity from which it had recently exploded.

No, Ramos *knew* he could not pull away from the weight of Coop's wrath, and so he quickly formed a plan that, instead of focusing on outrunning the danger, it would use a counter-balance that harnessed Coop's own awesome force and possibly allowed for him to escape from this encounter alive.

Working hard to remain calm, he allowed Coop's mass to bring him forward, and as he neared the Wolf's giant hands, Ramos twisted just slightly enough to bring the axe handle down on its head. This allowed him to slip past the massive beast and to own another second of life. But he knew that when he turned around, his life would be over. Fortunately for him, other men jumped into the fight, momentarily delaying his death. The new arrivals, though, were quickly broken by the fists that met them, but they had given Ramos time enough for one more chance at existence. He brought the axe handle down hard with both hands on the beast's skull, and watched as Coop fell to taste the floor.

He tried to get up, and Ramos continued to hit him until he couldn't.

Coop was dragged outside and put in the trunk of the car. Ramos drove off with him.

CHAPTER **26**

THE MOTEL

Another dirt road.

More dust.

An old motel sitting off in the woods.

A car parked off to the side.

The trunk swung open and Coop lay inside, beat to shit. His eyes were open already, though. He had planned on springing out of the trunk to massacre whoever opened it, but his body wouldn't comply with his demands. Hell, he could have jumped out onto the road a while ago just by grabbing the lever that opened the trunk lid from inside. All the cars had that now. But as he had rested in the dark metal box, he took a quick physical survey of his body and found that he could barely manage a fumble from his phalanges.

Not able to do much with himself, he allowed complacency to take over. The bumpy ride became soothing, and he was able to relax from the idea that at this point, he had nothing to worry about. He had no choices left to make. Whether he lived or died at the end of this car ride was not up to him, the consequences couldn't be changed. He waited as the car rumbled on, and when it finally stopped, he looked up to the opening trunk lid, not to escape, but to at least meet the eyes of the men who would bury him.

Coop saw a pair of hands reach down through the penetrating sun, and they grabbed him. He was pulled up into a sitting position, and a cooler was put down in front of him filled with ice. His captor pulled out a bottle of water and gave it to Coop, who drank it all – there was no sense in dying thirsty. Then, a chilled pint of whiskey was handed to him, and he drank that, too – there was even less sense in dying sober.

Eventually, Coop allowed his thoughts to move beyond the immediate need to mend his damaged meat suit, and he spoke to the person that had been quietly standing beside him since opening the trunk.

"Fuck you doing here?"

"Ramos called me," Woody replied in a semi-rehearsed explanation. "Said he needed help, so I came. He told me to drive you far enough away from people, so if you needed time to think, you could. I knew about this motel out here, so it's there if you need it. You look like shit."

Coop didn't want to talk, but there were questions. "Ramos called YOU? Why? You two don't have civil-type conversations. Woody, listen to me when I tell you that he's not someone you want to be around if you don't need to. He's dangerous to you."

"Fuckin' right, I know that!" said Woody and choked out a nervous laugh that Coop didn't care for. "Yeah, I know that. I really do. But see we talked, me and him, and we got things straightened out…"

"You and Ramos talked things out? When?"

Woody shook his head and Coop saw him fall back into his mind, remembering something. He looked into Woody's eyes to try and get a glimpse of what it was, but he couldn't see shit.

In the woods; Ramos was on top of Woody as he pulled his knife back and his arm came down. Thunk! The blade embedded itself in wood beside Woody's head. He could feel it touching his ear.

He yelled out "Ahhh, fuck! Why!"

Ramos pulled his face up close. "I told you. This is NOT the way I wanted it done. I wanted to fillet the skin off your bones, cretin, and then cut off your extremities one by one while you were still alive and conscious. I wanted to breathe in your suffering. But Sam saved you. She asked for a gift, and your life was the gift she asked for. And because I love her, she'll have what she asks."

Woody shivered. "Sam?" he croaked.

"She is my queen, my Pack Mother, and I spared your life to honor her. I don't like it, but I'm forcing myself to see it as a sacrificial thing… the more it hurts me, the greater the gift it must be. Point of view really is the most important thing for a man, ya know."

Woody understood, and he loved Sam for thinking to spare him. She didn't have to.

"But Woody," Ramos continued," You have to sign this, now." He pulled out a pad and pen and threw it on the ground. "This forfeits any right of parenthood or guardianship for Ally. That is MY child, and you know that. I've had tests done, but you already know the truth. You will come around and be known as Uncle Woody, because Ally, despite all your faults, loves you very much, and I won't take away things she loves. But I am and will be her father, Woody, and you will accept that."

"And if I don't?"

Ramos smiled, and shrugged. "Then I will find you, and I'll have you begging for death in seconds, but it won't come for days. You will disappear into a dark pit in the woods and never return. I will claim your life. Truly, I love that idea. A part of me wants you to push back on this, so I get what I want. But that's not what Sam and Ally want - they want you alive. And my job is to provide them whatever it is they want, and so I am going to forgo my pleasure for their happiness. Sign this."

Woody accepted this and bent down for the pad Ramos offered. Slowly, he pulled on the sheets to try and flatten them out so he can begin to read the document. Ramos looked at him and asked, "The fuck are you doing?"

"It's a contract. I'm reading it before I sign. You should always do that, and people never do. Like phone contracts? The shit that's in those things…"

He trailed off as Ramos handed him a pen. "Sign it."

Woody thought to explain to him how irresponsible that was, but wisely kept it to himself. He took the pen and signed the docs, and Ramos grabbed them immediately.

"We need to get those notarized?" asked Woody. "I know a guy that does it, we'll both need to be there, we could drive…"

"I got that covered." uttered Ramos as he tucked the papers into his back pocket. He nodded, then turned and disappeared back into the dark of the woods just as quickly as he had popped out of them.

Woody slumped down with his back to the tree and looked up at the knife that had almost taken his life. It was still embedded in the bark, bouncing a little, and still hot for action.

He sat there for a long time, just breathing and letting his new reality mold around him.

Eventually, he got up and pulled the knife from the tree, and he had kept it near him ever since. It was a frightening thing, that blade, but it also reminded him that he was alive.

Woody shook his head again. Coop knew he'd get nothing from him. "Thanks for the warning Coop. I'm leaving town for a while. Not for good, though. This is home."

"When are you leaving?"

"Now, actually. Found a ride that'll take me to the bus stop in town."

"Good luck to you. Stay safe. We'll see each other again." Coop knew they would.

Woody walked off towards the motel and Coop watched him get into the passenger seat of a waiting car. It drove off.

Eventually Coop got himself together and he checked into the motel. He took a shower, drank, and passed out naked on the floor. At some point, he woke up and crawled into the lone bed. He lay awake all the next day and stared up at the rotating fan. He was furious, naked, and sad, and confused.

Toward dusk, there was a knock on the door. Coop grumbled his way out of bed and stalked over to pull it open. Standing there was the lady that owned the motel. She was middle aged and slightly plump, but a damn good-looking lady. And what's more, she smelled nice.

She coolly gave Coop an examining glance; it wasn't the first time she'd seen a naked man answer the door. This one had more black and blues on him than she'd ever seen on a live person, but he was still nice to look at. She introduced herself. "Hey hon. I'm Patrice. You gonna be another night? Gotta get paid up, if we could."

"Sure." said Coop. Patrice stood in the open door and watched him pick up a pile of clothes on the floor and fumble through them for his wallet.

He pulled out a neat stack of bills, more than enough for his stay here. She walked into the room to meet him. He handed her the bills and she took them without counting.

"If you want," she said, pointing to his dirty suit, t-shirt and boxers, "I can get those cleaned and pressed. Have 'em waitin' for ya in the morning. A man walks taller when his suit's clean."

"My momma used to say that."

"She did? Smart lady."

Coop sat on the bed and his head lolled. Patrice moved slightly so that if he had looked up just then, he'd have seen her in front of him and known he could have her at his pleasure. But she saw his exhaustion and pulled back her invitation before it was noticed.

"Hon, you are whipped. When you eat last?"

"Been a minute."

"I'm gonna send Rhonda over with a meal, and some sweet tea."

"That'd be fine. Thank you."

"My pleasure. And Hon, seeing as you ain't gonna have clothes while I'm washing them, do me a favor. Wrap a towel around your fun bits when Rhonda gets here. She's pushing seventy and your bare ass might give her shakes."

Coop smiled. "No sweat."

Patrice bent down to pick up all his clothes, and she intentionally allowed her hands to brush against his legs. She was happy to see that his sex came alive at her touch.

"Thank you again, Patrice" Coop said as she walked out the door.

Rhonda showed up later, and Coop answered the door, again, butt ass naked. Rhonda came in to set down the tray of food, then stood back and gave him her appraisal of him. "You got the piss beat out you, huh?" she asked.

"I did. Yes ma'am."

"Um-hm. Well, I reckon the other guy's much worse off. You don't look familiar with losing."

"I've lost plenty."

"But others have lost more, haven't they?"

Coop laughed. This old lady wasn't nearly as fragile as Patrice made her out, and he'd wager she'd been a handful her entire life. It occurred to him that, had he asked her to stay with him, she would.

"You'll heal up fine. I would tend to your wounds, if you'd let me."

"Yes, good mother. I would let you, and I would appreciate it."

Coop knew it would be an insult not to let her serve him, to take care of him. He was the Pack Master here, he was the Alpha. He brought strength into their home, and they honored it.

As she doctored his wounds with a tender hand and strong medicine, he noticed she had an accent and asked where she hailed from. She didn't pontificate on that much, but she did let on that she was from a small town in Ireland and had come to the states years back because of some trouble. She fell in with Patrice, and had been working here for years.

"Patrice owns this place, yes?" The older woman finished dressing his wounds. He had already eaten the meal she had brought him and he felt some strength return.

"Since her husband left her years back," she answered.

"Sounds like a difficult man."

"He was a coward. And a fucktard. It was best that he left, she ain't got time for a man that's no' a man."

Coop nodded his understanding as Rhonda traced her hands around his body. "You'll heal well."

"I will today, thanks to you. Tell me, how do you fare?"

"I'm well, sir. Thank you. I've got years, but they've been strong ones. There are times, though, when it's good to know I'm still alive."

She looked at him, and he knew she begged his company.

He lifted her head up to him and she reached down to hold his manhood in her hands. The maiden of her youth became visible to him when he grew hard in her soft palms and she began to giggle helplessly.

Coop laid her down and took control; it was what she wanted. And when she lay before him with her clothes off and her hair down, he was ecstatic to find that not only was she a very healthy woman, she was a literal classic beauty. Her breasts were supple, her mound was vibrant and brilliantly defined by an exquisite pelt of lightened hair, and her smell was intoxicating.

He went down and feasted between her legs, and she moaned to demonstrate her pleasure. Later, she grabbed his hair to pull him up. "Your skill is admirable, sir, but... I am touched best when a man's in deep. That's where you'll please me."

He mounted her, penetrating the offered sweetness, and she pulled him in greedily. This is what she wanted, a man to be with. She locked her legs onto him, and he rode her full and hard. For a deeper insertion, he began to turn her over, but she said "Nay, just as you were," and he continued his downward rhythm.

Soon after, she exploded, and he felt her pleasure run down his thighs. She stretched her hands over her head, exposing her verdant, round peaks, and he saw beneath him the girl that she was.

He liked that, and he kept moving, kept driving himself into her. She raked her fingers up his ribcage and set her lips to his chest, flicking her tongue so that his nipples popped. He roared in delight and came powerfully into her.

After, he sat up and the lady dressed. He thanked her for the meal and her care.

"Thank you, sir, for your attention." She said.

"The pleasure was mine," he answered. When she left, he went and sat under a hot shower. He bathed, and allowed the water to renew his vigor. When he went back to bed, he slept soundly for many hours.

That evening, Patrice returned with a pressed suit, dinner, and a bottle of whiskey.

Coop smiled. "Please come in."

"You wrap a towel for Rhonda, like I asked?" she teased.

"No, I figured she'd appreciate an eyeful. She's a feisty one."

There was no talk, no formality. With Rhonda, it had been tradition, the way of things; Coop was giving payment for services, providing succor for her loyalty.

But with Patrice, it was about hunger, and dominance, and lust in its purest form.

He waited as she hung his clothes in the closet and set the dinner onto a small table. Finally, she poured two glasses of whiskey.

She walked to him, and they drank, staring at each other. His sex began to rise, and Patrice wrapped her arms around his waist and cupped his buttocks. Her hands slid down his legs as she lowered down on her knees and took him in her mouth. He hardened fully as her tongue bathed his cock, and she slid her fingertips gracefully under his testes.

She was ravenous, and planned to devour him. She squelched her lips off of him and stood to remove her clothes. Once free of her stifling vestments, she pushed him onto the bed. She crawled to him and continued to take him into her mouth. He touched her shoulder to signal he was almost done, but she kept on with increased fervor until he released himself fully into her mouth, and she continued sucking until every drop of him had been swallowed by her.

That was her offering, her submission, and Coop accepted it.

They got up naked together, had drinks, ate, spoke well and fellowshipped.

Then Coop, revitalized by the whiskey and the nourishment, and with the sight of Patrice's ample curves and heavy bosom that were ready for him, threw her on the bed and took her in many ways, and for many hours.

They slept deep that night, and well into the next morning.

When Patrice awoke, she sat on top of him and said, "I'd like you to come back, if you're able."

"I'll see that I do."

Coop showered and dressed, and walked out of that wonderful, unknown, motel with a purpose and a reckoning.

CHAPTER **27**

RECKONING

He drove to Sam's house. It was early afternoon. He sat in the car and looked up at the front porch, at the movie being played out in front of him. Sam and Ramos were sitting on the steps, holding hands, and drinking lemonade. It was too perfect.

Coop stared, deciding how real he felt it all was. He got out and stood by the car with the door open. Ramos and Sam stood to greet him, but were uncertain of his temper and so hung back.

Ally came running out of the house and jumped into Ramos's arms. "Daddy!" she yells, like she had been saying it for years. Had it always been here, just this way? Coop thought. How did I miss this?

Ramos put Ally down, and turned to face Coop. He was standing in front of his girls, and they fell into his shade behind him. He was there now, in his house, with his family. Ramos was the guardian, head of the Pack.

There was talk to be had, though. Some would be hard, some not so much. Coop's time at the motel allowed him to clear his mind and put sorts to errant thought. He was Alpha, those were his girls, but not anymore. Ramos had fought back hard in life for his rightful status, albeit he hadn't challenged Coop. Not yet, but there was a special place in the leather book Ramos carried that had been set aside specifically for Cooper Cornelius Happenstance.

It didn't have to be that way, but there was defiance in Coop that would not allow any intrusion into his way of life, and Ramos would never yield to a man he believed would separate him from Sam.

Cooper knew he and Ramos had things to work out, but there were circumstances that took priority over their issues of stature. The Captain had said he put them together because he felt he owed their families a debt. He had never said what that debt was, but Coop intuited that it was something of great importance, and he would make sure to know all about it very soon.

He slammed the car door and the two monsters of men walked toward each other, for a Reckoning.

END

About The Author

Christopher S. White lives in Fernandina Beach, FL with his wife, daughter, two dogs, and cat. He grew up in North Georgia, and graduated from The University of Georgia. This is his first book.

CPSIA information can be obtained
at www.ICGtesting.com
Printed in the USA
LVHW091317220721
693416LV00004B/91